THE
Earl's Untouched Bride

ANNIE BURROWS

Available from Harlequin® Historical and
ANNIE BURROWS

One Candlelit Christmas #919
"The Rake's Secret Son"
The Earl's Untouched Bride #933

DON'T MISS THESE OTHER
NOVELS AVAILABLE NOW:

#931 WANTED IN ALASKA—Kate Bridges
When outlaw Quinn Rowlan mistakenly kidnaps
Autumn MacNeil, he never expects the curvy, blond,
ambitious singer to make him feel so whole again....
Only she can help to clear his name in town.

#932 THE RAKE'S UNCONVENTIONAL MISTRESS—
Juliet Landon
Letitia Boyce paid no heed to London's available bachelors, for
book-learning and marriage rarely mixed. Every heiress in the
ton wanted notorious rakehell Lord Seton Rayne—so his sudden
kissing of unconventional Letitia took them both by surprise....
The thrilling conclusion to the Ladies of Paradise Road *trilogy!*

#934 THE VIKING'S DEFIANT BRIDE—Joanna Fulford
Viking warrior Earl Wulfrum has come to conquer—
starting with the beautiful, spirited Lady Elgiva. He must break
down the walls to his defiant bride's heart!
Just one look from a smoldering Viking and her fate is sealed....

Author Note

Recently I had the opportunity to look at some cover pictures from Harlequin Mills & Boon's very earliest publications. As a lover of all things historical, I found it fascinating that it was fairly easy to date each book, simply by the style of the cover art. The 1920s and 30s was replaced by a more patriotic and earnest tone during the war years. Then came a profusion of bright colors which reflected the hopes of a nation emerging from austerity and rationing.

Whatever decade we live in, though, one thing is certain. Though our lifestyles may change, the deepest needs of each human being remain the same. Each of us longs to feel valued—loved for ourselves, just as we are.

The hero and heroine of *The Earl's Untouched Bride* are both painfully aware of their own deficiencies. So aware that it is hard for either of them to believe another person can truly love them. I hope you enjoy reading their story, which is set against the turbulent times France and England had to face when Napoleon escaped from Elba and tried to reestablish his empire.

Chapter One

Giddings opened the door to find His Lordship standing upon the step, his face set in such rigid lines a shiver went down his spine. It was a relief when the Earl of Walton looked straight through him as he handed over his hat and coat, turning immediately towards the door to the salon. Thank God young Conningsby had taken it into his head to pass out on one of the sofas in there, instead of staggering back to his own lodgings the previous night. It was far better that it should be a man who could answer back, rather than a hapless member of staff, who became the butt of His Lordship's present mood.

But Charles Algernon Fawley, the ninth Earl of Walton, ignored Conningsby too. Striding across the room to the sideboard, he merely unstoppered a crystal decanter, pouring its entire contents into the last clean tumbler upon the tray.

Conningsby opened one eye warily, and rolled it in the Earl's direction. 'Breakfast at Tortoni's?' he grated hoarsely.

Charles tossed the glass of brandy back in one go, and reached for the decanter again.

'Don't look as though you enjoyed it much,' Conningsby observed, wincing as he struggled to sit up.

'No.' As the Earl realised the decanter was empty, his fingers curled round its neck as though he wished he could strangle it. 'And if you dare say I told you so…'

'Wouldn't dream of it, my lord. But what I will say is—'

'No. I listened to all you had to say last night, and, while I am grateful for your concern, my decision remains the same. I am not going to slink out of Paris with my tail between my legs like some whipped cur. I will not have it said that some false, painted jilt has made the slightest impact on my heart. I am staying until the lease on this apartment expires, not one hour sooner. Do you hear me?'

Conningsby raised a feeble hand to his brow. 'Only too clearly.' He eyed the empty decanter ruefully. 'And while you're proving to the whole world that you don't care a rap about your betrothed running off with some penniless artist, I don't suppose you could get your man to rustle up some coffee, could you?'

'Engraver,' snapped the Earl as he tugged viciously on the bell-pull.

Conningsby sank back into the sofa cushions, waving a languid hand to dismiss the profession of the Earl's betrothed's lover as the irrelevance it was. 'Judging by the expression on your face, the gossip-mongers have already been at work. It's not going to get any easier for you…'

'My mood now has nothing whatever to do with the fickle Mademoiselle Bergeron,' he snarled. 'It is her countrymen's actions which could almost induce me to leave this vile charnel house that calls itself a civilised city and return to London, where the most violent emotion I am likely to suffer is acute boredom.'

'But it was boredom you came to Paris to escape from!'

He let the inaccuracy of that remark pass. Staying in London, with his crippled half-brother, had simply become intolerable. Seeking refuge down at Wycke had not been a viable alternative, either. There was no respite from what ailed him there. The very opulence of the vast estate only served as a painful reminder of the injustice that had been perpetrated so that he could inherit it all.

Paris had seemed like the perfect solution. Since Bonaparte had abdicated, it had become extremely fashionable to hop across the Channel to see the sights.

Leaning one arm on the mantelpiece, he remarked, with an eloquent shudder, 'I will never complain of that particular malady again, I do assure you.'

'What is it?' Conningsby asked. 'What else has happened?'

'Another murder.'

'Du Mauriac again, I take it?' Conningsby's face was grim. The French officer was gaining a reputation for provoking hot-headed young Englishmen to duel with him, and dispatching them with a ruthless efficiency gleaned from his years of active service. And then celebrating his kill by breakfasting on broiled kidneys at Tortoni's. 'Who was it this morning? Not anybody we know, I hope?'

'On the contrary. The poor fellow he slaughtered before breakfast today was a subaltern by the name of Lennox.' At Conningsby's frown, Charles explained, 'Oh, there is no reason why you should know him. He was typical of all the others who have fallen by that butcher's sword. An obscure young man with no powerful connections.'

'Then how…?'

'He served in the same regiment as my unfortunate half-brother. He was one of those young men who constantly paraded through my London house, attempting to rouse him to some semblance of normality.' Sometimes it seemed as if an entire regiment must have marched through his hall at one time or another, to visit the poor wreck of a man who had once been a valiant soldier. Though few of them paid a second visit after encountering his blistering rejection. Captain Fawley did not want to be an object of pity.

Pity! If only he knew! If he, the ninth Earl, had been injured so badly, there would be not one well-wisher hastening to his bedside in an attempt to cheer him. On the contrary, it would be vultures who would begin to hover, eager to see who among them would gain his title, his wealth…

'At least he was a soldier, then.'

'He never stood a chance against a man of Du Mauriac's stamp, and the blackguard knew it! He sat there laughing about the fact that the boy did not look as though he needed to shave more than once a week! And sneered at his milk-white countenance as he faced him… God, the boy must have been sick with fright.'

Charles smote one fist into his palm. 'If only Lennox had asked me to be his second, I would have found a way to stop it!'

Conningsby eyed him with surprise. The only thing he had known about the Earl before his arrival in Paris was that, upon coming of age, he had caused a ripple through society by ousting his guardians from his ancestral home and subsequently severing all connections with that branch of his family. He had not known of a single man who dared claim friendship with the chillingly insular young lord. In Conningsby's capacity as a junior aide at the English embassy, he had dutifully helped him to find these lodgings in the Rue de Richelieu, and generally smoothed his entry into the social scene. It had been quite a surprise, the previous night, when the Earl had reacted as any man might on discovering the beautiful Parisienne to whom he had just proposed had run off with her lover. He had gone straight home to drown his sorrows. Though his head had proved stronger than Conningsby's.

'Couldn't have backed down, though, could he?' he ventured sympathetically. 'Wouldn't have wanted to live with an accusation of cowardice hanging round his neck.'

'Somebody should have found some way to save Lennox,' the Earl persisted. 'If only…'

He was prevented from saying anything further when the butler opened the door. 'There is a visitor for you, my lord.'

'I am not receiving,' Charles growled.

Giddings cleared his throat, and eyed Conningsby warily, before saying diffidently, 'The young person insists you would wish to see her.' He stepped forward and, in a voice intended only for his master, said, 'She says her name is Mademoiselle Bergeron.'

Charles felt as though he had been punched in the stomach.

While he struggled to draw breath, Conningsby, who had remarkably acute hearing, rose gingerly to his feet. 'She has in all probability come to beg your forgiveness…'

'She shall not have it!' Charles turned to grasp the mantelpiece with both hands, his shoulders hunched. 'I shall not take her back. If she prefers some artist to me, then she may go to him and welcome!'

'But there may have been some dreadful mistake. Let's face it, my lord, the Bergeron household last night was in such a state of turmoil, who knows what may have been going on?'

They had gone to escort Felice to a ball, where the engagement was to have been announced. They had found Monsieur Bergeron slumped in his chair, as though all the stuffing had been knocked out of him, and Madame Bergeron suffering from a noisy bout of hysterics upon the sofa. The only clear piece of information either of them had been able to glean was that she had turned off the wicked maidservant who had aided and abetted her ungrateful daughter to elope with a nobody when she could have married an English earl.

The Earl was breathing rather rapidly. 'I am not safe to see her.' He turned back to face the room, his entire face leached of colour. 'I may well attempt to strangle her.'

'Not you,' Conningsby assured him.

The Earl looked at him sharply, then straightened up. 'No,' he said, his face freezing into a chillingly aloof mask. 'Not I.' He went to one of the fireside chairs, sat down, and crossed one leg nonchalantly over the other. 'You may show Mademoiselle Bergeron in, Giddings,' he said, keeping his eyes fixed on the door.

Conningsby got the peculiar impression he had just become invisible. And, though he could tell the Earl would not care one way or another, he had no intention of becoming a witness to the impending confrontation. It was one thing helping a man to drown his sorrows in a companionable way. Hell, what man hadn't been in a similar predicament at one time or another? But becoming embroiled with some hysterical Frenchwoman, with his head in its present delicate state, was asking too much! He looked wildly round the room for some other means of escape than the door through which Mademoiselle Bergeron would shortly appear. The only other exit appeared to be through the windows.

It took but a second to vault over the sofa on which he'd spent the night and dive through the heavy velvet curtains.

'Mademoiselle Bergeron,' he heard Giddings intone, as he fumbled open the shutter bolts.

Charles experienced a spurt of satisfaction when she paused on the threshold, her gloved hand fluttering to the heavy veil draped from her bonnet.

Instead of rising to his feet, he deliberately leaned back in his chair and crossed his arms, eyeing her with unremitting coldness. She squared her shoulders, taking one faltering step forward. Then, to his complete astonishment, she broke into a run, flying across the room and landing upon her knees at his feet. Seizing his hand, she pulled it to her face, kissing it through the veil.

Impatiently, he snatched it back. Whatever she had been up to last night, he was not prepared to unbend towards her without a really good explanation. And probably not even then. To feel such strong emotions that they could reduce you to the state of mind where not even copious quantities of alcohol could anaesthetise them was something he did not care to experience again. He was just about to tell her so when she knelt back, lifting the veil from her face.

'Oh, thank you, milord! Thank you for letting me in. I was so afraid! You have no idea how unpleasant it is to walk the streets unescorted with feelings running so high…'

Charles reeled back in his seat. 'You are not…not…'

'Felice? No.' The young woman who knelt before him returned his look rather defiantly. 'I regret the deception, but I did not think you would agree to see anyone but her today. And so I led your butler to believe I was she. And, indeed, the deception was not so very great. You were expecting Mademoiselle Bergeron, and I am Mademoiselle Bergeron…'

'You are entirely the wrong Mademoiselle Bergeron,'

he snapped. How could he have mistaken the much shorter and utterly plain Heloise for her beautiful, glamorous, and entirely captivating younger sister? He couldn't blame the bonnet, though the peak of it did protrude from her face by over a foot, nor the heavy veil that was suspended from it, though it had concealed her features. He had wanted to see Felice, he acknowledged painfully. He had clung to the faint hope that there had been some dreadful mistake, and that she had come to tell him that she wanted no other man but him. And so he had seen what he wanted to see. What kind of fool did that make him?

Heloise swallowed nervously. She had been expecting a little antagonism, but the reality of facing a man whose heart had been broken was altogether more daunting than she had supposed it would be.

'No,' she persisted. 'I do not think you will find that I am when you hear what I have to propose…'

'I cannot imagine what you hope to accomplish by coming here and prostrating yourself in this manner,' he began angrily.

'Oh, no—how could you, when I have not yet explained? But you only need to listen for a very few minutes and I will tell you!' Suddenly very conscious that she was still kneeling like a supplicant at his feet, she glanced about the room.

'May I sit upon one of these so comfortable-looking chairs, my lord? This floor it is most hard, and really I do not see that you can take me at all seriously if I do not make some effort to look more rational. Only I did not know what was to become of me if you did not let me in. I was followed all the way from the Tuileries gardens by a contingent of the National Guard of the most vile manners. They refused to believe at all that I am a respectable female, merely visiting a friend of the family who also happens to be an English milord, and that they would be entirely sorry for accusing me of the things they did—for why should I not be entirely innocent? Just because you are English, that does not make me a bad person, or unpatriotic at all, even if I am not wearing either the white lily or the violet. If they are going to arrest anyone, it should have been the crowd who were brawling in the gardens, not someone who does not care at all that the emperor has gone, and that a Bourbon sits on the throne. Not but that they got the chance, because your so kind butler permitted me to enter the hall the moment he saw how things were, and even if you would not see me, he said there was a door to the back through the kitchens from which I could return home, after I had drunk a little something to restore my nerves…'

The Earl found he had no defence against the torrent of words that washed over him. She didn't even seem to pause for breath until Giddings returned, bearing a tray upon which was a bottle of Madeira and two glasses.

She'd risen to her feet, removed her bonnet and gloves, and perched on the edge of the chair facing him, twittering all the while like some little brown bird, hopping about and fluffing its plumage before finally roosting for the night.

She smiled and thanked Giddings as she took the proffered drink, but her hand shook so much that she spilled several drops down the front of her coat.

'I am sorry that you have been offered insults,' he heard himself saying as she dabbed ineffectually at the droplets soaking into the cloth. 'But you should have known better than to come to my house alone.' Far from being the haven for tourists that he had been led to believe, many Parisians were showing a marked hostility to the English. It had

started, so he had been reliably informed, when trade em-
bargoes had been lifted and cheap English goods had come
on sale again. But tensions were rising between die-hard
Bonapartists and supporters of the new Bourbon regime as
well. If factions were now brawling in the Tuileries
gardens, then Mademoiselle Bergeron might well not be
safe to venture out alone. 'I will have you escorted
home…'

'Oh, not yet!' she exclaimed, a look of dismay on her
face. 'For you have not heard what I came to say!'

'I am waiting to hear it,' he replied dryly. 'I have been
waiting since you walked through the door.'

Heloise drained the contents of her glass and set it down
smartly upon the table that Giddings had placed thoughtfully at her elbow.

'Forgive me. I am so nervous, you see. I tend to babble
when I am nervous. Well, I was only nervous when I set
out. But then, after the incident in the Tuileries, I became
quite scared, and then—'

'Mademoiselle Bergeron!' He slapped the arm of his
chair with decided irritation. 'Will you please come to the
point?'

'Oh.' She gulped, her face growing hot. It was not at all
easy to come to the point with a man as icily furious as the
Earl of Walton. In fact, if she wasn't quite so desperate, she
would wish she hadn't come here at all. Looking into those
chips of ice that he had for eyes, and feeling their contempt
for her chilling her to the marrow, Heloise felt what little
courage she had left ebb away. Sitting on a chair instead
of staying prostrate at his feet had not redressed their po-
sitions at all. She still had to look up to meet his forbidding features, for the Earl was quite a tall man. And she had
nothing with which to combat his hostility but strength of

will. Not beauty, or grace, or cleverness. She had the misfortune to have taken after her mother in looks. While Felice had inherited her father's even features and long-limbed grace, she had got the Corbiere nose, diminutive size, and nondescript colouring. Her only weapon was an idea. But what an idea! If he would only hear her out, it would solve all their difficulties at a stroke!

'It is quite simple, after all,' she declared. 'It is that I think you should marry me instead of Felice.'

She cocked her head to one side as she waited for his response, reminding him of a street sparrow begging for crumbs. Before he could gather his wits, she had taken another breath and set off again.

'I know you must think that this is preposterous just at first. But only think of the advantages!'

'Advantages for whom?' he sneered. He had never thought of little Heloise as a scheming gold-digger before. But then nor had he thought her capable of such fluent speech. Whenever she had played chaperon for himself and her sister she had been so quiet he had tended to forget she was there at all. He had been quite unguarded, he now recalled with mounting irritation, assuming, after a few half-hearted attempts to draw her out, that she could not speak English very well.

Though the look he sent her was one that had frozen the blood in the veins of full-grown men, Heloise was determined to have her say.

'Why, for you, of course! Unless… Your engagement to Felice has not been announced in England yet, has it? She told me you had not sent any notice to the London papers. And of course in Paris, though everyone thinks they know that you wished to marry Felice, you have only to say, when they see me on your arm instead of my sister,

"You will find you are mistaken," in that tone you use for giving an encroaching person a set-down, if anyone should dare to question you, and that will be that!'

'But why, pray, should I wish to say any such thing?'

'So that nobody will know she broke your heart, of course!' Her words, coupled with her look of genuine sympathy, touched a place buried so deep inside him that for years he had been denying its very existence.

'I know how her actions must have bruised your pride, too,' she ploughed on, astonishing him with the accuracy of her observations. Even Conningsby claimed he had not guessed how deep his feelings ran until the night before, when, in his cups, he'd poured out the whole sorry tale. But this girl, of whom he had never taken much notice, had read him like an open book.

'But this way nobody will ever guess! You are so good at keeping your face frozen, so that nobody can tell what you are truly feeling. You can easily convince everyone that it was my family that wished for the match, and that they put Felice forward, but all the time it was me in whom you were interested, for I am the eldest, or—oh, I am sure you can come up with some convincing reason. For of course they would not believe that you could truly be attracted to me. I know that well! And if any rumours about a Mademoiselle Bergeron have reached as far as London—well, I have already shown you how one Mademoiselle Bergeron may enter a room as another. Nobody else need know it was quite another Mademoiselle Bergeron you had set your sights on. If you marry me, you may walk round Paris with your head held high, and return home with your pride intact!'

'You are talking nonsense. Arrant nonsense!' He sprang from his chair, and paced moodily towards the sideboard. He had ridden out malicious gossip before. He could do so again. 'The connection with your family is severed,' he snapped, grasping the decanter, then slamming it back onto the tray on discovering it was still empty. He was not going to be driven from Paris because a few tattle-mongers had nothing better to talk about than a failed love affair. Nor would anything induce him to betray his hurt by so much as a flicker of an eyelid. 'I see no need to restore it!'

He turned to see her little face crumple. Her shoulders sagged. He braced himself for a further outpouring as he saw her eyes fill with tears. But she surprised him yet again. Rising to her feet with shaky dignity, she said, 'Then I apologise for intruding on you this morning. I will go now.'

She had reached the door and was fumbling her hands into her gloves when he cried out, 'Wait!' His quarrel was not with her. She had never given him a moment's trouble during the entire time he had been courting Felice. She had never voiced any protest, no matter where they had dragged her, though at times he had been able to tell she had been uncomfortable. All she had done on those occasions was withdraw into the shadows, as though she wished to efface herself from the scene completely. That was more her nature, he realised with a flash of insight. To have come here this morning and voiced that ridiculous proposition must have been the hardest thing for her to do. It had not been only the brush with the National Guard that had made her shake with fright.

He had no right to vent his anger on her. Besides, to let her out alone and unprotected onto the streets was not the act of a gentleman.

'*Mademoiselle,*' he said stiffly, 'I told you I would ensure you returned to your house safely. Please, won't you sit down again, while I get Giddings to summon a cabriolet?'

'Thank you,' she sighed, leaning back against the door. 'It was not at all pleasant getting here. I had no idea! To think I was glad Maman had turned off Joanne, so that it was an easy matter for me to sneak out without anyone noticing.' She shook her head ruefully. 'It is true what Papa says. I am a complete imbecile. When I had to pass that crowd in the Tuileries, I knew how stupid I had been. Then to walk right up to the door of an Englishman, on my own, as though I was a woman of no virtue…'

Seeing her tense white face, Charles felt impelled to check the direction of her thoughts.

'Please, sit down on the sofa while you are waiting.'

She did so, noting with a start that her bonnet still lay amongst its cushions. As she picked it up, turning it over in her hands as though it was an object she had never seen before, he continued, 'Whatever prompted you to take such drastic steps to come to my house, *mademoiselle*? I cannot believe you are so concerned about my wounded pride, or my—' He checked himself before alluding to his allegedly broken heart.

She turned crimson, suddenly becoming very busy untangling the ribbons of her bonnet. Her discomfort brought a sudden suspicion leaping to his mind.

'Never tell me you are in love with me!' The notion that this plain young woman had been harbouring a secret passion for him, while he had been making love to her sister under her very nose, gave him a very uncomfortable feeling. 'I had no idea! I did not think you even liked me!'

Her head flew up, an arrested expression on her face when she detected the tiniest grain of sympathy in the tone of his voice. 'Would you marry me, then, if I said I loved you?' she breathed, her eyes filled with hope. But as he returned her gaze steadily she began to look uncomfortable. Worrying at her lower lip with her teeth, she hung her head.

'It is no good,' she sighed. 'I cannot tell you a lie.' She sank back against the cushions, her whole attitude one of despondency. 'I'm not clever enough to make you believe it. And apart from that,' she continued, as Charles settled into his favourite fireside chair with a profound feeling of relief, 'I confess I did dislike you when you first came calling on Felice and she encouraged your attentions. Even though Maman said I was letting the family down by making my disapproval plain, and Felice insisted I was being a baby. But I couldn't help feeling as I did.' She frowned. 'Although, really, it was not you at all I did not like, so much as the idea of you. You see?'

He had just opened his mouth to reply that he did not see at all, when she continued, 'and then, when I got to know you better, and saw how much you truly felt for Felice, even though you hid it so well, I couldn't dislike you at all. Indeed, I felt most sorry for you, because I knew she never cared for you in the least.'

When she saw a flash of surprise flicker across his face, she explained.

'Well, how could she, when she had been in love with Jean-Claude for ever? Even though Maman and Papa had forbidden the match, because he has no money at all. I really hated the way you dazzled them all with your wealth and elegance and seemed to make Felice forget Jean-Claude.' Her face brightened perceptibly. 'But of course you hadn't at all. She merely used your visits as a smoke-screen to fool Maman into thinking she was obeying her orders, which gave Jean-Claude time to make plans for their escape. Which is all as it should be.' She sighed dreamily. 'She was not false to her true love.' She sat up straight suddenly, looking at him with an expression of chagrin. 'Though she was very cruel to you when you did not deserve it at all. Even if you are an Englishman.'

Charles found himself suddenly conscious of a desire to laugh. 'So, you wish to marry me to make up for your sister's cruel treatment of me? In fact because you feel sorry for me—is that it?'

She looked at him hopefully for a few seconds, before once more lowering her eyes and shaking her head.

'No, it is not that. Not only that. Although I should like to make things right for you. Of course I should. Because of my sister you have suffered a grievous hurt. I know you can never feel for me what you felt for her, but at least your pride could be restored by keeping the nature of her betrayal a secret. It is not too late. If you acted today, if you made Papa give his consent today, we could attend a function together this evening and stop the gossip before it starts.' She looked up at him with eyes blazing with intensity. 'Together, we could sort out the mess she has left behind. For it is truly terrible at home.' She shook her head mournfully. 'Maman has taken to her bed. Papa is threatening to shoot himself, because now there is not to be the connection with you he can see no other way out.' She twined one of the bonnet ribbons round her index finger as she looked at him imploringly. 'You would only have to stroll in and say, "Never mind about Felice. I will take the other one," in that off-hand way you have, as though you don't care about anything at all, and he would grovel at your feet in gratitude. Then nobody would suspect she broke your heart! Even if they really believe you wanted to marry her, when they hear of the insouciance with which you took me they will have to admit they were mistaken!'

'I see,' he said slowly. 'You wish to save your family

from some sort of disgrace which my marrying Felice would have averted. That is admirable, but—'

The look of guilt on her face stopped him in his tracks. He could see yet another denial rising to her lips.

'Not family honour?' he ventured.

She shook her head mournfully. 'No.' Her voice was barely more than a whisper. 'All I have told you is part of it. All those good things would result if only you would marry me, and I will be glad to achieve all of them, but—' She hung her head, burying her hands completely in the by now rather mangled bonnet. 'My prime reason is a completely selfish one. You see, if only I can persuade you to marry me, then Papa would be so relieved that you are still to pull him out of the suds that he will forget all about compelling me to marry the man he has chosen for me.'

'In short,' said Charles, 'I am easier to swallow than this other fellow?'

'Yes—much!' she cried, looking up at him with pleading eyes. 'You cannot imagine how much I hate him. If you will only say yes, I will be such a good wife! I shall not be in the least trouble to you, I promise! I will live in a cottage in the country and keep hens, and you need never even see me if you don't want. I shan't interfere with you, or stop you from enjoying yourself however you wish. I will never complain—no, not even if you beat me!' she declared dramatically, her eyes growing luminous with unshed tears.

'Why,' said Charles, somewhat taken aback by her vehemence, 'would you suspect me of wishing to beat you?'

'Because I am such a tiresome creature!'

If it hadn't been for the fact Heloise was clearly on the verge of tears, Charles would have found it hard not to laugh.

'Papa is always saying so. So did Gaspard.'

'Gaspard?'

'My brother. He said any man fool enough to marry me would soon be driven to beat me. But I feel sure…' her lower lip quivered ominously '…that you would only beat me when I *really* deserved it. You are not a cruel man. You are not cold, either, in spite of what they all say about you. You are a good person underneath your haughty manner. I know because I have watched you. I have had much opportunity, because you never took the least notice of me when Felice was in the same room. And I would not be afraid to go away with you, because you would not ever wish to beat a woman for sport like he would…'

'Come now,' Charles remonstrated, as the first tears began to trickle down her heated cheeks. 'I cannot believe your papa would force you to marry a man who would be as cruel as that…'

'Oh, but you English know nothing!' She leapt to her feet. 'He would very easily sacrifice me to such a man for the sake of preserving the rest of the family!' She was quivering from head to toe with quite another emotion than fear now. He could see that. Indignation had brought a decidedly militant gleam to her eye. She was incapable of standing still. Taking brisk little paces between the sofa and the fireplace, she did not notice that she was systematically trampling the bonnet, which had fallen to the floor when she had leapt to her feet. It occurred to him, when she stepped on it for the third time, that her sister would never have been so careless of her apparel. Not that she would have been seen dead in such an unflattering item in the first place.

'And, besides being so cruel, he is quite old!' She shuddered.

'I am thirty-five, you know,' he pointed out.

She paused mid-stride, running her eyes over him assessingly. The Earl's light blue eyes twinkled with amusement from a face that was devoid of lines of care. Elegant clothes covered a healthily muscled physique. His tawny hair was a little disarrayed this morning, to be sure, but it was neither receding nor showing any hint of grey. 'I did not know you were as old as that,' she eventually admitted with candour.

Once again, Charles was hard put to it not to burst out laughing at the absurdity of this little creature who had invaded the darkness of his lair like some cheeky little song bird hopping about between a lion's paws, pecking for crumbs, confident she was too insignificant to rate the energy required to swat her.

'Come, child, admit it. You are too young to marry anyone!'

'Well, yes!' she readily admitted. 'But Felice was younger, and you still wanted to marry her. And in time, of course, I will grow older. And by then you might have got used to me. You might even be able to teach me how to behave better!' she said brightly. Then, just as quickly, her face fell. 'Although I very much doubt it.'

She subsided into the chair opposite his own, leaning her elbows on her knees. 'I suppose I always knew I could not be any sort of wife to you.' She gazed up at him mournfully. 'But I know I would have been better off with you. For even if you are as old as you say, you don't...' Her forehead wrinkled, as though it was hard for her to find the words she wanted. 'You don't smell like him.'

Finding it increasingly hard to keep his face straight, he said, 'Perhaps you could encourage your suitor to bathe...'

Her eyes snapped with anger. Taking a deep breath, she flung at him, 'Oh, it is easy for you to laugh at me. You think I am a foolish little woman of no consequence. But this is no laughing matter to me. Whenever he comes close I want to run to a window and open it and breathe clean air. It is like when you go into a room that has been shut up too long, and you know something has decayed in it. And before you make the joke about bathing again, I must tell you that it is in my head that I smell this feeling. In my heart!' She smote her breast. 'He is steeped in so much blood!'

However absurdly she was behaving, however quaint her way of expressing herself, there was no doubt that she really felt repelled by the man her father thought she ought to marry. It was a shame that such a sensitive little creature should be forced into a marriage that was so distasteful to her. Though he could never contemplate marrying her himself, he did feel a pang of sympathy. And, in that spirit, he asked, 'Do I take it this man is a soldier, then?'

'A hero of France,' she replied gloomily. 'It is an honour for our family that such a man should wish for an alliance. An astonishment to my papa that any man should really want to take on a little mouse like me. You wonder how I came to his notice, perhaps?' When Charles nodded, humouring her whilst privately wondering why on earth it was taking Giddings so long to procure a cab to send her home in, she went on, 'He commanded Gaspard's regiment in Spain. He was...' An expression of anguish crossed her face. 'I was not supposed to hear. But people sometimes do talk when I am there, assuming that I am not paying attention—for I very often don't, you know. My brother sometimes talked about the Spanish campaign. The things his officers commanded him to do! Such barbarity!' She shuddered. 'I am not so stupid that I would willingly surrender to a man who has treated other women and children like cattle in a butcher's shop. And forced decent Frenchmen to descend to his level. And how is it,' she continued, her fists clenching, 'that while my brother died of hunger outside what you call the lines of Torres Vedras, Du Mauriac came home looking as fit as a flea?'

'Du Mauriac?' Charles echoed. 'The man your father wishes you to marry is Du Mauriac?'

Heloise nodded. 'As commander of Gaspard's regiment, he was often in our home when my brother was still alive. He used to insist it was I who sat beside him. From my hand that he wished to be served.' She shuddered. 'Then, after Gaspard died, he kept right on visiting. Papa says I am stupid to persist in refusing his proposals. He says I should feel honoured that a man so distinguished persists in courting me when I have not even beauty to recommend me. But he does not see that it is mainly my reluctance that Du Mauriac likes. He revels in the knowledge that, though he repels me, my parents will somehow contrive to force me to surrender to him!'

Heloise ground to a halt, her revulsion at the prospect of what marriage to Du Mauriac would entail finally overwhelming her. Bowing forward, she buried her face in her hands until she had herself under control. And then, alerted by the frozen silence which filled the room, she looked up at the Earl of Walton. Up until that moment she would have said he had been experiencing little more than mild amusement at her expense. But now his eyes had returned to that glacial state which had so intimidated her when first she had walked into the room. Except…now his anger was not directed at her. Indeed, it was as if he had frozen her out of his consciousness altogether.

'Go home, *mademoiselle*,' he said brusquely, rising to his feet and tugging at the bell pull. 'This interview is at an end.'

He meant it this time. With a sinking heart, Heloise turned and stumbled to the door. She had offended him somehow, by being so open about her feelings of revulsion for the man her father had decided she should marry. She had staked everything on being honest with the Earl of Walton.

But she had lost.

Chapter Two

It came as something of a shock, once the door had closed on Heloise's dejected little figure, when Conningsby stepped in over the windowsill.

'My God,' the man blustered. 'If I had known this room overlooked the street, and I was to have spent the entire interview wedged onto a balcony when I fully expected to be able to escape through your gardens...'

'And the curtains were no impediment to your hearing every single word, I shouldn't wonder?' The Earl sighed. 'Dare I hope you will respect the confidentiality of that conversation?'

'I work for the diplomatic service!' Conningsby bristled. 'Besides which, no man of sense would wish to repeat one word of that absurd woman's proposition!'

Although Charles himself thought Heloise absurd, for some reason he did not like hearing anyone else voice that opinion. 'I think it was remarkably brave of her to come here to try to save her family from ruin.'

'Yes, my lord. If you say so,' the other man conceded dubiously.

'I do say so,' said the Earl. 'I will not have any man disparage my fiancée.'

'You aren't really going to accept that outrageous proposal?' Conningsby gasped.

Charles studied the tips of his fingers intently.

'You cannot deny that her solution to my…uh…predicament, will certainly afford me a great deal of solace.'

'Well,' said Conningsby hesitantly, loath to offend a man of Lord Walton's reputation, 'I suppose she is quite a captivating little thing, in her way. Jolly amusing. She certainly has a gift for mimicry that almost had me giving myself away! Had to stuff a handkerchief in my mouth to choke down the laughter when she aped your voice!'

The Earl stared at him. Captivating? Until this morning he had barely looked at her. Like a little wren, she hid in the background as much as she could. And when he had looked he had seen nothing to recommend her. She had a beak of a nose, set above lips that were too thin for their width, and a sharp little chin. Her hair was a mid-brown, without a hint of a curl to render it interesting. Her eyes, though…

Before this morning she had kept them demurely lowered whenever he glanced in her direction. But today he had seen a vibrancy burning in their dark depths that had tugged a grudging response from him.

'What she may or may not be is largely irrelevant,' he said coldly. 'What just might prompt me to take her to wife is that in so doing I shall put Du Mauriac's nose out of joint.'

Conningsby laughed nervously. 'Surely you can't wish to marry a woman just so that some other fellow cannot have her?'

The Earl returned his look with a coldness of purpose that chilled him. 'She does not expect me to like her very much. You heard what she said. She will not even be surprised if I come to detest her so heartily that I beat her. All she wants is the opportunity to escape from an intolerable position. Don't you think I should oblige her?'

'Well, I…' Conningsby ran his finger round his collar, his face growing red.

'Come, now, you cannot expect me to stand by and permit her father to marry her off to that butcher, can you? She does not deserve such a fate.'

No, Conningsby thought, she does not. But then, would marriage to a man who only wanted revenge on her former suitor, a man without an ounce of fondness for her, be any less painful to her in the long run?

Heloise gripped her charcoal and bent her head over her sketchpad, blotting out the noise of her mother's sobs as she focussed on her drawing. She had achieved nothing. Nothing. She had braved the streets, and the insults of those soldiers, then endured the Earl's mockery, for nothing. Oh, why, she thought resentfully, had she ever thought she might be able to influence the intractable Earl one way or another? And how could she ever have felt sorry for him? Her fingers worked furiously, making angry slashes across the page. He had coaxed her most secret thoughts from her, let her hope he was feeling some shred of sympathy, and then spurned her. The only good thing about this morning's excursion was that nobody had noticed she had taken it, she reflected, finding some satisfaction in creating a most unflattering caricature of the Earl of Walton in the guise of a sleekly cruel tabby cat. She could not have borne it if anyone had found out where she had been. It had been bad enough when her *maman* had laid the blame for Felice's elopement at her door—as though she had ever had the least influence with her headstrong and pampered little sister!

With a few deft strokes Heloise added a timorous little mouse below the grinning mouth of the tabby cat, then set to work fashioning a pair of large paws. Folly—sheer folly! To walk into that man's lair and prostrate herself as she had!

There was a knock on the front door.

Madame Bergeron blew her nose before wailing, 'We are not receiving visitors today. I cannot endure any more. They will all come, you mark my words, to mock at us…'

Heloise rose to her feet to relay the information to their manservant before he had a chance to open the door. Since her seat was by the window, where she could get the most light for her sketching, she had a clear view of their front step.

'It is the Earl!' she gasped, her charcoal slipping from her suddenly nerveless fingers.

'It cannot be!' Her papa sprang from the chair in which he had been slumped, his head in his hands. 'What can he want with us, now?' he muttered darkly, peering through the window. 'I might have known a man of his station would not sit back and take an insult such as Felice has dealt him. He will sue us for breach of promise at the very least,' he prophesied, as Heloise sank to the floor to retrieve her pencil. 'Well, I will shoot myself first, and that will show him!' he cried wildly, while she regained her seat, bending her head over her sketchbook as much to counteract a sudden wave of faintness as to hide the hopeful expression she was sure must be showing on her face.

'*Noo!*' From the sofa, her *maman* began to weep again. 'You cannot abandon me now! How can you threaten to leave me after all we have been through?'

Instantly contrite, Monsieur Bergeron flung himself to his knees beside the sofa, seizing his wife's hand and pressing it to his lips. 'Forgive me, my precious.'

Heloise admired her parents for being so devoted to each other, but sometimes she wished they were not quite so demonstrative. Or that they didn't assume, because she had her sketchpad open, that they could behave as though she was not there.

'You know I will always worship you, my angel.' He slobbered over her hand, before clasping her briefly to his bosom. 'You are much too good for me.'

Now, that was something Heloise had long disputed. It was true that her mother should have been far beyond her father's matrimonial aspirations, since she was a younger daughter of the *seigneur* in whose district he had been a lowly but ambitious clerk. And that it might have been reprehensible of him to induce an aristocrat to elope with him. But it turned out to have been the most sensible thing her mother had ever done. Marriage to him had saved her from the fate many others of her class had suffered.

The affecting scene was cut short when the manservant announced the Earl of Walton. Raising himself tragically to his full height, Monsieur Bergeron declared, 'To spare you pain, my angel, I will receive him in my study alone.'

But before he had even reached the door Charles himself strolled in, his gloves clasped negligently in one hand. Bowing punctiliously to Madame Bergeron, who was struggling to rise from a mound of crushed cushions, he drawled, 'Good morning, *madame, monsieur.*'

Blocking his pathway further into the room, Monsieur Bergeron replied, with a somewhat martyred air, 'I suppose you wish to speak with me, my lord? Shall we retire to my study and leave the ladies in peace?'

Charles raised one eyebrow, as though astonished by this suggestion. 'Why, if you wish, of course I will wait with you while *mademoiselle* makes herself ready. Or had you forgot that I had arranged to take your daughter out driving this morning? *Mademoiselle*—' he addressed Heloise directly, his expression bland '—I hope it will not take you long to dress appropriately? I do not like to keep my horses standing.'

Until their eyes met she had hardly dared to let herself hope. But now she was sure. He was going to go through with it!

'B…but it was Felice,' Monsieur Bergeron blustered. 'You had arranged to take Felice out driving. M…my lord, she is not here! I was sure you were aware that last night she…'

'I am engaged to take your daughter out driving this morning,' he continued implacably, 'and take your daughter I shall. I see no reason to alter my schedule for the day. In the absence of Felice, Heloise must bear me company.'

For a moment the room pulsed with silence, while everyone seemed to be holding their breath.

Then Madame Bergeron sprang from the sofa, darted across the room, and seized Heloise by the wrist. 'She will not keep you waiting above ten minutes, my lord.' Then, to her husband, 'What are you thinking of, not offering his lordship a seat? And wine—he must have a glass of wine while he is waiting!' She pushed Heloise through the door, then paused to specify, 'The Chambertin!'

While Monsieur Bergeron stood gaping at him, Charles strolled over to the table at which Heloise had been sitting and began to idly flick through her sketchbook. It seemed to contain nothing but pictures of animals. Quite strange-looking animals, some of them, in most unrealistic poses. Though one, of a bird in a cage, caught his attention. The bedraggled specimen was chained to its perch. He could feel its misery flowing off the page. He was just wondering what species of bird it was supposed to represent, when something about the tilt of its head, the anguish burning in its black eyes, put him forcibly in mind of Heloise, as she had appeared earlier that day. His eyes followed the chain that bound the miserable-looking creature to its perch, and saw that it culminated in what looked like a golden wedding ring.

His blood running cold, he flicked back a page, to a scene he had first supposed represented a fanciful scene from a circus. He could now perceive that the creature that was just recognisable as a lion, lying on its back with a besotted grin on its face, was meant to represent himself. The woman who was standing with her foot upon his chest, smiling with smug cruelty, was definitely Felice. He snapped the book shut and turned on Monsieur Bergeron.

'I trust you have not made the nature of my interest in your elder daughter public?'

'Alas, my lord,' he shrugged, spreading his hands wide, 'but I did give assurances in certain quarters that a match was imminent.'

'To your creditors, no doubt?'

'Debt? Pah—it is nothing!' Monsieur Bergeron spat. 'A man may recover from debt!'

When Charles raised one disbelieving eyebrow, he explained, 'You English, you do not understand how one must live in France. When power changes hands, those who support the fallen regime must always suffer from the next. To survive, a man must court friends in all camps. He must be sensitive to what is in the wind, and know the precise moment to jump…'

In short the man was, like Talleyrand, '*un homme girou-*

ette', who was prepared, like a weather vane, to swing in whichever direction the wind blew.

Somewhat red in the face, Monsieur Bergeron sank onto the sofa which his wife had recently vacated.

'So,' Charles said slowly, 'promoting an alliance with an English noble, at a time when many Parisians are openly declaring hostility to the English, was an attempt to…?' He quirked an inquisitive eyebrow at the man, encouraging him to explain.

'To get one of my daughters safely out of the country! The days are coming,' he said, pulling a handkerchief from his pocket and mopping at his brow, 'when any man or woman might go to the guillotine for the most paltry excuse. I can feel it in the air. Say what you like about Bonaparte, but during the last few years I managed to hold down a responsible government post and make steady advancements, entirely through hard work and capability. But now the Bourbons are back in power, clearly bent on taking revenge on all who have opposed them, that will count for nothing!' he finished resentfully.

Charles eyed him thoughtfully. Monsieur Bergeron feared he was teetering on the verge of ruin. So he had spread his safety net wide. He had encouraged his pretty daughter to entrap an English earl, who would provide a safe bolthole in a foreign land should things become too hot for his family in France. And he had encouraged the attentions of his plain daughter's only suitor though he was an ardent Bonapartist. Every day Du Mauriac openly drank the health of his exiled emperor in cafés such as the Tabagie de la Comete, with other ex-officers of the Grand Armée. Much as he disliked the man, there was no denying he would make both a powerful ally and a dangerous enemy.

Finding himself somewhat less out of charity with his prospective father-in-law, Charles settled himself in a chair and stretched his legs out, crossing them at the ankles.

'Let me put a proposition to you.'

Monsieur Bergeron eyed him warily.

'I have my own reasons for not wanting my…er…disappointment to be made public. I wish, in fact, to carry on as though nothing untoward has occurred.'

'But…Felice has run off. That is not news we can keep quiet indefinitely. It may take some time to find her, if you insist you still wish to marry her…'

He made an impatient gesture with his hand. 'I am finished with Felice. But nobody knows for certain that it was her I intended to marry. Do they?'

'Well, no…'

'Then the sooner I am seen about in public with your other daughter, the sooner we can begin to persuade people that they were entirely mistaken to suppose it was Felice to whom I became engaged.'

'What are you suggesting?'

'Isn't it obvious? Since Felice is out of the picture, I will marry your other daughter instead.'

'But—but…'

'You can have no objections, surely? She is not contracted to anyone else, is she?' He held his breath while he watched the cogs whirring in Monsieur Bergeron's head. Heloise had spoken of proposals to which she had not agreed, but if her father and Du Mauriac had drawn up any form of legal agreement things might be about to get complicated.

'No, my lord,' Monsieur Bergeron said, having clearly made up his mind to ditch the potential alliance with the man whose star was in the descendant. 'She is free to marry you. Only…' He slumped back against the cushions, closing his eyes and shaking his head. 'It will not be a simple matter of substituting one girl for the other. Heloise has so little sense. What if she won't agree? Ah!' he moaned, crumpling the handkerchief in his fist. 'That our fortunes should all rest in the hands of such a little fool!'

Charles found himself rather indignant on Heloise's behalf. It seemed to him that it was Felice who had plunged her family into this mess, but not a word was being said against her. And, far from being a fool, Heloise had been the one to come up with this coldly rational plan which would wipe out, at a stroke, all the unpleasantness her sister had created.

'I beg your pardon?' he said coldly.

'Of course our family owes it to you to redress the insult my younger daughter has offered you. But I pray you won't be offended if I cannot make Heloise see reason.'

His brief feelings of charity towards the older man evaporated. He had no compunction about forcing his daughter into any marriage, no matter how distasteful it might be to her, so long as he stood to gain by it. If Charles hadn't already known that Heloise was all for it, he would have turned away at that point and left the entire Bergeron family to sink in their own mire.

'I am sure she will do the right thing,' he said, in as even a tone as he could muster.

'That's because you don't know her,' her father bit out glumly. 'There is no telling what the silly creature will take it into her head to do. Or to say. She is nowhere near as clever as her sister.'

Charles eyed Monsieur Bergeron coldly. He had encouraged Felice to ensnare him when she'd never had the slightest intention of marrying him. Heloise, for being, as she put it, too stupid to tell a lie, was castigated as being useless. On the whole, he found he preferred Heloise's brand of stupidity to Felice's sort of cleverness.

'A man does not look for a great deal of intellect in his wife,' he bit out. 'I am sure we shall deal well together. Ah,' he said, as the door opened and Heloise and her mother returned to the room. 'Here she is now, and looking quite charming.' Walking to her side, he bowed over her hand.

'Pray, don't overdo it,' she whispered, her eyes sparking with alarm.

Tucking her hand under his arm, and patting her gloved hand reassuringly, he smiled at her mother, who had also hastily donned her coat and bonnet. 'I am sure you will agree there is no need for you to act as chaperon, *madame*, since the news of my engagement to Heloise will soon be common knowledge.'

Her jaw dropped open as she reeled back. 'You wish to marry Heloise?' she gasped.

'Why not?' he retorted. 'I have already settled the matter with your papa,' he turned to inform Heloise. 'He thinks your family should make recompense to me for the insult your younger sister offered me. Since I have rather got used to the idea of returning to England with a bride, it might as well be you. And, before you raise any foolish objections, let me inform you that I expect your full co-operation.' He bent a rather stern eye on her. 'I have no wish to appear as an object for vulgar gossip. I do not want anyone to know your sister jilted me. You will explain, if you please,' he said, turning once more to Madame Bergeron, 'that naturally you are upset by Felice's running off with a totally unsuitable man, but that it has no bearing on the relationship which already existed between me and her older, better-behaved sister.'

The woman plumped down onto the sofa next to her husband.

'People have grown used to seeing the three of us about together over the last few weeks. And while Felice was always the more flamboyant of the two, if we but stick to our story we can easily persuade people that it was Heloise all along who was the object of my interest. She is much better suited to becoming my countess, since her manner is modest and discreet. What man of breeding would want to take an outrageous flirt to wife?'

'Heloise,' her father now put in, rather sternly. 'I hope you are paying attention to what his lordship is saying. As a dutiful daughter you must do all you can to protect the honour of this family. I expect you to submit to me in this, young woman! You will keep your mouth shut about how far things went between Felice and his lordship, and you *will* marry him.'

Meekly bowing her head, Heloise replied, 'Whatever you say, Papa.'

Not wishing to linger any longer with that pair of opportunists, Charles ushered Heloise to the door.

She stayed silent, her head bowed to conceal her jubilant expression from her parents, until they were outside. Her eyes ran over the smart two-wheeled carrick Charles had procured for the occasion with approval. She had recognised the vehicle the moment it had drawn up outside. He had borrowed it once before, from another English noble who had brought it over to Paris for the express purpose of cutting a dash in the Bois de Boulogne. When Charles had taken Felice out in it, he had hired two liveried and mounted servants to ride behind, ensuring that everyone knew he was *someone*, even if he had picked up his passenger from a modest little dwelling on the Quai Voltaire.

Borrowing this conveyance, which he could drive himself, giving them the requisite privacy to plan their strategy whilst contriving to look as though they were merely being fashionable, was a stroke of genius.

He tossed a coin to the street urchin who was holding the horses' heads, and handed her up onto the narrow bench seat.

'You were magnificent!' she breathed, turning to him with unfeigned admiration as he urged the perfectly matched pair of bays out into the light traffic. 'Oh, if only we were not driving down a public street I could kiss you. I really could!'

'We are already attracting enough notice, *mademoiselle*, by driving about without a chaperon of any sort, without the necessity of giving way to vulgar displays of emotion.'

'Oh!' Heloise turned to face front, her back ramrod-straight, her face glowing red with chagrin. How could she have presumed to speak in such a familiar fashion? Never mind harbour such an inappropriate impulse?

'You may place one hand upon my sleeve, if you must.'

His clipped tones indicated that this was quite a concession on his part. Gingerly, she laid her hand upon his forearm.

'I have decided upon the tale we shall tell,' he said, 'and it is this. Our alliance has withstood the scandal of Felice's elopement with an unsuitable young man. I am not ashamed to continue my connection with your family. After all, your mother came from an ancient and noble house. That your sister has lamentably been infected by revolutionary tendencies and run off with a nobody has nothing to do with us.'

The feeling of happiness which his put-down had momentarily quelled swelled up all over again. She had known that if anyone could rescue her it was the Earl of Walton! He had grasped the importance of acting swiftly, then taken her rather vague plan and furnished it with convincing detail. She had always suspected he was quite intelligent, even though he had been prone to utter the most specious drivel to Felice. What was more, he would never let her down by making a slip in a moment of carelessness, like some men might. He was always fully in control of himself, regarding men who got drunk and made an exhibition of themselves in public with disdain.

Oh, yes, he was the perfect man to carry her scheme through successfully!

'I was planning to announce my engagement officially at Lady Dalrymple Hamilton's ball last evening.'

'I know,' she replied. It had been his decision to make that announcement which had finally driven Felice to take off so precipitously. She had hoped to keep him dangling for another week at the very least. Heloise worried at her lower lip. She hoped Felice had managed to reach Jean-Claude safely. Although he had gone ahead to Switzerland, and secured a job with a printing firm, he had planned to return and escort Felice across France personally.

'No need to look so crestfallen. I do not expect you to shine in society as your sister did. I will steer you through the social shoals.'

'It is not that!' she replied indignantly. She might not 'shine', as he put it, but she had mingled freely with some of the highest in the land. Why, she had once even been introduced to Wellington! Though, she admitted to herself with chagrin, he had looked right through her.

He glanced down at the rim of her bonnet, which was all he could see of her now that she had turned her head away.

How shy she was. How hard she would find it to take

her place in society! Well, he would do all he could to smooth her passage. It was her idea, after all, that was going to enable him to salvage his pride. He would never have thought of something so outrageous. He owed her for that. And to start with he was going to have to smarten her up. He was not going to expose her to ridicule for her lack of dress sense.

'Deuce take it,' he swore. 'I'm going to have to buy you some more flattering headgear. That bonnet is the ugliest thing I think I've ever seen.' He leant a little closer. 'Is it the same unfortunate article you trampled so ruthlessly in my drawing room this morning?'

She looked up at him then, suddenly cripplingly conscious of how far short of the Earl's standard she fell. 'It is practical,' she protested. 'It can withstand any amount of abuse and still look—'

'Disreputable,' he finished for her. 'And that reminds me. While we are shopping, I shall have to get you a ring.'

His eyes narrowed as a look of guilt flickered across her mobile little features. No wonder she did not attempt to tell lies, he reflected. Her face was so expressive every thought was written clearly there.

'What is it?' he sighed.

'First, I have to tell you that I do not wish you at all to take me shopping!' she declared defiantly.

'You are unique amongst your sex, then,' he replied dryly. 'And what is second?'

'And second,' she gulped, the expression of guilt returning in force, 'is that you do not need to buy me a ring.' Holding up her hand to prevent his retort, she hastened to explain, 'I already have a ring.'

He stiffened. 'Our engagement may not have been my idea, *mademoiselle*, but it is my place to provide the ring.'

'But you already have. That is—' She blushed. 'The ring I have is the one you gave Felice. The very one that made her run away. She gave it to me.'

'The ring…made her run away?' He had chosen it with such care. The great emerald that gleamed in its cluster of diamonds was the exact shade of Felice's bewitching eyes. He had thought he was past being hurt, but the thought that she found his taste so deficient she had run to another man…

'Yes, for until that moment it had not been at all real to her,' he heard Heloise say. 'She thought you were merely amusing yourself with a little flirtation. Though I warned her over and over again, she never believed that she could hurt you. She said that nobody could touch your heart— if you had one, which she did not believe—and so you made the perfect smokescreen.'

'Is that estimation of my character supposed to be making me feel better?' he growled.

'Perhaps not. But at least it may help you to forgive her. It was not until you gave her that ring that she understood you really had feelings for her. So then of course she had to run away, before things progressed beyond hope.'

'In short, she would have kept me dangling on a string indefinitely if I hadn't proposed marriage?'

'Well, no. For she always meant to go to Jean-Claude. But she did not mean to hurt you. Truly. She just thought—'

'That I had no heart,' he finished, in clipped tones.

Inadvertently he jerked on the reins, giving the horses the impression that he wished them to break into a trot. Since they were approaching a corner, there were a few moments where it took all his concentration to ensure they were not involved in an accident.

'Oh, dear.' Heloise was gripping onto his sleeve with both hands now, her face puckered with concern. 'Now I have made you angry again, which is precisely what I wished not to do. For I have to inform you that when we are married, if you forbid me to contact her, knowing that I must obey I will do so—but until then I fully intend to write to her. Even if she has wronged you, she is still my sister!'

The moment of danger being past, the horses having been successfully brought back to a brisk walk, she folded her arms, and turned away from him, as though she had suddenly become interested in the pair of dogs with frills round their necks which were dancing for the amusement of those strolling along the boulevard.

'Ah, yes,' he replied, reaching over to take her hand and place it back upon his own arm. 'You fully intend to bow to my every whim, don't you, once we are married?'

'Of course! For you had no thought of marrying me until I put the notion in your head, so the least I can do is be the best wife you would wish for. I will do everything I can,' she declared earnestly. 'Whatever you ask, I will do with alacrity!' Pulling herself up short, she suddenly frowned at him suspiciously. 'And, by the way, why did you suddenly change your mind about me? When you made me leave, you seemed so set against it!'

'Well, your proposal was so sudden,' he teased her. 'It took me by surprise. Naturally I had to consider…'

She shook her head. 'No, I may have surprised you, but you had made up your mind it was an absurd idea.'

'So absurd, in fact,' he countered, 'that nobody would credit it. Nobody would believe I would take one Mademoiselle Bergeron merely to save face at being embarrassed by the other Mademoiselle Bergeron. And therefore they will have to believe that you were the object of my interest all along.'

When she continued to look less than convinced by his complete about-face, he decided it was high time he regained control of the conversation.

'Now, getting back to the ring. May I enquire, although I somehow feel I am about to regret doing so, why your sister left it with you? The normal practice, I should remind you, when an engagement is terminated, is for the lady to return the ring to the man who gave it to her.'

'I had it with me when I came to visit you this morning,' she declared. 'I was going to return it to you for her if you should not agree to my suggestion.'

'Indeed?' His voice was laced with scepticism. 'And yet somehow it remains in your possession. How did that come about, I wonder?'

'Well, because you were so beastly to me, if you must know! I told you the deepest secret of my heart and you laughed at me. For the moment I quite lost my temper, and decided I should do with it exactly as Felice said I ought to do! For you are so wealthy it is not as if you *needed* to have it back, whereas for me…'

She let go of his arm again, folding her own across her chest with a mutinous little pout which, for the first time in their acquaintance, made Charles wonder what it would be like to silence one of her tirades with a kiss. It would probably be the only way to stop her once she had built up a head of steam. Something in the pit of his stomach stirred at the thought of mastering her militant spirit in such a manner. He shook his head. It was not like him to regard sexual encounters as contests of will. But then, he frowned, when had he ever had to do more than crook his finger for a woman to fall obediently in line with his every whim?

'I take it you meant to sell it, then?'

Heloise eyed his lowered brows contritely.

'Yes,' she confessed. 'Because I needed the money to get to Dieppe.'

'Dieppe?' He shook himself out of his reverie. 'What is at Dieppe?'

'Not what, but who. And that is Jeannine!'

'Jeannine?' he echoed, becoming fascinated in spite of himself. 'What part does she play in this farce, I wonder?'

'She was Maman's nurse, until she eloped with Papa.'

'There seems to have been a great deal of eloping going on in your family.'

'But in my parents' case it was a good thing, don't you think? Because even if they were terribly poor for the first few years they were married, since my grandpapa cut her off entirely, she was the only one to survive the Terror because her family were all so abominably cruel to the *menu peuple*—the common people, that is. Jeannine was cast out, but she married a *fermier*, and I know she would take me in. I would have to learn how to milk a cow, to be sure, and make butter and cheese, but how hard could that be?'

'I thought it was hens,' he reflected.

'Hens?'

'Yes, you said when you married me you would live in a cottage so that you could keep hens. Now I find that in reality you would rather milk cows and make cheese.' He sighed. 'I do wish you would make up your mind.'

Heloise blinked. Though the abstracted frown remained between his brows, she was almost sure he was teasing her. 'I do not wish to milk cows at all,' she finally admitted.

'Good. Because I warn you right now that no wife of mine will ever do anything so plebeian. You must abandon all these fantasies about living on a farm and tending to live-stock of any sort. When we return to England you will move in the first circles and behave with the decorum commensurate with your station in life. You are not to go anywhere near any livestock of any description. Is that clear?'

For a moment Heloise regarded the mock sternness of his features with her head tilted to one side. She had never been on the receiving end of one of these teasing scolds before. Whenever he had been playful like this, she had never been able to understand how Felice could remain impervious to his charm.

'Not even a horse?' she asked, taking her courage in both hands and deciding to play along, just once. 'I am quite near a horse already, sitting up here in your carriage.'

'Horses, yes,' he conceded. 'You may ride with me, or a suitable companion in the park. A horse is not a farm animal.'

'Some horses are,' she persisted.

'Not my carriage horses,' he growled, though she could tell he was not really the least bit cross.

The ride in the fresh air seemed to be doing him good. He was far less tense than he had been when they set out. Oh, it was not to be expected that he would get over Felice all at once, but if she could make him laugh now and again, or even put that twinkle in his eye that she could see when he bent his head in her direction to give her this mock scold, she would be happy.

'What about dogs, then? What if I should go into some drawing room and a lady should have a little dog. Must I not go into the room? Or should I just stay away from it? By, say, five feet? Or six?'

'Pets, yes—of course you will come across pets from time to time. That is not what I meant at all, you little minx!'

Pretending exasperation he did not feel, to disguise the fact he was on the verge of laughter, he said, 'No wonder your brother said I should end up beating you. You would drive a saint to distraction!'

'I was only,' she declared with an impish grin, 'trying to establish exactly what you expected of me. I promised to behave exactly as you would wish, so I need to know exactly what you want!'

He laughed aloud then. 'You, *mademoiselle*, were doing nothing of the kind.' Why had he never noticed her mischievous sense of humour before now? Why had he never noticed what an entertaining companion she could be when she put her mind to it? The truth was, he decided with a sinking feeling, that whenever Felice had been in the room he'd had eyes for nobody else. With her sultry beauty and her vivacious nature she had utterly bewitched him.

Flicking the reins in renewed irritation, he turned the curricle for home.

Chapter Three

His eyes, which a moment ago had been twinkling with amusement, had gone dull and lifeless. It was as though he had retreated into a dark and lonely room, slamming the shutters against her.

She was positively relieved to get home, where her *maman* greeted her with enthusiasm.

'I never thought to have secured such a brilliant match for my plain daughter!' she beamed. 'But we must do something about your attire,' she said as Heloise untied the ribbons of the one bonnet she possessed. 'He cannot want people thinking he is marrying a dowd.'

Hustling her up the newly carpeted stairs to the room she had shared with Felice, her mother grumbled, 'We do not have time to cut down one of Felice's gowns before tonight. If only I had known,' she complained, flinging open the doors to the armoire, 'that you would be the one to marry into the nobility, we could have laid out a little capital on your wardrobe.'

Nearly all the dresses hanging there belonged to Felice. From the day the allies had marched into Paris the previous summer, what money her parents had been able to spare had been spent on dressing her sister. She had, after all, been the Bergeron family's secret weapon. She had flirted and charmed her way through the ranks of the occupying forces, playing the coquette to the hilt, whilst adroitly managing to hang onto her virtue, catapulting the family to the very heart of the new society which had rapidly formed to replace Napoleon's court.

'Nobody could have foreseen such an unlikely event,' Heloise replied rather dispiritedly, hitching her hip onto her bed.

She worried at her lower lip. What was her sister going to do now? She had left carrying only a modest bundle of possessions, and her young husband would not have the means to provide either the kind of dress allowance she had enjoyed for so long, nor the stimulating company of the upper echelons of society.

Heloise sighed. 'What about the lilac muslin?' she suggested. It was quite her favourite dress. She always felt that it made her look almost girlishly attractive, though the underskirt, which went with the full, shorter overdress, was embroidered about the hem with violets. Surely she could not be taken for a supporter of Bonaparte if she appeared in public on the arm of an Englishman?

'Where is His Lordship taking you tonight?' her *maman* enquired sharply.

'To the theatre first, and then on to Tortoni's for ices.'

Her mother clicked her tongue. 'Muslin to the theatre? I should think not!' she snapped, entirely overlooking the political symbolism of the violets, Bonaparte's emblem. 'When Felice went to the theatre with him she wore the gold satin!'

'I cannot compete with Felice, Maman,' Heloise remonstrated. 'Nor do I think it would be wise to try to be like her. Do you not think he might find it in poor taste if I did?'

'I had no idea,' her mother remarked sarcastically, 'that you had such a grasp of what is in men's hearts.' Flinging a bundle of Felice's discarded gowns to the bare boards, she gripped the iron foot-rail of the wide bed the girls had shared. 'Don't, I beg of you, do anything to make him change his mind about marrying you.'

'He has only taken me to save face,' Heloise pointed out. 'I know he still loves Felice. Nothing I do will matter to him.'

Her mother regarded the bleak look that washed over her daughter's features with concern.

'But you are going to be his wife, you foolish creature!' Coming round the side of the bed, her mother took her hand, chafing it to emphasise her point. 'Listen to me! And listen well! You will be going away to live in a foreign country, amongst strangers. You will be utterly dependent on your husband's goodwill. So you must make an effort to please him. Of course he will never fall in love with you—' she made a dismissive gesture with her hand '—the sister of the woman who betrayed him. Not even if you were half so beautiful or clever as she. But at least you can try not to antagonise him. You must learn to behave in a manner worthy of the title he is going to bestow on you. He will expect you to dress well and behave well, as a reflection of his taste. You must never embarrass him by displaying any emotion in public.'

He had only just informed her that displaying emotion in public was vulgar. So her mother's next words took on a greater power.

'Above all, you must never clamour for his attention if he does not wish to give it. You must let him go to his mistresses when he is bored with you, and pretend not to notice or to mind.'

A great lump formed in her throat. He would, of course, be unfaithful. She was the one who had instigated this marriage, and though he was disposed to go through with it, she knew only too well that it was not because he found her attractive.

How could he? Even her mother, who loved her as well as she was able, referred to her as her plain daughter.

'Mistresses?' she whispered, a sickening vision of a lifetime of humiliation unfolding before her.

'Of course,' her mother replied, stroking her hand soothingly. 'You are not blind. You know that is what men do. All men,' she said grimly, her thin lips compressing until they were almost white. 'Just as soon as they can afford it.'

Heloise's stomach turned over at the implication of her mother's words. Even her papa, who behaved as though he was deeply in love with her mother, must have strayed.

'If he is very considerate of your feelings he will conduct his affairs discreetly. But I warn you, if you make any protest, or even show that you care, he will be most annoyed! If you wish him to treat you well, you must not place any restrictions on his little *divertissements.*'

'I have already informed him that I will not interfere with his pleasures,' Heloise replied dully. And when she had told him that she had meant it. But now the idea that he could hasten to the arms of some other woman, when he could barely bring himself to allow her to lay her hand upon his sleeve, was unbelievably painful. Rising to her feet swiftly, she went to the open armoire. 'What about the grey shot silk?' she said, keeping her face carefully averted from her mother. 'I have not worn that for some time. I don't think His Lordship has ever seen me in it.'

Heloise did not particularly like the dress, for it had bad

associations. The first time Du Mauriac had asked her father if he might pay his addresses to his oldest daughter, he had been so proud that she had captured the interest of a hero of France that he had sent her to the dressmaker with the instruction to buy something pretty to wear when her suitor came calling. She had been torn. Oh, how pleasant it had been, to be able to go and choose a gown with no expense spared! And yet the reason for the treat had almost robbed her of all joy in the purchase. In the end she had not been able to resist the lure of silk, but had chosen a sombre shade of grey, in a very demure style, hoping that Du Mauriac would not think she was trying to dress for his pleasure.

'It is not at all the sort of thing Felice would have worn,' her mother remarked, shaking her head. 'But it will do for you. I shall get it sponged down and pressed.' She bustled away with Heloise's best gown over her arm, leaving her to her solitary and rather depressing reflections.

He had never seen her dressed so well, Charles thought with approval, when he came to collect her that evening. The exquisitely cut silk put him in mind of moonbeams playing over water. If only her eyes did not look so haunted. He frowned, pulling up short on the verge of paying her a compliment.

For the first time it hit him that she did not really wish to marry him any more than he wished to marry her. And she looked so small and vulnerable, hovering in the doorway, gazing up at him with those darkly anxious eyes.

She needed solid reassurance, not empty flattery.

Taking her hand in his, he led her to the sofa.

'May I have a few moments alone with your daughter before we go out?' he enquired of her parents. They left the room with such alacrity he was not sure whether to feel amused at their determination to pander to his every whim, or irritated at their lack of concern for their daughter's evident discomfort.

Heloise sank onto the sofa next to him, her hand resting limply in his own, and gazed up into his handsome face. Of course he would have mistresses. He was a most virile man. She would just somehow have to deal with this crushing sense of rejection the awareness of his infidelity caused her. She must learn not to mind that he frowned when he saw her, and stifle the memories of how his eyes had lit with pleasure whenever Felice had walked into a room.

'Heloise!' he said, so sharply that she collected he must have been speaking to her for quite some time, while she had not heard one word he had said.

Blushing guiltily, she tried to pay attention.

'I said, do you have the ring?'

Now he must think she was stupid, as well as unattractive. Her shoulders drooping, she held out her left hand obediently.

'Hell and damnation!' he swore. 'It's too big!'

'Well, you bought it for Felice,' she pointed out.

'Yes, and I would have bought you one that did fit if only you'd told me this one didn't! Why in God's name didn't you tell me, when I raised the subject this afternoon, that this ring was not going to be any good?'

'Because I didn't know it wouldn't fit. Although of course I should have known,' she ended despondently. Felice had long, strong, capable fingers, unlike her own, which were too slender for anything more strenuous than plying a needle or wielding a pencil.

'Do you mean to tell me that you had an emerald of this value in your possession and you were never tempted to try it on? Not once?'

'Oh, is it very valuable, then?' She looked with renewed interest at the jewel which hung from her ring finger. In order not to lose it, she knew she was going to have to keep her hand balled into a fist throughout the evening. 'I was not at all convinced it would get me all the way to Dieppe. Even if I'd managed to find a jeweller who would not try to cheat me, I fully expected to end up stranded halfway there.'

Her reference to her alternative plan of escaping Du Mauriac turned his momentary irritation instantly to alarm. He would do well to remember that he held no personal interest for her for his own sake at all. He was only providing the means, one way or another, for her to escape from an intolerable match with another man.

'Well, you won't be running off to Dieppe now, so you can put that notion right out of your head,' he seethed. Damn, but he hoped her distress was not an indication she was seriously considering fleeing from him!

Though he could see she was scared as hell of him right now. And no wonder. She had entrusted him with her entire future, and all he could do was berate her over the trifling matter of the fit of a ring!

'Come, now,' he said in a rallying tone. 'We struck an honest bargain this morning. It is in both our interests to stick with it.' He took her hands between his own and gave them what he hoped was a reassuring squeeze. 'We are in this together.'

Yes. She sighed. And so was Felice. He would never be able to keep from comparing her, and unfavourably. Just look at the way he was coaxing her out of the sulks in that patronising tone, as though she were a petulant child.

'It is easier for you,' she began. He was used to disguising his feelings behind that glacial mask he wore in public. But she had never been any good at dissembling.

'Why do you suppose that?' he said harshly.

'Because I won't know what to say to people!' she snapped. Had he forgotten already that she had told him she was hopeless at telling lies?

'Oh, come,' he scoffed. 'You ran on like a rattle in my drawing room this morning!'

'That was entirely different,' she protested. 'It does not matter what you think.' They were co-conspirators. She had no need to convince him she was anything other than herself.

Charles swiftly repressed the sharp stab of hurt these words inflicted. Why should he be bothered if she did not care what he thought of her? It was not as if she meant anything to him, either. He must just accept that playing the role of his fiancée was not going to be easy for her.

'Very well,' he nodded, 'you need not attempt to speak. I will do all the talking for us both. Providing—' he fixed her with a stern eye '—you make an attempt to look as though you are enjoying yourself tonight.'

'Oh, I am sure I shall—in my own way,' she assured him.

She loved studying how people behaved in social situations. Their posturing and jostling both amused and inspired her with ideas that went straight into her sketchbook the minute she got home.

A vague recollection of her sitting alone at a table littered with empty glasses, a rapt expression on her face as she observed the boisterous crowd at the *guingette* that Felice had dared him to take her to, sprang to Charles' mind. He began to feel a little calmer. The theatre was the best place he could have chosen for their first outing together *à deux*. She would be content to sit quietly and watch the performance.

Then she alarmed him all over again by saying mournfully, 'It was a stupid idea. I wish I had never mentioned it. Nobody looking at the two of us together will ever believe you wish at all to marry me.'

'Well, they will not if you carry on like this!' It was bad enough that Felice had jilted him; now Heloise was exhibiting clear signs of wanting to hedge off. What was wrong with the Bergeron sisters? He knew of half a dozen women who would give their eye teeth to be in their position. Why, he had been fending off females who wished to become his countess since his first foray into society!

'You came up with this plan, not I. And I expect you to play your part now you have wheedled me into it!'

'Wheedled?' she gasped, desperately hurt. She had not wheedled. She had put her proposition rationally and calmly…well, perhaps not calmly, for she had been very nervous. But he was making it sound as though she had put unfair pressure on him in some way.

'If that is what you think—' she began, sliding the ring from her finger.

His hand grabbed hers, thrusting the ring back down her finger.

'No, *mademoiselle*,' he said sternly, holding her hands captive between his own, his steely fingers keeping the ring firmly in place.

She took a breath, her brow furrowing in preparation for another round of argument.

There was only one sure way to silence her. And Charles took it.

She flinched when his lips met hers, rousing Charles' anger to new heights.

What was the woman doing proposing marriage if she could not even bear the thought of kissing him? Leaving go of her hands, he grasped her by the nape of the neck, holding her still, while he demonstrated his inalienable right, as her betrothed, to kiss her as thoroughly as he pleased!

Charles had taken her completely by surprise. She didn't know what to do. No man had ever kissed her before. Du Mauriac had tried, once or twice, but she had been expecting it from him, and had always managed to take evasive action.

But she didn't want to evade Charles, she discovered after only a fleeting moment of shock. What she really wanted, she acknowledged, relaxing into his hold, was to put her arms about him and kiss him back. If only she knew how!

Well, she might not know anything about kissing, but there was nothing to stop her from putting her arms about his neck. Uttering a little whimper of pleasure, she raised shaky hands from her lap and tentatively reached out for him.

'My God,' he panted, breaking free. 'I never meant to do that!'

Leaping to his feet, he strode to the very far side of the room. Hearing her little cry of protest, feeling her hands fluttering against his chest in an attempt to push him away, had brought him to his senses.

'I can only offer my sincere apologies,' he ground out between clenched teeth. He could not think what had come over him. What kind of blackguard chose that particular way to silence a woman?

He had accepted intellectually that one day he would have to get his heirs by Heloise. But judging from her shocked recoil it had been the furthest thing from her mind.

The fierce surge of desire that even now was having a visible effect on his anatomy was an unexpected bonus. When the time was right, he was going to enjoy teaching his wife all there was to know about loving.

Until then he must exercise great restraint. He would have to get her used to the idea of him before broaching the subject of heirs. He already knew how shy she was, and had realised she would need to feel she could rely on him. How could she do that if she was worried he was going to pounce on her at any moment?

'You need not fear that I shall importune you in that way again,' he grated, his back still turned to her while he desperately fought to regain mastery over his unruly body.

Heloise pressed her hand to her bruised lips, her heart sinking as swiftly as it had soared when he had seized and kissed her so excitingly. Why had he done it if he was now adamant he would not be doing it again? Had it only been some sort of experiment? To see if he could stomach touching her as a man should want to touch his wife? If so, it was evident he regretted giving in to the impulse.

It was a while before he could bear to so much as turn round and look at her! But at least it gave her the time to wipe away the few tears that she had been unable to prevent from trickling down her cheeks. For she would never let him see how humiliated his rejection made her feel. If he did not wish to kiss her, then she would not beg for his kisses. Never!

She got to her feet, determination stiffening her carriage. She would never let him suspect—not by one lingering look, one plaintive sigh—that she… She faltered, her hand flying to her breast.

No, this was too appalling! She could not be in love with him. She *must* not be in love with him. She was certain she had not lied when she had denied being in love with him that morning. Her feelings could not have changed so swiftly during the course of one day. Just because he had strolled into the drawing room and swept all her problems away with his marvellously insouciant declaration of intent to marry her. Not because she had felt a momentary rapport with him while they had gently teased each other during their carriage ride.

And yet she could not deny that since her *maman* had broached the subject of his infidelity she had been eaten up by jealousy.

No, that was not love! It was wounded pride that made her eyes smart so. It had to be.

Her abstracted air, coupled with the Earl's barely tamped down lust, created quite a stir when they entered the theatre arm in arm.

As soon as they were seated, Charles tore off a corner of the programme and wedged it under her ring. 'That should hold it in place for now.'

'Thank you,' she murmured, keeping her face averted. It was stupid to feel resentful because he was being so practical about everything. She sighed.

'*Mademoiselle*,' he murmured, 'I am about to put my arm along the back of your chair, and I do not want you to flinch when I do it.'

A shiver slid all the way down her spine to her toes at the warmth of his arm behind her shoulders. With him so close, every breath she took filled her nostrils with his clean, spicy scent. Though his arm was not quite touching her, she remembered the strength of it, holding her captive while he ravaged her mouth. She felt weak, and flustered, and utterly feminine.

'I promise I shall not do anything you will not like. Only I must sometimes seem to be…how shall I put it? …lover-like when we appear in public. I shall not go beyond the bounds of what is proper, I assure you.'

No, she reflected with annoyance. For he'd found kissing her such an unpleasant experience he had vowed never to do it again! This show of being 'lover-like', as he put it, was as much of a performance as what was going on upon the stage. But then, she reflected bleakly, she had known from the outset that all he wanted from her was the means to salvage his pride.

'Y…you may do what you like,' she conceded, feeling utterly wretched. 'I understand how important this show is to you.' Turning towards him, so that their faces were only a few scant inches apart, she declared, 'It was for this reason that you agreed to marry me, was it not? So that nobody would suspect you had been hurt. I think the worst thing you could endure is to have someone mock you.' Raising one hand, she laid it against his cheek. 'I trust you,' she said, resolving that, come what may, she would never be sorry to have given him this one source of consolation. 'However you decide to behave tonight, I will go along with it.'

Charles found it hard not to display his hurt. Go along with it, indeed! She could not conceal how nervous he made her. She was drawing on every ounce of courage she possessed to conceal her disquiet at his proximity. She had shuddered when he put his arm round her, tensed up when he had whispered in her ear.

Was it possible, he wondered, his heart skipping a beat, that she found him as repellent as Du Mauriac?

Regarding her nervously averted eyes, he refused to entertain that notion. She had come to him, after all. He had not put any pressure on her. She was just shy, that was all. He doubted many men had so much as flirted with her, let alone kissed her. She was as innocent as her sister had been experienced.

His expression bland, he murmured, 'We should take advantage of our relative privacy to organise the practical details of our wedding, don't you think?'

The sooner he secured her, the sooner he could stop worrying that she might run away.

By the end of the first act, by dint of keeping their heads close together and keeping their voices low, they had managed to agree upon a simple civic wedding. Conningsby, upon whose discretion he relied, would serve as his witness, and her parents would support Heloise. It would take next to no time to arrange it.

They had also managed to create the very impression Charles had sought. The audience, agog with curiosity, spent as much time training their opera glasses upon the unchaperoned young couple who appeared so intent on each other as they did upon the stage.

Heloise ordered a lemon ice once they finally managed to secure a table at Tortoni's. But she did not appear to be enjoying it much. She was still ill at ease in his company. The truth was that much of the behaviour upon which she had to judge him might well have given her a false impression of his character.

He shuddered, recalling that excursion beyond the city boundaries to the *guingette*, where ordinary working people went to spend their wages on food, drink and dancing. Felice had made it seem like such fun, and in its way it had been. But Heloise, he suddenly realised, watching as she daintily licked the confection from her spoon, had not only refused to join in the hurly-burly, but would never have cajoled him to attend such a venue. He would have to reassure her that he would never so browbeat her again.

'Since I have been in Paris,' he began, frowning, 'I have done things I would never consider for a minute in London. Things that are breaches of good *ton*.'

Heloise tried not to display her hurt that he should regard marrying her as a breach of ton. She already knew she was not at all the sort of wife an English earl ought to marry. His infatuation with Felice would have been much easier for society to forgive, given that she was so very enchanting. But nobody would be able to understand why he had picked up a plain little bourgeoise like her, and elevated her to the position of Countess.

'Allow me to be the first to congratulate you,' a voice purred. Dropping her spoon with a clatter on the table, she looked up to see Mrs Austell hovering over their table, her beady eyes fixed on Felice's emerald ring. 'Though I had heard…' She paused to smile like a cat that had got at the cream, and Heloise braced herself to hear whatever gossip had been noised abroad concerning the Earl and her sister. 'I had heard that you were going to make an announcement at the Dalrymple Hamilton ball.'

'Circumstances made it impossible for us to attend,' Charles replied blandly.

'Ah, yes, I hear there was some unpleasantness in your family, *mademoiselle*?'

Laying his hand firmly over hers, Charles prevented her from needing to answer. 'Mademoiselle Bergeron does not wish to speak of it.'

'Oh, but I am the soul of discretion! Is there nothing to be done for your poor sister? Too late to prevent her ruination, I suppose?'

'Oh, you have the matter quite out. The affair is not of that nature. The young man fully intends to marry my fiancée's sister. Has done for some considerable time. It is only parental opposition that has forced the silly children to feel they needed to run off together in that manner.'

Heloise marvelled that he could appear so unconcerned as he related the tale. Deep down, she knew he was still smarting. But it was this very *sang-froid* she had factored as being of paramount importance to her scheme. Why should she be surprised, she chastised herself, when he played the part she had written for him so perfectly?

'A little embarrassing for me to have an escapade of that nature in the family,' he shrugged, 'to be sure. But it is of no great import in the long run.' With a smile that would have convinced the most cynical onlooker, Lord Walton carried Heloise's hand to his lips and kissed it.

'Of course I never held to the prevalent opinion that you would make the younger Mademoiselle Bergeron your wife,' Mrs Austell declared. 'A man of your station! Of course you would prefer the more refined Mademoiselle Bergeron to her flighty little sister. Though I must warn you—' she turned to Heloise, a malicious gleam in her eye '—that you ought not to make your dislike of Wellington so apparent when you get to London. They idolise him there, you know. If anyone were to catch a glimpse of that scurrilous drawing you made of him...' She went off into a peal of laughter. 'Though it was highly entertaining. And as for the one you showed me of Madame de Stael, as a pouter pigeon!'

'I collect you have had sight of my betrothed's sketch-book?'

'Felice handed it round one afternoon,' Heloise put in, in her defence. 'When a few ladies connected with the embassy paid us a visit.'

'Oh, yes! Such a delight to see us all there in her menagerie, in one form or another. Of course, since the one of myself was quite flattering, I suppose I had more freedom to find the thing amusing than others, to whom *mademoiselle* had clearly taken a dislike.'

At his enquiring look, Heloise, somewhat red-faced, admitted, 'I portrayed Mrs Austell as one of the birds in an aviary.'

With a completely straight face, Charles suggested, 'With beautiful plumage, no doubt, since she always dresses so well?'

'Yes, that's it,' she agreed, though she could tell he had guessed, even without seeing the picture, that all the birds portrayed on that particular page had been singing their heads off. If there was one thing Mrs Austell's set could do, it was make a lot of noise about nothing.

'And dare I ask how you portrayed Wellington?'

But it was Mrs Austell who answered, her face alight with glee. 'As a giraffe, if you please, with a great long neck, loping down the Champs-Elysées, looking down with such a supercilious air on the herd of fat little donkeys waddling along behind!'

'For I see him as being head and shoulders above his contemporaries,' Heloise pleaded.

'Oh, I see!' Mrs Austell said. 'Well, that explains it. Have you seen your own likeness among your talented little betrothed's pages, my lord?' she simpered.

'Why, yes,' he admitted, feeling Heloise tense beneath his grasp. 'I feature as a lion in a circus, if you please.'

'Oh, of course. The king of the beasts!' she trilled. 'Well, I must not take up any more of your time. I am sure you two lovebirds—' she paused to laugh at her own witticism '—would much rather be alone.'

'As soon as you have finished your ice,' Charles said, once Mrs Austell had departed, 'I shall take you home. Our "news" will be all over Paris by the morning. Mrs Austell will convince everyone how it was without us having to perjure ourselves.'

He was quiet during the short carriage ride home. But as he was handing her out onto the pavement he said, 'I trust you will destroy your sketchbook before it does any more damage?'

'Damage?' Heloise echoed, bemused. 'I think it served its purpose very well.'

'There are pictures in there that in the wrong hands could cause me acute embarrassment,' he grated. He had no wish to see himself portrayed as a besotted fool, completely under the heel of a designing female. 'Can I trust you to burn the thing yourself, or must I come into your parents' house and take it from you?'

Heloise gasped. She had only one skill of which she was proud, and that was drawing. It was unfair of him to ask her to destroy all her work! It was not as if she had made her assessment of her subjects obvious. Only someone who knew the character of her subject well would know what she was saying about them by portraying them as one type of animal or another.

It had been really careless of her to leave that sketchbook lying on the table when she had gone up to change. She had not been gone many minutes, but he had clearly found the picture she had drawn of him prostrate at her sister's feet, while she prepared to walk all over him. And been intelligent enough to recognise himself, and proud enough to resent her portrayal of him in a position of weakness.

He was not a man to forgive slights. Look how quickly he had written Felice out of his life, and he had loved her! Swallowing nervously, she acknowledged that all the power in their relationship lay with him. If she displeased him, she had no doubt he could make her future as his wife quite uncomfortable. Besides, had she not promised to obey his slightest whim? If she argued with him over this, the first real demand he had made of her, she would feel as though she were breaking the terms of their agreement.

'I will burn it,' she whispered, her eyes filling with tears. 'I promised you, did I not, that I would do my best to be a good wife, and never cause you a moment's trouble? I will do whatever you ask of me.' However it hurt her to destroy that which she had spent hours creating, the one thing in her life she felt proud to have achieved, her word of honour meant far more.

'Heloise, no—dammit!' he cried, reaching out his hand. That had been tactless of him. He should have requested to examine the book, and then decided whether to destroy the one or two sketches which might have caused him some discomfort. Or he should have been more subtle still. He should have asked if he could keep the whole thing, and then ensured it was kept locked away where nobody could see it. Not demand her obedience in that positively medieval way!

But it was too late. She had fled up the steps to her house, the sound of her sobs sending a chill down his spine.

How had the evening gone so wrong? He had decided she needed reassurance, and what had he done? Bullied and frightened her, and sent her home in floods of tears.

If he carried on like this she might still decide to run away to her farm in Dieppe. And where would that leave him?

Chapter Four

Heloise gazed wide-eyed around the mirror-lined interior of the most expensive and therefore the most exclusive restaurant in Paris.

'Most people come to Very Frères to sample the truffles,' Charles had informed her when they had taken their places at a granite-topped table in one of the brilliantly lit salons.

That seemed inordinately foolish, considering the menu contained such a staggering variety of dishes. 'I will have the *poulet à la* Marengo.' She leaned forward and confided, 'Although it is much cheaper in the Trois Frères Provencaux.'

'You do not need to consider the expense,' he pointed out. 'I am a very wealthy man.'

Heloise shifted uncomfortably as his gaze seemed to settle critically upon her rather worn lilac muslin. 'I am not marrying you for that.'

'I know,' he acknowledged. 'But you must admit having a wealthy husband will make your lot more tolerable.'

'Will it?' she replied in a forlorn little voice. She really

could not see that it mattered how wealthy her husband
was when he was in love with someone else. Someone he
could not have. And when she would only ever be a poor
second best.

'Of course,' he replied briskly. He had decided to make
amends for his overbearing attitude the previous evening
by spoiling her a little. And demonstrating that he was
prepared to consider her feelings. 'I appreciate that you
may find certain aspects of marrying me more uncomfortable than I had at first assumed.' If he didn't want her
bolting to Dieppe, he would have to persuade her that
marriage to him would be nothing like the picture she had
painted of being chained down by Du Mauriac.

'I shall not forbid you from pursuing your own pleasures.' He did not want her worrying he would be forever
breathing down her neck. 'Nor shall I expect you to hang
on my arm.' He would not force her to any event that she
would rather not attend. He knew that her rather retiring
nature might make it hard for her to hold her own with
some of the people with whom he routinely crossed swords
during the course of his public life. However, he did not
want her to feel he saw her shyness as a failing. 'It is not
done for a man to be seen about too much with his wife,'
he explained. 'And though we must live in the same house,
there is no reason we may not live virtually separate lives.'

Her heart fluttered in panic. It sounded as if he meant
to deposit her in some house in a foreign country, where
she knew nobody, and leave her to fend for herself.

'D…don't you want people to think we have a true
marriage?'

He felt touched that she could still think of his image,
when she must have so many reservations about the new
life she was about to embark upon.

'We must be seen about together occasionally, yes,' he acknowledged. 'Just once every se'en night or so should be sufficient.'

She bit her lip. She could hardly complain if he could not face wasting more than one evening a week on her. Hadn't she rashly declared she would go and live in a cottage and keep hens if he did not wish to be burdened with her company?

'Do you have a house in the country, my lord?' she asked. The hens were seeming increasingly attractive.

'That is far too formal a way to address me now we are to be married,' he countered, puzzled by her abrupt change of subject. He had done what he could to put her at ease. Now it was time to take things to a more intimate level. 'You had best call me Walton. Or Charles.'

'Ch…Charles,' she stammered, the familiarity of his name catching on her tongue.

'And may I call you Heloise?'

She nodded, rendered speechless at the warmth of the smile he turned on her for acceding to this small request.

'I hope you will like Wycke.'

'Wycke?'

'Although I have a house in London, where I reside whilst Parliament is in session, Wycke is my principal seat, and it is where…' Where the heirs are traditionally born, he refrained from finishing. Regarding her upturned, wary little face, he wondered with a pang if there would ever come a time when he would be able to tackle such a delicate subject with her.

Though, legally, he already had an heir.

'There is one rather serious matter I must broach with you,' he said firmly. It was no good trying to shield her from everything. There were some things she would just have to accept. 'I have someone…residing with me in Walton House—that is, my London home.'

Heloise attacked the tender breast of chicken the waiter had set before her with unnecessary savagery. She had wondered just how long it would be before he raised the topic of his mistress. Of course she would not voice any objections to him visiting such a woman. But if he expected her to let his mistress carry on living with him, then he was very much mistaken!

'Indeed?' she said frostily.

'He is not going to be easy to get along with, and on re-flection I recommend you had better not try.'

He? Oh, thank goodness—not a mistress.

Then why should she not try to get along with this guest? Heat flared in her cheeks. Of course—she was not good *ton*, and this person was clearly someone whose opinion he valued.

'Whatever you say,' she replied dully, taking a sip of the *meursault* that had somehow appeared in her glass when she had not been attending.

'And, while we are on the topic, I must inform you there are several other persons that I do not wish you to associate with.'

'Really?' she said bleakly. She was not good enough to mix with his friends. How much more humiliation did he intend to heap on her? 'Perhaps you had better provide me with a list?'

'That might be a good idea,' he replied in an abstracted manner. In marrying him, Heloise would become a target through which his enemies might try to strike at him. It would be unfair to leave her exposed when, with a little forethought, he could protect her. Some people would take great pleasure in making her as uncomfortable as possible simply because she was French. Others would be livid that she had thwarted their matrimonial ambitions towards him. 'Those you need to be wariest of are certain members of my family.'

She knew it! He was downright ashamed of her! What further proof did she need than to hear him warn her that his own family would be her bitterest enemies?

'You see, I have severed all connection with certain of them—'

Catching the appalled expression on her face, he pulled up short.

'Beware, Heloise,' he mocked. 'Your husband is a man notorious for being so lacking in familial feeling that even my closest relatives are not safe from my cold, vengeful nature.'

She was so relieved to hear that his forbidding her to mix with these people was not because he was ashamed of her that she could easily dismiss the challenge aimed at her with those bitter words. Whatever had happened in the past was nothing to do with her! It was her future conduct that mattered to him.

'Of course I would not have anything to do with people who would say such things about you,' she declared, with a vehemence that shook him.

'Your loyalty is…touching,' he said cynically.

'I will be your wife,' she pointed out with an expressive shrug, as though matrimonial loyalty went without saying. Her declaration effectively stunned him into silence.

'Shall we stroll awhile?' he eventually recovered enough to say, when they had finished their meal.

Heloise nodded. At this hour of the evening, the brightly lit central quadrangle of the Palais Royale would be crowded with Parisians and tourists looking for entertainment of all sorts. From the restaurants in the basements and the shops beneath the colonnade, to the casinos and brothels on the upper floors, there was something in the arcades to cater for all tastes. Strolling amongst the pleasure-seeking crowds would be one way of demonstrating that he was not in the least broken-hearted.

They had barely stepped outside when she heard an angry and all too familiar voice crying, 'Hey, Heloise— stop!'

Looking across the square, in the direction from which the voice hailed, she saw Du Mauriac bearing down on them like an avenging whirlwind.

To her consternation, rather than retreating into the relative safety of the restaurant, Charles continued to stroll nonchalantly towards the most dangerous man in Paris.

'Didn't you hear me calling you?' he snarled, coming to a halt directly in front of them. His black moustache bristled in a face that was mottled red from wine and anger. Heloise tried to detach her hand from Charles' arm. The waiters would not deign to help, but many of the diners in Very Frères were Englishmen, who would be bound to come to their aid if she could only get to them.

But Charles would not relax his grip.

Eyeing the lean figure of her former suitor with cool disdain, he drawled, 'My fiancée does not answer to strangers shouting in the street.'

'Fiancée!' Ignoring Lord Walton, Du Mauriac turned the full force of his fury on the slender form cringing at his side.

'Y…yes,' she stuttered.

'Do not let this fellow unsettle you, my sweet. I will deal with him.'

'Your sweet?' The Earl's endearment drew Du Mauriac's fire down upon himself. 'She is not your sweet. Everyone knows you are in love with her sister! Not her! What could a man like you want with a little mouse like her?'

'Since you speak of her in such a derogatory manner,' he replied stiffly, 'it is clear you care little for her either. So what exactly is your problem?'

'You have no notion of what I feel for Heloise. Before you came to France, with your money and your title, she was going to be my wife! Mine! And if she had an ounce of loyalty she would be mine still. But it is the same with so many of her sort. They can wear the violet on their gowns, but their heart is filled only with greed and ambition.'

The confrontation between a slender officer in his shabby uniform and an obviously wealthy Englishman, in the doorway of such an exclusive restaurant, was beginning to attract the attention of passers-by.

'I collect from your agitation,' Charles said, finally relinquishing his vice-like grip on her hand, so that he could interpose his own body between her and Du Mauriac, 'that you were once an aspirant to Mademoiselle Bergeron's hand?'

Heloise was too shocked by these words to think of running for help. Charles knew exactly how things had stood between them. So why was he pretending differently? Oh, she thought, her hands flying to her cheeks. To conceal her part in the plot! He was shielding her from Du Mauriac's wrath. Her heart thudded in her chest. It was wonderful to know Charles was intent on protecting her, but did he not know Du Mauriac would calmly put a bullet through a man on far flimsier quarrel than that of stealing his woman?

'I fully understand,' Charles said in an almost bored tone, 'if the harsh words you level at this lady stem from thwarted affection. Being aware that you French are apt to be somewhat excitable, I also forgive you your appalling lapse of manners. Though naturally were you an Englishman it would be quite another matter.'

Du Mauriac laughed mockingly. 'I insult your woman and you stand there and let me do it, like the coward you are. What must I do to make you take the honourable course? Slap your face?'

The Earl looked thoughtful. 'You could do so, of course, if it would help to relieve your feelings. But then I would be obliged to have you arrested on a charge of assault.'

'In short, you are such a coward that nothing would induce you to meet me!'

Heloise gasped. No gentleman could allow another to call him a coward to his face. Especially not in such a public place.

But Charles merely looked puzzled. 'Surely you are not suggesting I would wish to fight a duel with you?' He shook his head, a pitying smile on his face. 'Quite apart from the fact I do not accept there is any reason for us to quarrel, I understand your father was a fisherman of some sort? I hate to have to be the one to break it to you, but duelling is a *gentleman's* solution to a quarrel.'

'I am an officer of the French army!' Du Mauriac shouted.

'Well, that's as may be,' Charles replied. 'Plenty of upstarts are masquerading as gentlemen in France these days. I,' he said, drawing himself up a little, 'do not share such republican ideals. A man is a gentleman by birth and manners—and frankly, sir, you have neither.'

Du Mauriac, now completely beside himself, took a step forward, his hand raised to strike the blow that would have made a duel inevitable. And met the full force of the Earl's left fist. Before he knew what had hit him, the Earl followed through with a swift right, leaving the notorious duellist lying stretched, insensible, on the gravel path.

'I am so sorry you had to witness that, Heloise,' the Earl said, flexing his knuckles with a satisfied smile. 'But it is well past time somebody knocked him down.'

Heloise was torn by a mixture of emotions. It had been quite wonderful to see Du Mauriac floored with such precision. And yet she knew he was not a man to take such a public insult lying down. At least, she thought somewhat hysterically, only while he was unconscious. As soon as he came to he would be hell-bent on revenge. If he could not take it legitimately, by murdering the Earl under the guise of duelling with him, then he would do it by stealthy means. It would be a knife in the ribs as he mounted the steps to the theatre, or a shot fired from a balcony as they rode along the boulevard in the borrowed carrick. She could see the Earl's blood soaking into the dust of some Parisian street as she held his dying body in her arms.

She burst into tears.

Putting one arm around her, Lord Walton pushed a way through the excited crowd that was milling round Du Mauriac's prone form.

It had been a tactical error, he acknowledged as he bundled her into a cab, to deal with Du Mauriac while she was watching. Gentlemen did not brawl in front of ladies. Displays of masculine aggression were abhorrent to them. But it had seemed too good an opportunity to pass up! Wellington had forbidden officers of the occupying forces to engage in fisticuffs in public places. He had stipulated that the sword was the weapon of gentlemen, and Du Mauriac had taken advantage of that order to murder one young Englishman after another. Only a man like Walton, who was exempt from Wellington's orders, was free to mete out the humiliating form of punishment that such a scoundrel deserved.

But witnessing what an aggressive brute she was about to marry had clearly devastated Heloise. By the time they reached the Quai Voltaire she had worked herself into such a pitch he had no option but to carry her into the house and hand her over to the care of her mother, while he went in search of some brandy.

'He will kill him, *Maman*,' Heloise sobbed into her mother's bosom. 'And then he will take his revenge on me. Whatever shall I do?'

'We will bring the wedding forward to tomorrow,' her mother said, comforting Heloise immensely by not decrying her fears as groundless. 'And you will leave Paris immediately after the ceremony.'

'What if he should pursue us?' Heloise hiccupped, sitting up and blowing her nose.

'You leave that to me,' her mother said with a decisive nod. 'He has plenty of enemies who want only a little push to move against him, and we can keep him tied up long enough for you to escape France.'

'But I thought you wanted me to marry him!'

'And so I did, my dear.' Her mother absently stroked a lock of hair from her daughter's heated forehead. 'When I thought you could get no other suitor, and when I thought Bonaparte's ambition would keep him away from Paris, fighting for ten months of the year. But I would never have permitted you to go on campaign with him. Besides,' she concluded pragmatically, 'Bonaparte is finished now. Of what use is a man like Du Mauriac when he has no emperor to fight for?'

The moment Charles heard Madame Bergeron suggest that, due to Heloise's state of nerves, it might be better to bring the wedding forward, he completely forgot his determination that nothing would induce him to leave Paris before the lease on his apartment had run its course. Nothing mattered except making sure of Heloise.

'I will go and order the removal of my own household,' he said, rising from his chair and pulling his gloves on over his bruised knuckles. It would take some time to pack up the house and arrange transport for his staff. But he could leave all that in Giddings' capable hands. He could most certainly leave immediately after the wedding ceremony. It only required his valet to pack an overnight case.

At first he assumed that once she had spoken her vows, and signed all the necessary documents, he would feel easier in his mind. But it was not so. Every time he glanced at the tense set of her pale face he wondered if she still considered the dairy farm at Dieppe a preferable option to being leg-shackled to a man of whom she was growing increasingly afraid. He was not being fanciful. She had admitted almost as soon as they had set out that she had left her one decent dress behind because it brought back bad memories.

It was the one she had been wearing the night he had forced that kiss on her.

Before long, he realised he was not going to be able to relax until he had her on board ship and out into the Channel. While they were in France there were innumerable ways for her to wriggle out of his grasp.

It was a great relief when, about ten miles out of Paris, her head began to droop. She couldn't have slept a wink the night before to be sleeping so soundly in the jolting carriage. She must have been scared stiff of leaving her family and her country behind, and going to live amongst strangers. She made no demur when he tucked her wilting form against his shoulder, and once he was certain she was fully asleep he took the liberty of putting his arm round her, and settling her into a more comfortable position. She was so tiny, tucked against his heart. So frail a creature.

Surely there must be some way he could get her to see he was not a monster? Just a man who wanted to be her friend and protector. But how? When so far all he had done was bully and frighten her?

She did not wake until well into the afternoon.

'Where are we?' she yawned, pushing herself upright.

'Abbeville. Since you were sleeping so soundly, I took the opportunity to press on. We have been able to cover far more ground than if we had needed to keep stopping to see to your comfort.'

His matter-of-fact tone brought her sharply to her senses. For a blissful moment, as she had come awake within the cradle of his powerful arms, she had mistaken the fact that he had allowed her to use his broad chest for her pillow as a mark of tenderness.

'You will have your own suite of rooms tonight,' he said, plunging her deeper into gloom. Of course he would not want any real intimacy with her. Their marriage was only for public show.

She was not very much surprised when a meal was brought to her own little parlour, or when she ate it alone. He had barely spoken a handful of words to her all day. On seeing the meagre amount of luggage she had packed, instead of appreciating her ability to travel light he had made a sarcastic comment about having to arrange credit at various smart outfitters once they arrived in London. After that Charles had turned from her and gazed fixedly out of the window.

The hotel was naturally first class, and the maid

provided to help her prepare for bed was both efficient and friendly. But Heloise knew she would not sleep a wink, no matter how soft the feather mattress was. She had dozed in her husband's arms nearly all day, and now she was wide awake—and as troubled as she had been the night before.

She had nobody but herself to blame for her predicament. She had approached Charles and offered to be the means by which he could salve his wounded pride. She should not feel offended that he cared so little for her that he would not even fight a duel when she was insulted in a public square. Besides, she had not wanted him to fight a duel. She could not bear to think of him being injured or, worse, killed on her account.

She would not be able to rest properly until he was safely in England, where Du Mauriac would not dare follow, she reflected, chewing at a fingernail.

Anyway, she had worked out, during the long sleepless hours of the previous night, that the quarrel in the Palais Royale had not been about her at all, no matter what words the men had used. Charles had clearly known far more about Du Mauriac than she had told him, else how would he have been able to sneer at his parentage? And another thing—it had only been when she had told him Du Mauriac was the suitor she wished to escape that he had shown any inclination to take her proposition seriously.

She shivered at the cold, calculating way Charles had behaved. He must have studied Du Mauriac closely to have taken the very course which would hurt him most. He had stolen his woman, refused to acknowledge him as a social equal, then knocked him down in a public place, rendering him an object of ridicule.

She drew the coverlet up to her chin, the cold seeping into her very soul. Felice had said he had no heart. He had warned her himself that his nature was so cold and vengeful he could sever the ties to his own family without a qualm.

No. She shook her head. Felice had been wrong. And when Charles himself had informed her of his nature there had been something in his eyes—almost as though he was taunting her with the description she had heard applied to him so often.

His treatment of Du Mauriac had been cold and vengeful, that was true. But Du Mauriac was a vile man who fully deserved all that Charles had done to him. And as for that business about cutting ties with the family who had raised him…well, yes, that did sound bad. But, knowing what she did of Charles, she would not be a bit surprised to learn that it was they who had done something dreadful, and that rather than expose them he'd let the gossip-mongers make what they would of it all.

She was startled out of her reverie when someone pushed her bedroom door open. This might be a first-class inn, but clearly some people lodging here had no manners. She was just opening her mouth to scream her objection at having her room invaded when she realised it was only Charles, entering not from the corridor but from a connecting door to another bedroom.

'I am not a monster, Heloise,' he sighed, stalking towards her. 'You do not need to clutch the sheet up to your chin as though you fear I mean to ravish you. I can assure you, nothing is further from my mind.'

Relief that it was not some stranger about to assault her had her sagging into the pillows. Though his words rankled. Did he think she was a complete fool? She knew all too well that when he wanted a woman he would go to one of his mistresses.

'I only came to inform you of the fact that I will not be making demands of that nature upon you. I said from the start that you are far too young to be married at all, leave alone face motherhood.' He bent over her and placed a per-functory kiss on her forehead. 'Goodnight, Lady Walton,' he said.

'Goodnight, Charles,' she replied, betraying by only the very slightest quiver in her lower lip her feeling of hu-miliated rejection.

She would not cry until he had left the room. He detested any display of emotion. She could only imagine how disgusted her complete breakdown the night before must have made him. But it probably accounted for his distant behaviour with her today. She must not make the mistake of showing such lack of breeding again. Even if he never came to care all that much for her, she would do her utmost to be the kind of wife he wanted—compliant and undemonstrative.

To prove that she could do this, she tried a shaky smile. To tell the truth, she did feel a measure of relief. She was totally unprepared for a wedding night with a husband who regarded her as a necessary evil. Or to endure the ordeal of being deflowered by a man who would regard it as a duty to be performed in the cold-blooded way he seemed to live the rest of his life.

Lord Walton ripped off his cravat the moment he entered his room, and flung it aside to land he knew not where. He felt as though he could not breathe. God, how scared of him she had looked! And how relieved when he had told her he had no intentions of claiming his husbandly rights!

He strode to the side table and poured a measure of brandy into a tumbler. Then slumped into a chair, staring into its amber depths. He would find no solace there, he reflected, swirling the liquid round and round, warming it to release its fragrant fumes. The one time he had attempted to use alcohol as an anaesthetic it had failed him miserably. All it had done was make him feel sorry for himself. He had spouted the most maudlin nonsense to a virtual stranger, and woken with a thick head in the morning. He would need a clear head the next morning. If they could make an early enough start they would reach Calais and be sailing for home on the evening tide.

Providing Heloise did not fly from him during the night. Starting to his feet, he crossed to the chamber door. And paused with his hand on the latch.

Perhaps the gentlemanly thing to do would be to let her go.

Heloise deserved a man who could love and nurture her, not scare and bully her.

Dammit, why was it so impossible to behave rationally around her? He ran a hand over his brow.

Seeing her sitting in that bed, chewing her nails like a frightened, lonely child, had made him want to take her in his arms and comfort her. But he knew it would not have worked. He was the last person she would want to seek comfort from. He was the worst of her problems. Besides, the feel of her slight body, snuggled trustingly against his in the coach, had filled him with most unchivalrous longings. Right this moment he wanted her with a ferocity that made him disgusted with himself.

God, what had he done? What was he to do?

Determined to prove she was capable of behaving correctly, Heloise sat bolt upright in the carriage all the way to Calais. In spite of the fact she had spent most of the night crying into her pillow, she was not going to repeat the mistake of yielding to exhaustion and falling asleep on a husband who seemed to regard any form of touching as an intrusion on his personal dignity.

She had served her purpose—giving him the opportunity to take revenge on Du Mauriac and concealing the chink in his armour that was his love for Felice. And now he did not know quite what to do with her.

He was avoiding her as much as he could. When they got to Calais, he left her in the carriage while he arranged their passage, then installed her in a private parlour to await the sailing while he went off for a walk. On the few occasions when he had deigned to speak to her, he had done so with such icy civility she just knew he regretted giving in to the rash impulse to marry her.

And who could blame him? No one was more unsuitable to be the wife of such a man than she!

By the time he came to inform her it was time to embark, she was trembling so badly she had to cling to his arm for support.

Just as they reached the companionway, a messenger dashed up to them. 'Countess of Walton? Formerly Mademoiselle Bergeron?' he panted.

When she nodded, he reached into his pocket and pulled out a letter. 'Thank heaven I reached you in time.' He grinned. 'Urgent, the sender said it was, that I got this to you before you left France.' His mission complete, the man melted back into the crowd that thronged the quayside.

'You had better open it at once,' she heard Charles say, and he pulled her slightly to one side, so that they did not impede other passengers from boarding.

'It is from my mother,' she said, after swiftly scanning the few lines of hastily scrawled script. 'Du Mauriac is dead.'

Translating for Charles, she read, "'…the Royalist officials sent to arrest him employed such zeal that many Bonapartists rushed to his aid. In the ensuing brawl, somebody stabbed him. Nobody knows yet who it was…'"

She clutched the letter to her bosom, her eyes closing in relief. Charles was safe.

'What violent times we live in,' Charles remarked, wondering why it felt as though the dock had lurched beneath his feet.

Heloise had only married him to escape Du Mauriac's clutches. What a pointless gesture she had made. If only she had waited a few days, and not panicked, she would not have had to make that ultimate sacrifice.

'Dear me,' he observed. 'You need not have married me after all.'

Chapter Five

Oh, poor Charles! He was already smarting from taking on a wife he did not really want, and now he had learned that at least part of his reason for doing so had ceased to exist.

But, instead of betraying his annoyance, he held out his arm and said in an icily polite voice, 'Will you come aboard now, madam?'

Oh, dear. She gulped. How he must wish he could just leave her on the quayside and go back to England alone. But he was too honourable even to suggest such a thing. Laying her hand upon his sleeve, she followed him up the gangplank, her heart so leaden in her chest she wondered it could keep beating.

He showed her to the cabin he had procured for the voyage, then informed her that he was going on deck. His face was frozen, his posture rigid, and she ached for his misery. It hurt all the more to know she was the cause of it!

Charles hardly dared breathe until the last rope was cast off and the ship began to slide out of the harbour. She had not made a last desperate bid for freedom. Even when the coast of France was no more than a smudge on the horizon, she remained resolutely belowdecks.

Avoiding him.

He paced restlessly, heedless of the spray which repeatedly scoured the decks.

His conscience was clear. After a night spent wrestling with it, he had deliberately given her several opportunities to give him the slip during the day. Why had she not taken them? She was not staying with him because she was avaricious, nor was she all that impressed by his title.

The only thing that might explain her resolute determination to stick to their bargain was the fact she had given her word. Did it mean so much to her? He pictured her eyes, burning with zeal when she had promised to be the best wife she knew how to be, and accepted that it must.

It was a novel concept, to link a woman with integrity. But then Heloise, he was beginning to see, was not like any woman he had ever known.

Below decks, Heloise groaned, wishing she could die. Then he would be sorry. She whimpered, reaching for the conveniently positioned bucket yet again. Or would he? No, he would probably just shrug one shoulder and declare that it was a great pity, but after all he could always marry someone else. It was not as though he cared for her—no, not one jot. How could he, to leave her to endure such suffering alone?

Not that she wanted him to see her in such a demeaning state, she amended, heaving into the bucket for what seemed like the hundredth time.

Oh, when would this nightmare be over? How long before she could leave this foul-smelling cupboard and breathe fresh air again?

Never, she realised, after an eternity had rolled and pitched relentlessly past. Though she could hear the sounds of the hull grating against the dock, of officers shouting commands and sailors running to obey, she was too weak to so much as lift her head from the coarse cotton pillow.

'Come, now, my lady,' she heard her husband's voice say, none too patiently. 'We have docked. It is high time to disembark—Good God!'

The evidence of Heloise's violent seasickness finally caught his eyes.

'Go away,' she managed resentfully when he approached the bunk, stern purpose in his eyes. He was a brute to insist she get up and move. Later, once the ship had remained steady for several hours, she might regain the strength to crawl. 'Leave me here to die,' she moaned.

'Nobody has ever yet died of seasickness,' he said briskly, swinging her into his arms. It was amazing how cheerful he felt to discover it was seasickness which had kept her belowdecks, when he had been imagining her lying there weeping for her lost freedom. 'I know it must have been unpleasant for you, but you will be right as a trivet once you get upon dry land.'

'Unpleasant?' she protested. 'I have never suffered anything so horrid. How could you be so cruel as to force me to go to sea in a storm? I think—' she hiccupped down a sob '—that I hate you.'

'I am sure you don't mean that,' he reproved her mildly. Although he wasn't at all convinced. 'Besides, the sea was scarcely more than a bit choppy.' He consoled himself with the reflection that, even if she did hate him, nothing but the direst distress would ever induce her to endure another sea voyage.

He had planned to push on to London straight away, but

he could not force Heloise to travel in her weakened state. He told the coachman to stop at the first hotel that could offer a suite of rooms.

He left her to herself for as long as he could. But when night fell concern for her had him knocking on her door and marching in before she had time to deny him admittance.

She was sitting up in bed, looking much better. Indeed, the nearer he got to the bed, the rosier her cheeks grew…

He checked in the middle of the room, biting down on a feeling of irritation. Did she think he was crass enough to insist on his marital rights, after she had been so ill? But before he could begin to defend himself Heloise blurted out, 'Oh, I am so sorry, Charles, about what I said.'

'What exactly that you said are you apologising for?' He frowned, drawing a chair to her bedside and settling himself on it.

'For saying that I hate you! I thought you meant to force me to walk off that ship and try to behave like a lady, when all I wished to do was die. I never guessed you were going to pick me up and carry me. And I had spent the entire voyage cursing you, so it was hard to get myself out of thinking that everything was entirely your fault. Indeed, at that precise moment I think I did hate you. But of course now I have calmed down I fully accept it is not your fault that I have seasickness. And you weren't at all cruel to force me to go on that ship. It would only have been cruel if you had known how ill I would be—and how could you, when I never knew myself? For I have never been on a ship before!'

'Nor will you ever set foot on one again,' he said with determination.

She shuddered. 'Indeed not.'

He paused. 'You know, of course, that means you can never return to France.'

They eyed each other warily as the import of his remark sank in, each convinced the other must regret this truth, and each equally determined to conceal their hurts.

It was Charles who ended the impasse, by leaning back, crossing one leg over the other, and declaring, 'Since you do not hate me at this precise moment, perhaps this would be a good time to discuss our mode of life together?'

Recalling the way he had indicated he wished her to keep herself amused, and not interfere with his no doubt hectic social life, Heloise forced herself to nod, waiting to hear what further layers of humiliation he meant to heap on her.

'I don't wish to raise any speculation about my marriage by appearing to pack you off to the country as though I did not like you.' She would have to live with him in London, just to begin with, to prevent any speculation regarding their union. Not that he cared what people said about him. But he did not want her exposed to the sort of malicious gossip that was bound to hurt her. 'The season has not yet properly begun, but that will give you time to procure a suitable wardrobe and settle into your new role. I expect it will take you some time to find your feet, socially speaking, but until you have acquired your own circle of acquaintance I will ensure you always have a trustworthy escort to any event you may wish to attend.

'Naturally, I do not expect you to understand the British political system. All I expect from you is to be charming to those I introduce as my political allies, and reserved towards my opponents. Even though you may not like them, I shall expect you to be hospitable to the more important party members to whom I shall make you known, and their wives, when I have occasion to invite them to any of my homes. Do not worry, however, that I shall expect much of you as a hostess. I have excellent staff running all my properties, and a sterling secretary to whom you may apply, should you find yourself floundering in the political shoals.'

Heloise listened to that patronising little speech with growing indignation. If it would not give rise to the very speculation he wished to avoid, he would as soon pack her off to one of his country houses. Her poor little brain was no match for the intricacies of the English political system. She was not to interfere in the management of any of his households, which were all running exactly as he wished. And if she had any questions, he wished her to apply to his secretary rather than bother him!

'Heloise?' he prompted, when she had been sitting in simmering silence for several minutes. He sighed. She clearly felt overwhelmed by the idea of being a leading figure in society. 'You must tell me if there are any gaps in your education which may cause you difficulties.' He had no intention of throwing her in at the deep end and letting her sink or swim as best she could.

'G...gaps?' she gasped, flashing him a look so indignant even he could not misinterpret it.

'Don't fly into the boughs with me,' he retorted, annoyed that she should cling to her hostility when he was doing all in his power to smooth her entry into society. 'If you cannot dance then I need to know, so that I may engage a dancing master for you. If you cannot ride then there is no point in me acquiring a horse for you to show off its paces in the park. I would instead purchase a barouche, or landaulet, and employ extra grooms to take you about.'

Her cheeks flushing, she hung her head. 'I beg your pardon, my lord,' she said, as humbly as she could. She had to admit he was trying to make the best of a bad job. He was prepared to employ as many staff as it would take to ensure she would be able to carry off the role he expected her to play. Just so long as he didn't have to be personally involved.

'I have learned to dance,' she flashed at him. 'Though you probably never saw me stand up whenever we went to balls in Paris. For not many men have ever asked me to dance, and when I was with you it was in the role of chaperon, so it was not at all appropriate. As for the horse, it is true that I cannot ride.'

'Should you like to learn?'

'Do you wish me to?'

'I should never object to any activity which would give you pleasure, Heloise,' he said wearily. It was clear that he was not going to win his wife's trust overnight. And her mention of how he had neglected her, whilst showering attentions on her sister, reminded him she had a deep well of resentment from which to draw. 'I bid you goodnight.'

He placed a chaste kiss on her forehead and retreated before things deteriorated any further. She might declare she did not hate him, but she had withdrawn sufficiently to start calling him 'my lord' again.

All he could do was keep sufficient distance for her to forget to regard him as a tyrant, whilst maintaining a watchful eye on her. She would learn, eventually, that she could trust him.

Wouldn't she?

London was not at all like Paris. The streets and squares through which their carriage passed were so clean and orderly, giving an overall air of prosperity. She frowned. Although perhaps it was just that her husband inhabited one of the better areas. This, she surmised as the carriage drew to a halt outside an imposing mansion, whose doorway was flanked by two massive pillars supporting a portico, was probably the equivalent of the 'court' end of Paris. There were probably overcrowded and dirty alleys somewhere. It was just that as an English countess she would never set foot in them.

A footman dressed in blue and silver livery handed her from the coach, and she entered her new home on her husband's arm. Oblivious to the interested stares of the servants who had gathered to greet their new mistress, Heloise gazed in awe at the lofty dimensions of the hall. A marble staircase swept upwards, branching at a half-landing to serve the two wings of the first storey, then continued up by several more flights, as far as she could see. Light flooded in through a domed skylight at the very top. Walton House reminded her of one of the better hotels in Paris, though it was shocking to think one man lived here alone. In Paris, a house like this would be divided into several apartments, which would be leased to tourists to provide an income for the impoverished nobles who clung to the upper floors.

An upper servant approached, bowing. 'Begging your pardon, my lord, but Captain Fawley has requested the honour of making the acquaintance of your Countess.'

'Has he, indeed?' Handing over his gloves and hat, Charles wondered what new start this might be. 'How does the Captain fare today?'

'Restless, my lord,' the footman replied, wooden-faced.

'My lady,' Charles said to Heloise, placing his hand under her elbow. 'A word in private, if you please?'

Drawing her into a little ante-room, he shut the door to ensure total privacy. 'I have little time to explain, but I would request a further favour of you. I had planned on sparing you the worst of Captain Fawley's temper, but on this one occasion I would ask that you bear me company and back me up in whatever I say. Can you do that for me?'

'This Captain Fawley…he is the man you wished me not to meet, who lives here with you?'

'I have no time to explain it all, but the salient facts are these: Captain Fawley is my brother. He hates me. He hates the fact that since he was invalided out of the army he has been forced to depend on me. I fear he will use your presence in my life as an excuse to try to strike out on his own. He must not do so, Heloise.' He took her by the shoulders, his eyes burning with an intensity she had never seen before. 'He must stay in Walton House!'

'Of course I will do whatever it takes to prevent him from leaving, if that is your wish,' she replied, though it all seemed very strange to her. Whatever could have gone wrong between them? Was this to do with the rift Charles had referred to before, with certain of his family?

'Robert—that is Captain Fawley—occupies a suite of rooms at the rear of the house, on the ground floor,' he explained as he steered her out of the little ante-room and across the hall. 'His condition when I first brought him back from the Peninsula made it imperative that he not have to attempt stairs. Also, I had hoped that installing him in these particular rooms would encourage him to make free of the place. They have a private entrance, leading to the mews, which would have made it easy for him to come and go as he pleased.'

They reached a set of panelled doors, upon which Charles knocked. To her surprise, he did not simply enter, but waited until the door was opened by a stocky servant, dressed in a plain black coat and stuff breeches.

'Ah, Linney,' Charles said, 'I believe Captain Fawley has expressed an interest in meeting my bride?'

'Indeed he has, m'lord,' the stocky man replied, his own face as impassive as her husband's. Why, then, did she get the impression that both of them saw this as a momentous occasion?

It took Heloise's eyes a moment or two to acclimatise to the gloom that pervaded the room she walked into. Lit only by the flames of a roaring fire, it was clearly the domain of a man who did not care what his visitors might think. Her nose wrinkled at the smell of stale sweat, unwashed linen and general neglect that hung in the over-heated room. Unfortunately, it was the exact moment her eyes came to rest on a figure sprawled on a scuffed leather sofa, to one side of the soot-blackened fireplace.

For a second her heart seemed to stop beating. The man who regarded her with piercingly hostile black eyes was so very like Gaspard that she uttered a little cry and ran to him, her hands outstretched.

Leaning on his shoulders, she planted a kiss on each cheek, before sitting down next to him. When he flinched, she said, 'Oh, dear—should I not have done that? I have embarrassed you. It is just that you are so like my own dear brother.' In spite of herself, her eyes filled with tears. 'Who I will never see again. But now I find my husband has a brother, so I have a brother again, too.'

Somewhat overcome, she reached into her reticule for a handkerchief. While she was busy blowing her nose, she heard Charles cross to the fireplace.

'You haven't embarrassed me as much as I fear you have embarrassed yourself,' Captain Fawley snarled. 'Linney, perhaps you would be so good as to draw back the curtains?'

In silence, the manservant did as he was bade. Sunlight streamed in, illuminating the livid burns down one side of the Captain's face, head and neck, which the length of his unkempt hair did little to conceal. The left sleeve of his threadbare jacket was empty; the lower part of his left leg was also missing.

Perplexed, Heloise said, 'Why will drawing the curtains make me embarrassed?'

Captain Fawley laughed—a harsh noise that sounded as though it was torn from his throat. 'You have just kissed a cripple! Don't you feel sick? Most pretty women would recoil if they saw me, not want to kiss this!' He indicated his scarred face with an angry sweep of his right hand.

But, 'Oh!' said Heloise, her face lighting up. 'Do you really think I am pretty? How much more I like you already.'

The stunned look on Captain Fawley's face was as nothing compared to what Charles felt. Her face alight with pleasure, Heloise really did look remarkably pretty. He could not think why he had never noticed it before. Her eyes sparkled with intelligence, she had remarkably thick, lustrous hair, and a dainty little figure. She did not have the obvious attractions of her sister, but she was far from the plain, dull little creature he had written off while his eyes had been full of Felice. 'Captivating', Conningsby had said of her. Aye, she was. And she would be a credit to him once he had her properly dressed.

There was a certain dressmaker in Bond Street whose designs would suit her to a tee...

'You cannot mean that!' Robert began to curse.

A few minutes of such Turkish treatment was all he would permit Heloise to endure, then he would escort her to the safety of her rooms.

'Why not?' Unfazed, Heloise untied the ribbons of her bonnet and placed the shapeless article on her lap. Charles had a vision of wresting it from her hands, throwing it off a bridge into the Thames, and replacing it with a neat little crimson velvet creation, trimmed with swansdown.

'Well, because I am disfigured,' Captain Fawley said. 'I am only half a man.'

She cocked her head to examine him, in the way that always put the Earl in mind of a cheeky little sparrow. She missed nothing—from the toe of Robert's right boot to the puckered eyelid that drooped into the horrible scarring that truly did disfigure the left side of his face.

'You have only lost a bit of one leg and a bit of one arm,' she said. 'Not even a tenth of you has gone. You may think of yourself as nine-tenths of a man, I suppose, if you must, but not less than that. Besides—' she shrugged '—many others did not survive the war at all. Gaspard did not. I tell you now, I would still have been glad to have him back, and nothing would have prevented me from embracing him, no matter how many limbs he might have lost!'

'But you must want me to leave this house,' he blustered. 'And once an heir is on the way—' he rounded on Charles '—you can have no more excuses to keep me imprisoned here!'

Before he could draw breath to reply, Heloise said, rather stiffly, 'Is it because I am French?'

'Wh…what?'

'You reject my friendship because I am French. In effect, all this nonsense about being disfigured is the flim-flam. You don't want me for your sister.'

Faced with an indignant woman, Captain Fawley could do nothing but retreat from his stance, muttering apologies. 'It is not your fault you are French. You can't help that. Or being married to my half-brother, I dare say. I know how ruthless he can be when he wants his own way.' He glared up at Charles.

'Then you will help me?' Again, her face lit up with hope. 'Because Charles, he says it is not at all fashionable for a husband to hang on his wife's arm all the time. I have heard in Paris all about the season in London, with the masquerades, and the picnics, and the fireworks, which he will not at all want to take me to, even if I was not his wife, because such things are all very frivolous and not good *ton*. But I would like to see them all. And he said I may, if I could find a suitable escort. And who would be more proper to go about with me than my own brother? And then, you know, he says I must learn to ride…'

'Well, I can't teach you to ride! Haven't you noticed? I've only got one leg!'

Heloise regarded his left leg with a thoughtful air. 'You have only lost a little bit of the lower part of one leg. You still have your thigh, and that, I believe, is what is important for staying in the saddle. Do I have that correct? You men grip with your knees, is that not so? Whereas I—' she pulled a face '—must learn to ride side-saddle. I will have to hang on with my hands to the reins, and keep my balance while the creature is bouncing along…'

'Well, there you have it!' Captain Fawley pointed out. 'You have both hands. I have only one, and—'

'Oh, don't tell me you are afraid of falling off!' she mocked.

Charles suddenly felt conscious of holding his breath. For weeks before he had gone to Paris he had known Robert had regained most of his health and strength. There had been nothing preventing him from getting out and resuming a normal life but his own black mood. Had they all failed him by tiptoeing round his sensibilities?

'A brave soldier like you?' Heloise continued relent-lessly. 'You are full of…of… Well, it is not polite to mention what you are full of!'

Captain Fawley turned for support to his brother. 'Tell her, Charles. Tell her that I just can't—'

Charles cut him off with a peremptory wave of his hand. 'You had as well give in graciously. Once she has the bit between her teeth, there is no stopping her. You cannot argue with her logic because it is of that singularly female variety which always completely confounds we mere males.' So saying, he swept her a mocking bow.

Robert sank back into the cushions, looking as though he had been hit by a whirlwind. Heloise was still watching him, her head tilted to one side, a hopeful expression on her face. And all of a sudden the dour cripple let out a bark of genuine laughter.

'I quite see why you married her, Walton.'

'Indeed, she left me no choice.'

'Very well, madam. I will come with you when you start your riding lessons,' he conceded. Then he frowned. 'Since I expect we will both fall off with monotonous regularity, I recommend we take our lessons early in the mornings, when nobody will be about to see us.'

She clapped her hands, her face lighting up with joy. Something twisted painfully inside Charles. Nothing he had ever done or said to her had managed to please her half so well.

'I dare say,' he said brusquely, 'you would like to see your rooms now, madam wife, and freshen up a little?'

Heloise pulled a face at Robert. 'What he means, no doubt, is that I look a mess, and that also he wishes to take me aside to give me a lecture about my appalling manners.'

'No, I am sure not,' Robert replied, regarding the stiff

set of Walton's shoulders with a perplexed frown. 'Your manners are delightfully refreshing.'

Heloise laughed at that, but once they had quit Captain Fawley's suite she turned anxious eyes on her husband.

He made no comment until he had taken her to the suite of rooms he'd had his staff prepare for his bride. On sight of them, Heloise gasped aloud. She had her own sitting room, with a pale blue Aubusson carpet upon which various comfortable sofas and chairs were arranged. Her bedroom, too, was carpeted almost to the wainscot. With a smile, Heloise imagined getting up in the morning and setting her bare feet on that, rather than the rough boards of the little room she had shared with her sister. No shutters on any of the windows, she noted, only heavy dark blue velvet curtains, held back with self-coloured cords.

'I hope you like it—though of course if there are any alterations you wish to make, you have only to say.'

Heloise spread her hands, shrugging her utter bewilderment at such opulence. 'How could I not like this?' she managed to say, when it became apparent that her husband was waiting for her to say something.

It seemed to have been the right thing to say, for some of the tension left his stance. 'I will ring and ask for refreshments to be served up here in your sitting room,' he said, crossing to the bell-pull beside the chimney breast. 'You may rest assured I shall not intrude upon your privacy. This is your domain. Just as the rooms downstairs are Robert's. The only time I shall enter, save at your express invitation, will be to bid you goodnight. Every night,' he finished sternly.

So that the servants would believe they were a normal husband and wife, she assumed. She sighed as a group of them came in and laid out the tea things. She supposed she should be grateful he wanted things to look right. At least she would get to see him once each day. Otherwise, the place being so vast, they might not bump into each other from one end of the week to the other.

Once the servants had retreated, Charles said, 'Come, Heloise, I can see you are bursting with questions. I have a little time to spare to indulge your curiosity before I must be about other business.'

There was no point in questioning their living arrangements. She had promised not to be a nuisance. But she would like to know what on earth had happened between the two Fawley brothers for them to come to this.

'Why does your brother accuse you of imprisoning him here? Is this something to do with the rift in your family you spoke of to me?'

'You do not need to have tea served if you do not like it,' he remarked, noticing the grimace of distaste with which she had set down her teacup after taking only one sip. 'The kitchen can provide anything you wish for.'

'Don't you wish to tell me? Is that why you talk about tea? If you do not want me to know about your family secrets then you only need to say, and I will not pry any further!'

'That is not the issue!' This was not a topic he found it easy to discuss. She would have to make do with a succinct account of the facts. 'Robert's mother was my father's second wife,' he bit out. 'In their zeal to protect me from her influence, when my father died the people he had nominated my guardians sent her back to her own family—with a modest annuity and penalties attached should she try to inveigle herself back into my life.'

'What was she, then, Robert's mother?' Heloise asked, fascinated. 'Something scandalous? An actress, perhaps, or a woman of easy morals?'

Charles smiled grimly. 'Worse than that, in the opinion of my stiff-rumped maternal relatives. She was a doctor's daughter.'

At Heloise's complete bafflement, he continued, 'She was, with her middle-class values, the kind of person who might have influenced me into thinking less of my consequence than they thought I should. They reminded me that my real mother was the Duke of Bray's granddaughter, and set about instilling me with pride in my true lineage. Rigorously.'

Heloise shook her head. What a miserable little boy he must have been. But worse was to come.

'I did not even know that I had a brother until, when I came of age, I began to go through all the family papers with my lawyers, instead of just ratifying them as my guardians assumed I would. I discovered that Robert had been born some five months after my father's death. Instead of having him raised with me, and acknowledged as second in line to my inheritance, they consigned him to the care of his mother's family. By the time he was sixteen, so vehemently did he hate my mother's relations that he began to refuse even the meagre allowance they had arranged for him. Instead he requested they purchase him a commission, so that he could make his own way in the world without having any need for further contact with relatives who had made no secret of the fact they wished he had not been born. Which they did—hoping, no doubt, that his career would be short and bloody. It was not long after that when I discovered his existence. And by then he was beyond my reach. He neither wanted nor needed anything from the brother he had grown up hating.'

'Oh, Charles,' she said, her eyes wide with horror. 'How awful. What did you do?'

He looked at her with eyes that had grown cold. 'I did as I was trained to do. I acted without emotion. I severed all connection with those who had systematically robbed me, my stepmother and my brother of each other.'

'And what,' she asked, 'happened to Robert's mother?'

'She scarcely survived his birth. The story he had from his family was that she died from a broken heart, at the treatment meted out to her whilst she was still in shock at being widowed.'

No wonder Charles appeared so hard and cold. The one person who might have taught him to embrace the softer emotions had been ruthlessly excised from his orbit. Then his relatives had taught him, the hard way, that there was nobody upon whom he could rely.

No wonder he had been able to shrug off the loss of a fiancée with such panache. Her betrayal was nothing compared to what he had already experienced.

And yet, in spite of all that, he had never stopped reaching out to the brother who repaid all his overtures with bristling hostility.

'Oh, Charles,' she cried, longing to take him in her arms and hold him. Tell him he was not alone any more. She was there.

She had begun to stretch out her hands towards him before recalling what a futile gesture it was. She could not be of any comfort to him, for he was only tolerating her presence in his life. Besides, he had already expressed his dislike of her propensity for being demonstrative.

'I am so sorry,' she said, swallowing back the tears she knew he would disparage, and folding her hands in her lap with a feeling of resignation. He had only confided in her so that she might understand the situation, and not create further difficulties with his brother.

He made that very clear by turning on his heel and stalking from the room.

What further proof, thought Charles, seeking the solitude of his own bedchamber, did he need that she now considered him more repulsive than Du Mauriac? Even though her heart had been moved by his tale, she hadn't been able to bring herself to so much as touch his arm through his coat sleeve. But she had run to Robert and managed to kiss him. On both cheeks.

Chapter Six

'I have brought my bride to you for dressing,' the Earl informed Madame Pichot, upon entering her establishment the following morning. 'She needs everything.'

Madame Pichot's eyes lit up. 'Walking dresses, day dresses, ballgowns, nightrail?' She swallowed. 'A court dress?'

'Naturally.' By the time such a grand toilette was complete, and Heloise had practised walking in the hoops, he would have found someone to present her in Queen Caroline's drawing room. It was not so great a hurdle as obtaining vouchers for Almacks. If she offended one of the six patronesses of that exclusive club, or if they decided her background failed to meet their exacting standards for membership, she would never be truly a part of the *haut ton*.

Noting Heloise's rather worn coat and battered bonnet, Madame Pichot ventured, 'I could have one or two items delivered later today, or possibly first thing tomorrow. Just to tide milady over, of course...'

The Earl nodded acquiescence. Heloise would find it

easier to think of herself as an English countess once she shucked off the serviceable clothing of a French bureaucrat's daughter.

'In future, should we require your services, you will present yourself at Walton House at my wife's convenience.'

'Of course, my lord,' replied the dressmaker, somewhat startled by the statement Heloise knew had been made primarily for her benefit. Whatever had been her habit formerly, a countess did not deign to visit a dressmaker's. She sent for such people to wait on her in the privacy of her own home.

'My wife will wear pastel colours. Rose and powder-blue—and, yes, this primrose satin would suit my wife's colouring.' He fingered one of the swatches an assistant had brought for his inspection.

'Oh, but with *madame*'s dark hair and eyes, she could wear striking colours. This crimson would look ravishing.'

'I don't want her going about looking like a demi-rep,' he curtly informed the somewhat abashed modiste.

Heloise had just taken a breath to object and say that she was quite capable of selecting her own gowns, thank you very much, when her mother's warning rang loud in her memory. He would want her to look the part she had persuaded him she could play. That he had no confidence in her dress sense might be somewhat insulting, but then, he was the one picking up the bills. Feeling like a child's dress-up doll, she meekly tried on the few gowns that were already made up, and had never been collected by other clients, while Charles and the modiste between them decided which could be altered to fit, and which did nothing for her.

A trip to a milliner followed, and then to the bootmakers, where she had her feet measured for a last.

'You must be growing tired,' Charles eventually declared, when all his efforts to spoil his wife had met with supreme indifference.

Felice would have been in ecstasy to have had so much money spent on a wardrobe of such magnificence, not to mention his undivided attention in selecting it. But Heloise, he was coming to realise, cared as little for such fripperies as she did for him. He was not going to reach her by showering her with the kind of gifts that would win most women over.

'I have other business to attend to for the rest of the day,' he told her. 'But I shall be in for dinner this evening. Will you dine with me?'

Heloise blinked in surprise. He had spent hours with her today already. She had assumed he would have something better to do with his evening. But he had actually asked her to dine with him!

Struggling to conceal her elation, she had just taken a breath to form a suitably controlled reply when he added, 'Or would you rather remain in your room?'

Was that a veiled way of telling her that was what he wished her to do? Did he hope she would take the hint?

Well, she was blowed if she was going to take all her meals in her rooms as if…as if she were a naughty child!

'I will dine with you,' she said, with a militant lift to her chin.

As though she were about to face a firing squad, he thought, hurt by her response to a simple invitation.

'Until tonight, then.' He bowed, then stalked away.

The evening was not a success. Charles made polite enquiries about how she had spent the rest of her day, while they sat sipping sherry in an oppressively immaculate ante-room. He looked relieved when the footman came to inform them dinner was ready. She soon realised this was because they would no longer be alone. A troupe of footmen served a staggering variety of dishes, whisked away empty plates, poured wine, and effectively robbed the event of any hint of intimacy.

Her heart did begin to pound when Charles leaned forward, beckoning to her, indicating that he wished to whisper something to her. Only to plunge at his words.

'At this point it is the custom for ladies to withdraw. I shall join you in the drawing room when I have taken some port.'

Feeling humiliated that he'd had to remind her of this English custom, Heloise followed one of the younger footmen to a vast room that was so chilly her arms broke out in goose pimples the moment she stepped over the threshold. She sat huddled over the lacklustre fire for what seemed like an eternity before Charles joined her.

'Should you like to play cards?' he suggested. 'Some people find it helps to pass the time until the tea tray is brought in.'

He could not have made it clearer that this was the last way he wished to spend his evening.

'I enjoy cards as little as I care to pour that vile drink, which is fit only for an invalid, down my throat,' she replied rather petulantly.

'Most husbands,' he replied frostily, 'take themselves off to their clubs, where they find companionship and amusements they cannot find at home, leaving their wives free of their burdensome presence.'

As Heloise stormed up the stairs, she decided never to set foot in that horrible drawing room again. If Charles would rather go off to his club, then let him go! She did not care, she vowed, slamming her sitting room door behind her, almost knocking over one of the silly little tables dotted about the floor as she stormed across the room to fling herself onto the sofa.

She glared at it, and the collection of ornaments it held with resentment. She hated clutter. She would have to get a footman to move it against the wall, out of the way. After all, Charles had said she could do as she pleased up here.

A militant gleam came to her eye and she sat up straight. He had meant she could decorate as she pleased. But she could do much more than that. She dared not ask him for a proper drawing table, knowing how much he disapproved of her sketches, but if, under the pretext of reorganising her rooms, she had that one large desk moved to a spot between the two windows, to catch the maximum daylight…

Her spirits began to lift. Drawing was more than just a hobby to her. She could lose herself for hours in the fantasy world she created on paper. It had been a solace to her in Paris, where she had been such a disappointment to her parents. How much more would it comfort her here in London, as an unwanted bride?

Her fingers were already itching to draw Madame Pichot, with her peculiar accent that would only pass for French in England. She reminded her of a drawing she had seen in the Louvre, of a creature whose eyes stood out on stalks and which was said to change colour to match whatever type of background it walked across.

Though how she was to locate a really good shop where she could buy pencils, paper and brushes without Charles finding out, leave alone how she would pay for her materials, would pose quite a problem.

It was very late when Charles came up to bid her goodnight, as he had warned her he would do.

'Do you have everything you need?' he enquired politely.

'Yes, thank you,' she replied in an equally polite tone, her fingers plucking listlessly at the quilt.

'Then I will bid you goodnight,' he said, barely brushing his lips across her forehead.

Heloise glared at his back as he left, barely suppressing the urge to fling some pillows at it. She was not a child for him to come and kiss goodnight in that insufferably condescending manner! She was surprised he did not tuck her in and pat her on the head while he was about it!

But the sad truth was she was as inexperienced as a child. She had no idea how to encourage her husband to regard her as a woman rather than a girl. And there was no female to advise her. Her worst fear was that if she did try to breach his reserve she might only succeed in alienating him completely. She heaved a sigh as she sank down under the covers. At least *he* appeared content with the present situation.

Several evenings passed in an equally unsatisfactory manner before Heloise discovered a chink in Charles' armour.

When they met before dinner, and he enquired, as he always did, how she had spent her day, she told him that several outfits had arrived, and she had spent the afternoon trying them on.

'Was the riding habit among them?'

'Yes, and it is…' She bit her tongue. The pale blue gown with its silver frogging had instantly put her in mind of his servants' livery, and had made her crushingly aware that he only regarded her as just one more of his chattels. 'It is very pretty,' she finished in a subdued tone.

'If you are still determined to learn to ride, I could arrange for you to begin lessons with Robert tomorrow morning.' He frowned into his sherry glass for a few seconds, before saying softly, 'I bought him a lovely bay mare, very soft about the mouth, for Christmas. He has never even been to look her over. I shall be for ever in your debt—' he flicked her a glance '—if you could goad him into taking some form of exercise.'

'Of course!' she cried, immensely flattered that he had entrusted her with such an important mission. 'He must not stay in those dark rooms and moulder away.'

The rigid formality of the dining room was completely unable to dampen her spirits that night. For now she had a plan.

If she could be the means to help poor Robert get out of his rooms, Charles would be pleased with her. Riding lessons would only be the start. He could take her shopping for art supplies. And, though he might be sensitive about his scars, surely she could get him to take her to Vauxhall Gardens to watch the fireworks one evening? Buoyed up by the prospect, she received her husband's goodnight kiss with complaisance. Even though he was dressed in his evening clothes, and clearly on his way out.

One day, she vowed, snuggling down beneath the covers, he would take her with him on one of these forays into London's night life from which he had so far excluded her. If all went well with Robert in the morning, it might be quite soon!

The sound of the outer door slamming, not once, but twice, roused Charles from the pile of invitations he had been poring over in his study early the next morning. As the season got under way, more and more people were expressing an interest in meeting his bride. But he had no intention of exposing her to this collection of rakes, cynics, and bitches, he vowed, tossing a handful of gilt-edged invitations into the fire. It said something about his social circle that he thought it unlikely he would ever find a house into which he could take his vulnerable young bride without risk of having her confidence ripped to shreds.

'Stop right there!' he heard Robert bellow, just as he emerged from the study. Heloise, the back of her powder-blue riding habit liberally stained with mud, was fleeing up the stairs.

She did not even pause, but ran along the corridor to her rooms, from whence echoed the sound of yet another slamming door.

Robert, red-faced, had stopped at the foot of the staircase, clutching the newel post.

'Problems?' Charles drawled softly.

Robert spun round so swiftly the heel of his false leg slipped on the marble floor and he nearly lost his balance.

'Go on, then—order me to leave your house!' he panted.

Charles leaned against the doorjamb, folding his arms across his chest. 'Why do you suppose I should wish to do that?'

'Because I have insulted your bride,' Robert flung at him. 'I swore at her. Comprehensively and at length! You must have seen that she was crying when she fled up the stairs!'

Frowning, Charles pushed himself from the doorframe and advanced on his brother. 'If you have insulted her, it is for you to put right. This is your home. I shall not evict you from it.'

Glowering, Robert spat, 'And just how do you propose I make the apology? Crawl up all those stairs?'

Charles regarded the false leg his brother had, for the first time to his knowledge, strapped onto his mangled knee joint. Heloise was amazing. She had only been here a matter of days, and already she'd cajoled Robert out of his rooms, into his false leg, and onto the back of a horse.

'No,' he mused. 'Until she calms down, I dare say all that will happen is that she will inform you she hates you. Far better to wait until she has had time to reflect on her own part in your quarrel. I suggest you join us for dinner tonight, and make your apologies then.'

'Dinner?' Robert blustered. 'I had as well crawl to her suite now as to attempt ascending to any other rooms on the upper floors!'

'Then I will order dinner for the three of us in the little salon,' he replied, indicating a room across the hall. His heart beating with uncomfortable rapidity, he waited for Robert to protest that nothing would make him sit down and eat with the man who had been instrumental in causing his mother's death. Instead, he only glared mutinously before hobbling back to his own rooms and slamming the door behind him.

Upstairs, Heloise was blowing her nose vigorously. It was no good feeling sorry for herself. That her first riding lesson had been such a fiasco was not what upset her the most, though that had been bad enough. What really hurt was her failure to gain any ground with Robert at all. Charles would be so disappointed with her.

Startled by a tap on the door, she blew her nose again, annoyed to find her eyes were watering afresh.

'May I come in?'

Charles stood in the doorway, ruefully regarding his wife's crestfallen appearance. 'Was it the horse, or my brother?'

Waving admittance to the footman who hovered behind him, bearing a tray of what looked like His Lordship's finest brandy, Charles advanced into the room.

'I thought you might feel in need of a little restorative,' he explained, as the young man placed the silver salver on an elegant little table beside the sofa she had flung herself on when first she had come to her room. 'And, since I know of your aversion to tea, I thought I would supply something more to your liking.'

'You are m…most k…kind,' Heloise half sobbed, as Charles stooped to pick her riding hat up from the floor, where she had flung it not five minutes before. The feather that adorned the crown had snapped. He ran his fingers over it with a frown.

'Why is your hat on the floor? Is your dresser not in attendance?'

'I have not rung for her. I don't want her!' she snapped. Since he was already disappointed in her, she had nothing to lose by admitting she could not live up to his exacting standards. 'If I wish to throw my hat on the floor and…and stamp on it, then I have no wish to have her tutting at me as though I am a naughty child. It is my hat, after all, and I can do with it as I see fit!'

Instead of reprimanding her for her childish outburst, he merely smiled and remarked, 'I'll buy you another one,' tossing the crumpled headgear to the footman as he exited the rooms.

'I don't want another one,' Heloise said, perversely irritated by his magnanimity in the face of her tantrum. 'I am never getting on another horse again as long as I live.'

'I thought you scoffed at people who disliked falling from horses. I seem to remember you saying—'

'Yes, I remember very well what I said. If the horse had been trotting, or even walking, it might not have been so humiliating. But the horrid creature was standing perfectly still when I fell off. If I can fall off a stationary horse, which is being held at the head by a groom, I cannot think how much worse it will be should the brute try to move.'

'Are you badly hurt?' Charles frowned, suddenly wondering whether her tears and her evident discomfort might stem from more than wounded pride. 'Should I send for a doctor?'

So, after a perfunctory check, he was going to palm her off on another person? If they had the relationship a husband and wife ought to have, he would be running his hands over her bruises right now, assuring himself that nothing important was damaged. Instead of which he had handed her a drink, with a mocking smile twisting his lips.

'I don't need a doctor.' She sighed. I need a husband. A husband who would put his arms round me and tell me everything is all right, that he is not ashamed of his stupid little wife, or disappointed in her failure to help poor Robert.

Mutinously, she went to the bellrope and tugged on it viciously. 'I wish to change out of these clothes now,' she informed him. 'And take a bath. Unless there is anything else you wish to say to me?'

Charles bowed politely, remarking, 'Only that I hope, when your temper has cooled a little, you will endeavour to mend fences with Robert. I have invited him to dine with us this evening. It is the first time that he has agreed to do so. I would not wish it to be his last.'

Heloise glared at the door through which he departed. Not a word of thanks for her efforts, abortive though they had been. Only a stern warning to watch her behaviour at dinner this evening, so as not to offend his precious brother any further. He had not even bothered to find out what the boor had said to upset her!

Nothing she ever did would please him.

Very well, then, she would start pleasing herself. She

tore at the silver buttons of her riding habit with trembling fingers. She would dismiss the horrible dresser who looked down her nose at her. As a pair of housemaids came in, carrying towels and cans of hot water, she eyed them speculatively. Her husband seemed to employ dozens of staff. If she could not find one amongst them with whom she could strike up a tolerable relationship, then she would advertise for an experienced lady's maid and begin to conduct interviews. If nothing else, it would give her something to fill the endless monotony of her days.

And as for tonight... Oh, Lord! She sank into the steaming fragrant water of her bath and bowed her head over her raised knees. Charles would be watching her like a hawk. Robert would resent her for being the catalyst that had forced the two men to eat at the same table. She would be like a raw steak being fought over by two butcher's dogs.

By the time she entered the little salon Robert and Charles were already there, sitting on either side of the fireplace, sipping their drinks in a silence fraught with tension. Both, to her surprise, looked relieved to see her.

'I believe I owe you an apology,' Robert said, struggling to his feet.

She merely raised one eyebrow as she perched on the edge of the third chair which had been set before the hearth.

'All right, dash it! I *know* I owe you an apology. I should never have used such language to a female...'

'Not even a French female?' she replied archly, accepting the drink the footman handed to her. 'Who is not even of noble birth, is an enemy of your country, and most probably a spy to boot?'

Flushing darkly, Robert muttered, 'If I said any of those things to you this morning...'

'If?'

'All right. I admit I said a lot more besides the swearing I have reason to apologise for! But don't you think it is pretty disgusting behaviour to laugh at a cripple?'

'Oh, I was not laughing at you, Robert.' Heloise reached a hand towards him impulsively, her eyes filling with tears. 'No wonder you got so cross, if that was what you thought. It would indeed have been the most unforgivable behaviour if that was so!'

'But you were laughing…'

'It was the horse! When you went to climb onto him from the right side it looked so surprised. I have never seen such an expression on an animal's face before.' A smile twitched her lips at the memory. 'And it turned to stare at you, and it tried to turn round to place you on what it thought was the correct side, and the groom was dodging about under its head, and you were clutching onto the saddle to stop from falling off the mounting block…'

'I suppose it must have looked pretty funny from where you were sitting,' Robert grudgingly admitted. 'Only you have no idea how I felt—too damned clumsy to mount a slug like that, when I've always been accounted a natural in the saddle.'

'I'm sorry, Robert. But you have to admit I received just punishment for my thoughtlessness.'

He barked out a harsh laugh. 'Aye. You should have seen her, Walton. Laughed herself right out of the saddle. Lost her balance and landed on the cobbles at my feet…'

'With you swearing down at me while I was struggling to untangle all those yards of riding habit from my legs…'

'And the grooms not knowing where to look, or how to keep their faces straight…'

'It sounds better than the pantomime,' Charles put in

dryly. 'Ah, Giddings, it is good to see you back with us. I take it your presence indicates that our dinner is ready?'

Charles had tactfully arranged for the meal to be brought to a small round table set in the alcove formed by the bay windows, so that Robert had very little walking to do.

Linney took a position behind Robert's chair. When Charles' footman approached him with a tureen of soup, the man took it from him, ladling a portion into a bowl for his master himself. For the first time it occurred to Heloise just how difficult it must be to eat a meal with only one arm, and how demeaning it must be for a man in his prime to have to rely on someone else to cut up his food for him. How he must hate having others watching the proof of his disability.

Desperate to introduce some topic of conversation— anything to break the strained silence which reigned at the table—she asked Giddings, 'Did I not meet you in Paris?'

Although he was somewhat surprised to be addressed, the butler regally inclined his head in the affirmative.

'How was your trip back to England? I hope your crossing was smooth?'

'Indeed, once I was at sea I felt heartily relieved, my lady,' he unbent enough to admit.

'Did you dislike France so much?'

The butler looked to his lordship for a cue as to how he should answer. Instead, Charles answered for him.

'You have evidently not heard the news, my lady. Bona-parte has escaped from Elba. On the very eve of our marriage, he landed at Cannes with a thousand men and began his march on Paris.'

'Damn the fellow!' Robert put in. 'Has there been much fighting? King Louis must have sent troops to intercept him?'

Charles again gestured to Giddings, which the butler interpreted correctly as permission to tell his tale himself.

'The last I heard, every regiment sent for the purpose of arresting him joined him the minute they saw him in person.'

'It is no surprise, that,' Heloise said darkly. 'He has a way with the soldiers that makes them worship him.'

'By the time I reached Calais,' Giddings continued, 'fugitives from Paris were catching up with me, telling tales of the desperate measures they had taken to get themselves out of the city before he arrived. The price of any sort of conveyance had gone through the roof.'

'Thank heavens we married when we did,' Charles remarked. 'Else we might have been caught up in that undignified scramble.'

'Is all you can think of your precious dignity?' Robert retorted. 'And how can *you*—' he rounded on Heloise '—be so bacon-brained as to worship that Corsican tyrant?'

'I did not say *I* worship him!' Heloise snapped. First Charles had made light of the convenience of their marriage, and now Robert had jumped to a completely false conclusion about her. 'Do you think I want to see my country back in a state of war? Do you think any woman in France is ready to see her brothers and sweethearts sacrificed to Bonaparte's ambition? It is only men who think it is a fine thing to go about shooting each other!'

'Now, steady on, there,' Robert said, completely taken aback by the vehemence of her reply, and the tears that had sprung to Heloise's eyes. 'There's no need to fly into such a pucker…'

'Not at the dining table,' put in Charles.

'Oh, you!' She flung her napkin down as she leapt to her

feet. 'All you care about is manners and appearances. Men in Paris might be fighting and dying, but all you can do is frown because I speak to a servant as if he is a real person, and say what I really think to your so rude beast of a brother!'

'This is neither the time nor place—'

'When will it *ever* be the time or the place with you, Charles?' she cried. Then, seeing all hope torn from her— not only for her marriage, but also for her country—she burst into sobs and left the room.

For a few moments the brothers sat in an uneasy silence.

'Dammit, Walton,' Robert said at last, flinging his spoon down with a clatter. 'I didn't mean to upset her so.'

'I dare say she is anxious over the safety of her parents,' Charles replied abstractedly. Did she really think he was so shallow all he cared about was good manners? 'Giddings, give Her Ladyship an hour to calm down, then take a tray up to her room. As for you—' he turned to Robert with a cool look. '—I suggest you finish your meal while you consider ways to make amends for insulting my wife and making her cry for the second time in one day.'

Chapter Seven

'Charles, you will never guess what has happened!'
Heloise greeted her husband, when he came in to bid her
goodnight several nights later.

She was not clutching the sheets nervously to her chest
for once, Charles observed. Sadly, the robe which matched
the gossamer-fine nightgown she wore was fastened
demurely across her breasts, rather than lying provocatively across the ottoman. Though she was getting used to
him visiting her room, she had no intention of inviting him
into her bed.

Still, it was a small step in the right direction. There were
other indications that she was gaining confidence in her
position as his wife, too. She had ordered some lower
footmen to rearrange her furniture without asking his permission. She had dismissed the dresser and the maid he had
engaged for her. Then, as though wondering just how far she
dared push him, she had promoted the scrubby little girl who
cleaned the grates and lit the fires to the position of her maid.

She had then gone to Cummings and asked how she
might go about doing some personal shopping.

Was that what had put the sparkle in her eyes tonight? Discovering from his secretary what a generous allowance he had arranged for her to have?

He took his seat at her bedside with a vague feeling of disappointment.

'Robert is going to take me to Vauxhall Gardens to see the fireworks! Is that not wonderful?'

His disappointment evaporated. Her pleasure stemmed from mending a quarrel with his brother rather than a so far concealed streak of avarice.

'He said that he cannot take me anywhere by daylight, but if we kept to shadowy walks, so that nobody can raise objections to the state of his face, it might not be too bad. Charles, this is something I do not understand.' Her brow puckered with confusion. 'Nobody looks askance at a soldier on the boulevards of Paris, no matter how grotesque his injuries!'

'But you have had conscription in France for many years. Everybody feels more personally involved in the war. Anyone's brother or husband could easily suffer the same fate as those poor wretches.' He sighed. 'Heloise, you must understand that most people are basically selfish. They come to town to enjoy themselves. They want to gossip and flirt and dance. Seeing a man like Robert is a reminder that life can be ugly and brutal. And they don't want reminders that outside their charmed circle men are fighting and dying to ensure their freedoms.'

Heloise felt a twinge of guilt. She herself had become so preoccupied with her husband, and how she could win his approval, that she had not spared Bonaparte a thought for days.

'I trust you have not fixed tomorrow evening for your outing to Vauxhall?' Charles frowned. It had suddenly occurred to him that it would look very odd if her first outing in public was taken in the company of her brother-in-law. He rapidly reviewed the entertainments available to him for the next evening.

And wondered why he had never thought of it before.

'You will be accompanying me to the theatre.' It had worked well for them in Paris. Why should it not work here?

'I…I will?' Finally, *finally* he was going to permit her to appear in public as his bride!

And people would look at how small and plain she was, and wonder why on earth he had married her when he could have had any woman for the lifting of his finger.

Charles watched the joy drain from her face.

'Is the primrose satin ready?' he asked tersely, refusing to voice his hurt.

It was not her fault she regarded an outing with him as a duty to be borne, when a trip to Vauxhall Gardens with his half-brother filled her with eager anticipation.

When she nodded, he said, 'Wear it tomorrow.' Without further comment, he gave her the kiss which was always the prelude to leaving her room.

It was only after he had gone that she allowed herself to feel resentful that he had not bothered to thank her for getting Robert to venture out of doors. Nobody else had succeeded in so much as rousing him out of his rooms for months. But could Charles unbend towards her enough to applaud her achievement? Not he!

But she still, foolishly, studied his face for some sign of approval as she descended the stairs the following evening, dressed according to his dictates. She felt a little uncomfortable in the high-waisted gown which would have left her arms completely bare were it not for the matching gloves that came past her elbows. The neckline glittered with the most intricate beadwork Heloise had ever seen. The motif of thistle-heads and leaves was picked up in the self-coloured stitching on her gloves, and repeated around the three flounces on her skirts.

'Come into my study for a moment before we leave,' he said, crooking his finger imperiously. His guarded expression told her nothing. 'I have something I wish to give you.'

She followed him, her stomach feeling as though a nest of snakes had taken up residence there. She was thrilled he was taking her out, desperate to be a credit to him, terrified she would let him down, and agonisingly conscious of every single one of her physical deficiencies.

Walking to his desk, he opened a large, square leather case which had been lying on it, and pushed it towards her across the polished mahogany surface. Inside, nestling on a bed of black velvet, was a parure consisting of necklace, bracelet, earrings and an aigrette of pale yellow gems, in a rather heavy and elaborate setting of gold. From another box, which he produced from his pocket, he took a matching ring.

'I wished to have given you this sooner, but on returning to London and examining it I found it needed cleaning.'

'Oh?' Her eyes filled with tears as he slid the ring, which fitted perfectly, onto her finger. He had bought Felice a ring that matched her eyes. When he had given it to her, he had said no jewel could compare with them. He had merely had some old baubles he'd had to hand cleaned up for his plain and undeserving wife.

Still, at least she understood now why he had ordered her to wear the primrose satin. There were not many fabrics that could complement such unusually coloured gems as the ones he lifted from the box and fastened in her ears.

'Perfect,' he said, standing back to admire the effect of the earrings glittering against the curtain of his wife's dark hair.

Heloise stiffened her spine, stifling her momentary pang of self-pity. She had always known she was a second-best wife. Of course she would only get second-hand jewels! What had she expected? That her husband would begin to act out of character and forget that she was not the woman he had wanted to marry?

He was being very kind, considering the way she had acted since being installed in his home. He had never, for example, upbraided her for the scene she had created at dinner, when she knew such behaviour was what he deplored above all else. He had merely sent her food up to her room.

Because he was, she suddenly realised, a kind man underneath those chillingly controlled manners. It was why she had never really been able to stay afraid of him for longer than a minute at a time. Why she had been able to confide in him from the very first. She had even been secure enough to give way to the childish temper tantrums that her brother had predicted would drive any husband to give her a beating.

Charles would never beat her. He did not, she saw with a sinking heart, care enough about her to lose that glacial self-control.

'I couldn't have you going out without any jewellery, could I?' he said, fastening the necklace round her throat.

'No, I suppose not,' she replied. He might not care about her much, but he cared about his own reputation. His Countess could not appear in public without adequate adornment. The dress, the jewels—they were just the costume that made her look the part she was playing.

Charles was rather perplexed by Heloise's response. He

had just hung diamonds worth a king's ransom around her neck, and instead of going into raptures she seemed weighed down.

Could she be nervous at suddenly having so much wealth displayed upon her person? She had never owned much jewellery before.

Nor wanted it. She had not even been tempted to try on the emerald ring that had been her sister's.

'These are yours by right as my wife, you know, Heloise.' The set of yellow diamonds had been in his family for generations, handed down to each new bride upon her wedding—except for the ring, which was given upon the occasion of the betrothal. 'It never felt right that you had to wear that ring I bought in Paris.'

'I shall never wear it again,' she vowed. It must remind him of all he had lost! And while she had been complaining to herself of all that she did not have, she had entirely forgotten that her husband was still trying to recover from his broken heart. He was so good at disguising his emotions that it took moments like this to remind her how much he must still be hurting.

'What are we going to see at the theatre tonight?' she said, deciding that he would be more comfortable if they talked about trivial matters.

'The *beau monde*,' he quipped, taking her arm and leading her to the door. He was glad he had taken that moment to reassure her. Now that she had got over her initial reluctance to accept the family heirlooms, she might even be able to enjoy herself a little. 'As in Paris, we go to the theatre to see who is in the audience, not what is being performed upon the stage. I expect that during the intervals persons wishing for an introduction to my new Countess will besiege our box. They will probably think,' he remarked dryly, 'that they will be able to get to me through you. I hope you will not be taken in.' He frowned. 'It would be best if you did not associate with anyone without checking their credentials with me first.'

Heloise was virtually silent all evening. At first, Charles wondered if he had said something to offend her. She had lifted her chin as he'd handed her to her seat, and stared fixedly at the stage throughout the first act. Fortunately, this had left her oblivious to the stir her appearance, decked in the Walton diamonds, had created.

Gradually, he recognised that this was the Heloise he had first become acquainted with. The quiet, reserved girl that nobody noticed. Who observed but did not participate. This public Heloise was a far cry from the termagant who yelled at his brother, flounced out of rooms, slammed doors, and rattled on without pausing to draw breath.

He welcomed her return when they got into the carriage to go home.

'Charles,' she breathed, leaning forward and tapping his knee with her ivory-handled fan. 'Who was that dreadful man—the great big dark one who accosted us in the corridor during the interval?'

He smiled wryly. He had assumed it would be easier to control exactly whom he permitted to approach her if they went for a stroll, rather than sitting passively in their box and letting the importunate besiege them.

'Lord Lensborough,' he replied, no doubt in his mind as to who she meant.

The Marquis had stood directly in their path, blocking their progress. And when he had said, 'Allow me to felicitate you upon your marriage,' his hostility had been unmistakable.

'Is he one of the family you won't speak to because of what they did to Robert?'

'Far from it. If anything, he regards himself as Robert's champion. His own brother, who serves in Robert's former regiment, was so concerned about the Turkish treatment I would mete out, he wrote begging Lensborough to watch over him.'

'Oh. I am so sorry.' Heloise laid one gloved hand upon her husband's sleeve.

'For what?' It was ridiculous, he reflected with a frown, that his spirits should lift just because she had forgotten herself so far as to reach out and touch him.

'That people should so misunderstand you. What do they think you mean to do with Robert? Is he not your brother? Your heir?'

'Alas, from Lord Lensborough's reaction this evening, I fear they suspect that I mean to cut him out by siring an heir of my own. Through you.'

'Well, that just goes to show,' she said, snatching back her hand, remembering his reaction when she had made such an impulsive gesture once before, 'how silly they are.' Couldn't they see how devoted Charles was to his brother? Didn't they understand how outraged he had been by the way his guardians had tried to cut him out of the succession?

Charles sighed. The reminder that she would one day have to face this distasteful duty as a wife had brought about an instant withdrawal.

But at least when he went to her room later, to bid her goodnight, she seemed to be in good spirits.

'Thank you for this evening, Charles,' she said prettily, when he bent to bestow a chaste salutation on her forehead. 'I did enjoy it.'

'Really?' He frowned. 'I thought you seemed…abstracted.'

'Oh, well…' She fidgeted nervously with the ties of her robe, her cheeks flushing pink as she averted her eyes from his.

Ah! She was relieved it was over. But she did not wish to wound him by confessing as much.

She wanted him gone. Very well, he would oblige her! He would not force his unwelcome presence on her a moment longer. Turning on his heel, he stalked from the room.

Heaving a sigh of relief, Heloise flung back the covers and went to the desk which she had converted to a drawing table. She had nearly given the game away then. It was just that there had been so many odd people at the theatre. And the knowledge that there was, at last, a fresh sheaf of drawing paper and a selection of really good-quality pencils hidden in a box beneath her bed was like a tonic fizzing through her veins. Now that she was a countess, with an army of staff at her disposal, she did not have to search the shops for what she wanted. She simply sent her maid, Sukey, with a list, and *voilà!* After an hour or so the girl returned with exactly what she requested! And, since Sukey was so grateful for the meteoric rise in her status, she would rather cut her own throat, she had breathed dramatically, than ever betray Her Ladyship's confidence.

Heloise only felt a small twinge of conscience for continuing with a pastime Charles frowned upon. So long as he did not find out, it could not hurt him.

And so many ideas had flooded to her while she had been studying the crowds tonight. *Beau monde!* She scoffed as she pulled a stool to her desk and lit the two lamps she had placed there for moments such as this. There was nothing *beau* about the manners of some of those people! They ignored the efforts of the actors upon the stage for the most part, which was rude, since they had clearly gone to a great deal of effort for the entertainment of an audience that was interested only in its own members. Except for certain of the men, when the pretty young dancers came on. Then it was all tongues hanging out and nudging elbows, and comments which she was certain were coarse, though fortunately she had not been able to hear them. And as for that obnoxious marquis, who harboured such uncharitable thoughts towards both Charles and herself…well! She had seen the plump little blonde sitting beside him in his own private box, giving him sheep's eyes. A woman who was clearly not his wife. And he had the temerity to look askance at *her*!

Dawn was filtering through her curtains before Heloise began to yawn. Her excitement had driven her to fill page after page with initial sketches. Later, when she had the interminable hours of daylight to fill, she would add the detail and bring the scenes to life with judicious touches of watercolour paint. Yes… She yawned again, sloughing off her robe and letting it drop to the floor. There was much to be said about an evening spent at the English theatre.

And tonight the pleasure gardens of Vauxhall would provide even more material for her portfolio.

Robert was to dine with them both before taking her out. Charles had sent a note to inform her.

This time there were no arguments. There was scarcely any conversation at all. It was as though all three of them were determined to say nothing that might spark another confrontation.

Eventually, Charles remarked, 'I shall not be dining at home for the next few evenings, Lady Walton. I warned you before we married that I have an interest in politics. And at this particular time, with Bonaparte on the rampage again, you will appreciate that I must be busy in the affairs of my country.'

Of course she understood. In Paris, it was in the private salons of influential hostesses that statesmen decided which line they were going to take in public. Similar meetings must go on in London.

She nodded. Robert scowled.

She was not surprised when, the second they got into Walton's private carriage, which he had put at their disposal for the outing, Robert blurted, 'He's not going to back those fools who want to try and appease Bonaparte, is he?'

'I do not know,' she shrugged. They never talked about anything. 'All I know is what you heard him say. Charles will be too busy to bother with me for a while.'

Robert looked perplexed. 'I'm sure he did not mean that. You must admit, Bonaparte escaping like that, and winning over the army that was sent to arrest him, has caused the deuce of a panic all over Europe.'

She turned bleak eyes in his direction, though she could only make out his silhouette. Somehow, in the darkness of the jolting carriage, it was easy to let her hurt spill out. 'It is not a question of him suddenly being busy. He has never wanted to spend more time with me than he has to.'

'Cold-hearted wretch,' she heard Robert growl.

'No, you must not say such things,' Heloise protested. 'Really, he is most kind to me…'

'Kind! To leave you alone in your room, night after night, while he goes out on the town? Oh, don't think because I stay in my rooms I don't know what goes on in this house. The way he neglects you. Look.' He leaned forward, his earnest expression illuminated for a second as they passed under a street lamp. 'I may not be able to introduce you to the elevated set my brother belongs to, but I do have friends in town. You'd probably enjoy yourself a deal more with them, anyway, than at the stuffy *ton* gatherings Walton frequents. I'll…' He drew in a breath, as though steeling himself to go on. 'I'll introduce you to them. I will not,' he stipulated, 'escort you to picnics, or go boating, or anything of that nature. But once you get to know a few people you'll have no shortage of invitations to all the sorts of things females of your age enjoy.'

Sitting back, and running a hand over his perspiring brow, he grumbled, 'Why Walton hasn't seen to it himself beats me.'

Heloise was torn. On the one hand she wanted to defend Charles' actions. And yet there was no doubt she could use Robert's misapprehension to get him to renew contact with the friends he had shut himself away from for far too long.

It would take something as radical as his ingrained hatred for his brother for him to run the gauntlet of public reaction, she began to realise as the evening wore on. She lost count of the number of dandies who lifted their lace handkerchiefs to their noses as they sauntered past, eyes swiftly averted. She grew furious with the females who placed troubled hands to their breasts, as though the very sight of Robert was too distressing for their delicate sensibilities. She was beginning to wish she had not dragged Robert out and exposed him to such a cruel and humiliating reception.

Spying a bench, positioned in a secluded nook for the convenience of clandestine lovers, Robert limped to it and sat down heavily. His false leg might have been fashioned by the most skilled craftsman Walton could hire, but learning to walk in it was clearly no easy matter.

'Oh, Lord,' Robert moaned. 'Here comes another one of 'em.'

Heloise sat forward, to look round Robert and see who he meant, and spied Lord Lensborough strolling towards them, the plump blonde on his arm.

'I thought he was your friend.'

'No,' replied Robert shortly.

As he drew level with them, Lord Lensborough paused, eyeing them closely.

'My lady,' he said, bowing slightly. 'Captain Fawley. How…interesting to see you here, of all places.'

The blonde giggled, alerting Heloise to the fact that his sneering words could as well mean this particular secluded bench as Vauxhall Gardens. Beside her, she felt Robert stiffen.

'A word in private, if you please, Lensborough?' Robert growled.

The Marquis sloughed the blonde from his arm, taking a seat on the far side of Robert. The blonde seemed inured to such cavalier treatment, wandering off a few paces without expecting to be introduced, let alone take part in the general conversation. Indignant on her behalf at such rudeness, Heloise got to her feet, deciding she would go and introduce herself.

'Hello,' she said, offering her hand to the startled blonde.

Warily, she looked to Lord Lensborough for her cue. But since he had his head close to Robert, and they were engaged in such deep conversation that they were oblivious to what she might be doing, she protested, 'You didn't ought to be talking to the likes of me—a great lady like you.'

'Well, if I did not I would be sitting being ignored. Since you are being ignored as well, we might as well amuse each other, don't you think?'

The blonde smiled uncertainly.

'I saw you at the theatre yesterday evening, did I not?' Heloise asked, since the blonde still seemed unwilling to initiate any conversation.

'Yes, and I saw you too. With your husband. The Earl. Ever so nice you looked. That gown was from Madame Pichot's, wasn't it?' When Heloise nodded, she went on, 'Oh, I should love to have a gown from her. Your husband is ever so generous, ain't he? Mrs Kenton was always saying it, and when I saw those rubies he gave her...' She trailed off, suddenly looking guilty. 'I shouldn't be mentioning the likes of Mrs Kenton, or what your husband gives her,' she continued, hanging her head. 'Jasper is always telling me I talk too much...'

'It is of no matter to me.' Gritting her teeth, Heloise smiled bravely at Lord Lensborough's ladybird. 'Men of his rank always have mistresses.'

When the nameless blonde smiled in obvious relief, Heloise knew that the simple creature had just inadvertently revealed the name of Charles' mistress. She had always known he would have one. But it was a shock, all the same, to find out her name at a moment when she was least expecting it.

Feeling a little sick, she turned back to Robert.

'I wish to return home now,' she said, pointedly ignoring the Marquis, who had so far done the same to her.

'I shall be only too glad to take you. I'm devilish tired.'

To her surprise, as Robert struggled to get up, the Marquis also rose to his feet, and made her a respectably deep bow. Pinning her with an intent look, he said, 'I have issued an invitation to you and my young friend for an evening at Challinor House. Quite informal. A little supper, some hands of cards…'

Though she felt certain the last thing the Marquis wanted was to have her enter his home, she also knew he had Robert's welfare at heart.

'I don't mind taking you to play cards at Lensborough's,' Robert admitted gruffly. 'But not the supper.'

She winced at the memory of Linney cutting up Robert's food for him. 'It sounds delightful. I love above all things to play cards,' she lied.

Her ineptitude at the card table was one of the faults for which her father had frequently berated her. But people were so fascinating when they forgot company manners to concentrate on their game. Far more interesting than the little pieces of board she held in her hand, or the points she should have been counting in her head. However, Robert needed to believe she wished to play, and wanted his escort.

Bowing to her with a tight smile, the Marquis gathered up his companion and took his leave.

Neither of them was very talkative on the way home. Robert's face had the waxy pallor of a man close to exhaustion. And Heloise was wrestling with the turbulence of her thoughts.

She was not sorry, now, that she had let Robert think badly of Charles. It would motivate him to take her out, so that she could make her own friends. Which would leave Charles free to live his own life.

With his Mrs Kenton.

Somehow she would learn to cope. At least if she concentrated on helping Robert to regain his self-esteem it would stop her wallowing in her own unhappiness. It would be her mission, she decided, squaring her shoulders.

It was not until they made to go their separate ways, in the hall of Walton House, that he turned to her and said, in a voice hoarse with emotion, 'My brother is a prize idiot not to see what a treasure you are. If he won't treat you as he should, then, dammit, I will!'

'Oh, Robert,' she said, rather tearfully. Nobody could force her husband to grow fond of her. 'It is enough that you agree to take me out now and again. I have been…' She paused as her breath hitched in her throat. 'So lonely since I came to London.'

Impulsively, she flung her arms round him, almost causing him to overbalance.

'I say—steady on!' Robert laughed.

'I cannot help it,' she declared with feeling. 'You are the only friend I have.'

Neither of them heard the door to the small salon close quietly as Charles withdrew behind it. He had been a little anxious all evening about how Heloise would cope with his irascible brother. Given the way things usually turned out whenever Heloise tried to 'help' his brother, he had been preparing to go and pour oil onto troubled waters. He had not, he thought, recoiling from the scene he had just witnessed, expected to see his brother make a declaration of that sort to his wife—nor for her to respond so enthusiastically!

Nor had he expected the searing pain that left him gasping for breath.

For a few moments he gripped the edge of the mantel, leaning his forehead against the cool marble and taking deep, steadying breaths, while his heartbeat gradually returned to something like normal.

Why in Hades was he so upset?

It was not as if he was in love with Heloise. It was a proprietorial thing. That was all. He had always felt the same disgust when one of his mistresses had shown affection for another man while under his protection.

Had he made it clear to Heloise, when laying down the terms of their union, that, while he was willing to let her lead her own life, he would not tolerate her taking a lover? At least not until after she had given him an heir.

It probably hurt all the more that it was his own brother who had so effortlessly breached the defences he had lain siege to weeks ago. He laughed bitterly. All he'd had to do was trim his hair, put on clean linen, and take her to watch some fireworks!

He strode to the salon door and flung it open. The scene he had witnessed was only the opening round in the dance that went on between a man and a woman. He would have to make Heloise understand that it must progress no further, he thought, as he pounded up the stairs to her room.

He gave only a peremptory knock before striding into her bedroom. She was not yet in bed, but standing by her dressing table in the act of disrobing.

At his entrance, the maid uttered a little shriek, her hands flying to her cheeks. Heloise's gown, already half undone, slithered to the floor, leaving her standing in just a flimsy chemise. She had already removed her shoes and stockings.

He had never seen so much of her. Slowly, his blood thickening, he examined every perfect inch of her—from her flushed cheeks, down her slender arms, past her shapely calves and ankles to the ten naked toes she was curling into the soft blue carpet. She was exquisite. And he wanted to stake his claim right now.

'Sukey,' she said in a reedy voice, 'hand me my wrap, then you may leave us.' Whatever Charles wanted must be important for him to be displaying such an uncharacteristic lack of manners.

His eyes flicked upwards. She was fastening the belt tightly, with fingers that trembled.

Moodily he paced to her desk, looking blindly at the sheets of paper scattered on it, seeing only the anxiety in her eyes when he had invaded the sanctuary of her bedroom.

'I am writing a letter to my sister,' she said, breathy with panic as she gathered the loose pages and stacked them neatly together before he got a chance to glimpse any of the sketches she had been working on lately.

Stuffing the pages into a drawer, she turned to him warily.

'You did not forbid me, so I have written several times. I suppose that now you will tell me I must stop?' she finished gloomily.

She still thought of him as a tyrant, he realised, reeling from her. Hadn't he made any progress with her at all? If she still believed he would forbid her contact with her family, no wonder she turned to his brother for comfort.

'Heloise,' he ground out, seizing her by her shoulders, 'didn't I tell you that all I want is for you to be happy as my wife?'

'N…no, you didn't,' she stunned him by stammering.

'Of course I did!' He paced away from her, running his fingers through his hair. He had made it absolutely clear, on more than one occasion. Hadn't he? 'Well, I am telling you now!' he exclaimed.

Why, when he had just told her he wanted her to be happy, was she shrinking from him like that?

There must be something he could do to drive that scared look from her face. Perhaps he could begin by reassuring her that he did not, as she assumed, frown on her corresponding with her sister.

'If you want to write to your sister, of course you may. Has Felice replied to your letters?' he said, in as calm a tone as he could muster. 'How is she?'

'She reached Switzerland safely, and—' she swallowed, loath to be the one to break the news '—she has married Jean-Claude.'

Charles struggled to find something else to say. How did a man go about gentling a nervous female? He didn't know.

He only knew that he had to get out of here before he tore the damned wrapper that she was clutching to her throat like a shield from her perfect, enticing young body, and proved conclusively that he was the monster of her imagination.

Muttering an oath, he beat a hasty retreat.

'Whatever has got into His Lordship?' Sukey said, as she emerged timidly from the dressing room, where she had taken refuge. 'I've never seen him in such a pucker.'

'I have no idea.'

All she did know was that for the first time since their marriage he had not kissed her goodnight. No. Tonight, with thoughts of Felice running through his mind, he could not bear to touch her at all.

He was probably already on his way to his Mrs Kenton, to seek the solace his unappealing wife was too naïve to know how to offer.

'No idea,' she repeated dully.

Chapter Eight

'I do not agree!' Heloise returned her soup spoon to the bowl, the consommé untouched.

Robert glowered at her across the table. 'I suppose you think all the other European nations should just let Bonaparte take up where he left off, then?'

'That was not what I said!'

It was at moments like this that she was at her most attractive, Charles reflected, sipping his wine. And he only ever saw her this animated these days when Robert was around.

On the few occasions she could spare time from her increasingly hectic social life to accompany him to a ball, or rout, she behaved with extreme modesty and decorum.

He got the 'public' Heloise.

Not this vibrant, intelligent woman who held such passionate views.

She picked up her spoon again, her mind so fully locked in the tussle with Robert she didn't notice that she spattered droplets of consommé across the snowy damask tablecloth.

'I just meant that there might not need to be another war. There has not been any fighting in France...'

'Only because anyone who might have opposed Bonaparte's return has turned tail and fled. Why do you think he's amassing an army, you silly goose? Do you think he means to march them up and down the Champs-Elysées to entertain the tourists?'

'There are no tourists left in Paris,' Charles pointed out pedantically. 'They have all run for their lives.'

Heloise and Robert turned to stare at him, his wife's face creased with frustration, his brother's lip curling in contempt.

Flicking his finger to Giddings, Charles indicated it was time to remove the cooling soup and bring on the next course.

To all intents and purposes things could not be progressing better. He had wanted Heloise to make her own way in society. He had wanted Robert to get well.

He had not imagined the two events, taken in tandem, would make him feel like an intruder in his own home.

'There was no need for the tourists to flee,' Heloise said to him carefully. 'Your Whig politicians are pressing to make the treaty with Bonaparte...'

'While the allies gathered in Vienna have just declared him an outlaw!' scoffed Robert.

Charles frequently heard them bickering like this when they returned home of an evening. He was growing increasingly resentful that it was Robert with whom she felt easy enough to speak her mind. But that was nothing to what he felt when he heard them laughing together.

What kind of fool resented hearing his wife enjoying herself? Or watched his own brother's return to health and vigour with a sense of dread?

His lips twisted in self-mockery as he dug into a dish of lamb fricassee.

Heloise took only a small portion of the stew, which was

on tonight's menu so that Robert would have at least one dish from each course that he could manage for himself. She glowered at him as Linney spooned onion sauce onto his plate. She wished Charles would not invite Robert to dine with them quite so often. He ruined all her attempts to impress her husband with her increasing grasp of British politics. She had spent hours poring over the newspapers and questioning Cummings, to no avail. Robert took her up on every point, arguing with her until she became hopelessly enmired and tripped herself up. Confirming her husband's opinion she was the greatest idiot he had ever met. She only had to see the mocking way he was smiling now to know what he thought of her intellectual capabilities.

Well, she would soon wipe that smirk off his face!

'So—this masquerade you take me to at the Opera House this evening. Will it be very disgraceful?'

She had the satisfaction of causing Robert to choke on his wine. He had lectured her at length upon the importance of *not* telling her husband where they were headed tonight. Charles would strongly disapprove of his wife disporting herself at a venue where ladies of quality simply did not venture, he had warned her.

'Of course it would be,' he said hastily, 'if anyone was to find out you had gone there. But I've taken all the precautions necessary to protect your reputation. We will both be wearing masks and cloaks, and travelling in a plain carriage.'

Though he addressed the last part of this to his half-brother, Charles' face remained impassive.

'I say, you don't mind me taking Heloise there, do you?' Robert put in uneasily.

'If it amuses her to go to such places—' he shrugged

'—who am I to deny her? I have told her she may enjoy herself exactly as she pleases.'

She felt as if he had slapped her. Robert was always saying how generous it was of her husband to leave the Walton coach and driver at her disposal, but she knew better. He didn't care how many servants he had to pay to keep her out of his hair. Oh, he went through the motions of squiring her to at least one event 'every se'en night or so', as he'd put it, 'for form's sake'. But she knew, from the very way he carried himself on those occasions, that he was not enjoying her company.

'Well, then,' she said, rising to her feet and tossing the napkin to the table, 'I shall go and fetch my cloak. Tonight, Robert, you will get the proof that all I have been saying is correct.'

Charles went cold inside. Had he just inadvertently given his wife the go-ahead to commence an affair with Robert by saying she could do as she pleased?

He heard Robert's chair scrape back, heard him mutter that he would wait for Heloise in the hall, but all he could see was her face—the defiant look in her eyes as she said, 'Tonight, Robert.'

Sweat broke out on his brow.

Tonight.

Around him the footmen were clearing away the dishes, removing the cloth, pouring the port.

He had instinctively known they couldn't be lovers. Not yet. Apart from the fact Robert was scarcely fit enough, Heloise was not the kind of woman to break her marriage vows so quickly.

She had never been able to deal in deceit. Her father had said it was because she was too stupid, but he liked to think it was because she was too honest.

But if he didn't do something to put a spoke in Robert's wheel it would happen. How could Robert not desire her when she turned those flashing eyes up at him, or laughed at one of his sarcasms? She was so full of life. It was all any man could do to keep his hands off her. And she was clearly growing increasingly fond of him. It was only natural. They were far closer in age, their tastes seemed to mesh...

He was damned if he was going to sit at home and let his brother seduce his wife out from under him!

Leaving his port untouched, he rose from the table and, like a man on a mission, made his way up to his rooms. He had purchased a domino and mask for a private masquerade himself, the previous autumn. If his valet knew where to lay his hands on the outfit, he would track his wife and brother down at the masquerade and observe them undetected. The grotesque devil's mask that would cover his upper face was of red satin, matching the lining of the black velvet domino. He would look nothing like his usual civilised, conventional self in that disguise. Hell, he scarcely recognised himself any more. What kind of jealous fool stalked his wife and spied on his half-brother?

After the dire warnings Robert had given her, Heloise was surprised to discover the Opera House was not the shabby, ill-lit lair of her imagination, but a rather elegantly appointed theatre. Four tiers of boxes, decorated in white and gold, surrounded a stage upon which people in a variety of disguises were dancing.

'It's still not too late to turn back,' Robert urged her. 'So far you have not stepped over that invisible line which separates you from scandal. But if you set so much as a toe across it, I warn you, you will unleash consequences so dire...'

She tossed her head. 'I am no coward, to cringe at the threat of these vague consequences! But if you are afraid…'

Robert drew himself up. 'If I am wary, it is not on my own account, I assure you.'

'Isn't it?' she taunted. 'Isn't it truly the prospect of the rejection of females that has you quaking like a blanc-mange tonight? For I cannot believe you are suddenly afraid of what Charles might do—not after some of the places you have been taking me to…'

'Only because you asked me to!' he protested, twitching her simple black domino over her evening gown. 'For God's sake, if we are going to stay, keep yourself covered up,' he urged, taking her arm and tugging her towards one of the boxes on the lowest tier. 'And don't do anything or say anything that might give anyone a clue as to who you are. If you think you can shock Walton into taking more notice of you, you need your head examining!'

She almost laughed aloud at Robert's misapprehension. She had long since given up any hope of making Charles regard her with anything more than bored indifference.

But Mrs Kenton was a different matter.

She was not going to permit That Woman to sneer at her and pity her and crow over her for being the one who had Charles in her bed every night!

It had been Nell, Lord Lensborough's plump blonde mistress, who had introduced the two women one evening, when Heloise had gone unaccompanied to a small party being held by one of Robert's friends. At the last minute he had confessed he was not feeling up to it, but, at the look of disappointment on her face, had told her there was nothing to stop her going alone.

From the outside, the house had looked completely respectable. It had only been once she had stepped inside she'd realised she ought not to have gone. The guests had nearly all been young, single military gentlemen, who had already been growing rather boisterous. She had intended to say hello to her host, a Mr Farrar, and slip away, when Nell had come bounding up to her. The dear silly creature had noticed her looking a little flustered upon coming into a room of virtual strangers without a male escort, and decided to look after her. Being slightly foxed, she had seen nothing untoward in introducing her to the statuesque brunette who'd stood at her side. For a split second neither lady had been sure how to react.

It had been Heloise who had recovered first. Later, when she had gone over the evening's events, she had been proud of the way she had behaved.

She had smiled gaily, holding out her hand to Mrs Kenton, who had been looking as if she wished to strangle poor Nell.

'Is it not fortunate for us both that Charles is not here? This is exactly the sort of scene which he would dislike above anything!'

'Indeed he would,' Mrs Kenton had replied faintly, taking Heloise's hand in a limp grasp.

Seeing Nell's brow finally pleating with concern, Heloise went on, with false bravado, 'I assure you, I do not in the least mind meeting the lover of my husband. It is only what I expected when I married an Englishman. It would be silly of me to pretend I do not know he has a mistress.'

And now that she had seen her she could understand exactly what drew Charles to this woman. Although she was a good deal older than Felice, she had the same dark hair, the same graceful carriage, even a sultry set to her lips that put her strongly in mind of her sister when she was not in the best of moods.

'At least he does not have two, like Lord Wellington,' she prattled on. 'Or parade them about in public while shunning his poor little wife. Why he brought her to Paris at all nobody could in the least guess, if he meant to humiliate her in that fashion!' Finally she paused to breathe, desperately hoping the bright façade she had adopted was successfully hiding her despondency.

For Mrs Kenton was wearing the ruby necklace. The stones were magnificent, gleaming like fire against the woman's milk-white skin, the large, central stone dipping provocatively into a cleavage that made Heloise fully conscious of her total inadequacy to compete in the bedroom stakes.

'Although I suspect, myself, that he wished to prove he had beaten Bonaparte upon all suits, and probably had no idea he had hurt her. Men!' she finished on a false laugh, fluttering her fan before her flushed cheeks.

'It is very…open-minded of you to say so,' Mrs Kenton said, with a puzzled frown.

'Oh, no—I am a realist, me. And it seems silly to pretend not to know how the world works.'

A knowing expression flickered across Mrs Kenton's face. She purred, 'Or to pretend that you don't mind?'

Heloise responded with a shrug. 'Why should I mind?'

The older woman's eyes narrowed on the parure Heloise was wearing, her expression growing positively feline.

'Why, indeed? He is such a generous man that any woman with an ounce of sense would always forgive his little…lapses.' She leaned forward conspiratorially. 'You are wise to pretend not to mind about me, my dear, just as I shall pretend not to mind about you. The one thing he cannot abide is a woman making a fuss. He hates to feel he might be losing control of a situation.' She chuckled—

a low, throaty sound. 'Well, you know how far he takes his *desire* for mastery.' She fanned herself, raising her eyebrows meaningfully. 'My, I grow heated just thinking about his skill between the sheets. It more than compensates for the coldness of his public manners, as I am sure you would be the first to agree.'

Heloise turned and stalked away. Round one had definitely gone to the courtesan. Though she wanted nothing more than to leave the party at once, she refused to let it look as though Mrs Kenton had driven her away.

The second bout was fought with rather more subtlety. Mrs Kenton followed Heloise to the lady's retiring room, where she had been trying to hide until a sufficient amount of time had passed to make it look as though she was not running away.

Pretending she did not know anyone else was in the room, Mrs Kenton remarked to Nell, who was with her, 'Isn't it a good thing that Walton's poor little wife is able to look after herself?'

Nell blinked owlishly, hiccupped, and subsided onto a sofa.

'Otherwise, who knows what would become of her? Everyone knows he is bored with her already.'

'Well, I like her,' Nell protested.

'As do I!' Mrs Kenton quickly put in. 'Which is why I feel so sorry for her. He never goes anywhere with her if he can avoid it. One can only wonder why he married her in the first place!'

That remark had struck her to the core. Charles had only married her to save face, and at her own suggestion. But it had been to no avail. The whole of London could already see that it was a mismatch!

Well, one thing they would not see. And that was a

bride who was not completely content with her lot. Heloise had determined there and then to prove to the whole world that nobody need feel in the least sorry for her. Particularly the patronising Mrs Kenton. From that moment she had taken pains to attend the sorts of places she was most likely to run into the woman, and demonstrate that not only did she know exactly what she was to her husband, but that it didn't affect her in the least. She would show them all she was a sophisticated Parisienne, well acquainted with, and impervious to, the base nature of men.

This bravado had carried her, over the next few days, to all sorts of places she had not enjoyed visiting in the least. But she would not back down. Not while that woman flaunted the rubies her husband had given her, while all she had to show for the marriage were some antiquated crystals he'd got out of a cupboard and dusted down so she would not look as though she had nothing! And if she could face down her husband's mistress at every turn, Robert could learn to deal with his own demons.

'Robert,' she said now, more gently, laying a gloved hand on his arm, 'your limp will not deter a woman who has a good heart.'

'Nor my face?' he scoffed.

'Ah, but tonight it is covered.' She reached up to adjust the set of his white velvet mask, which matched her own. 'Any woman you approach will see only your eyes, burning with admiration for her. She will see how determined you are to approach her, and she will think, My, how he must want me. You will not give her commonplace flatteries about the colour of her hair, or the magnificence of her figure—*non*! You will tell her that no other woman has such beauty of spirit. You will see beneath the trappings to the very heart of her. And her heart, it will be in your hands before the end of the very first dance.'

'I shall sound like a complete coxcomb if I dish out that kind of cant,' Robert grumbled. 'Then I'll probably catch my false leg in her skirts and trip her over.'

'Ah, no! The coxcomb is the one who pays tribute too prettily, not meaning half of what he says. You will let your lady see that you need her. Every woman wants to feel she is the only one who can answer the needs of her lover's heart.'

'Sounds like a load of hokum to me,' huffed Robert from the dark corner of the box where he was hunched. 'Shall I prove it? Shall I do as you have suggested, and make a complete fool of myself?'

'That,' replied Heloise with some asperity, 'was the whole reason for coming to a masked ball. So that you could try out the technique on some girl who does not in the least matter to you, rather than make the cake of yourself before your friends. There!' Heloise took his arm and indicated a female in a pink domino, who was casting them an occasional look from a box directly across the stage from where they sat. 'She is looking your way again. Go and ask her to dance!'

The masked damsel shot him a coy look, before turning away and fanning herself with vigour.

'Hell, what have I got to lose?' Robert finally said, pushing himself out of the chair.

It was not until he had left her alone in her box that Heloise realised just how vulnerable she was to the attentions of the masked revellers who leered at her over its edge. This was not the first time since embarking on her private little battle with Mrs Kenton that Heloise had felt completely out of her depth. But it was the first time she had sensed she could be in real danger. Even in private gaming hells there was a code of conduct which ensured her personal safety. But here the drunken bucks who made free with the females clearly felt they had the right to do so. For the type of females who came to such a place did not expect the same consideration as would a lady of quality. Indeed, she had not seen any woman here display reluctance towards any advances made upon her.

It was quite terrifying when a large male, clad in a black silk domino topped with a red devil's mask, stepped over the edge of the box without so much as a by-your-leave.

The domino parted as he took the chair beside her, revealing the stuff knee breeches of a tradesman.

'All alone, my pretty?' he slurred. 'How about a kiss?' He lurched forward, assailing her nostrils with gin fumes.

'Non!' she gasped, shrinking back into her chair.

'French, hey?' the stranger responded, cocking his head to one side. 'Not a good time to be a Frenchwoman in London, is it? Though you are the prettiest one I've ever seen. Let me see you better,' he said, reaching for the strings of her mask.

'You must not!' she cried, rapping him over the knuckles with her fan. It was imperative that her mask remain in place. Charles would be furious if he ever found out she had revealed her face at such a place as this!

'Why not?' The man chuckled, his hands dropping to her waist. 'It's what you've come here for, isn't it? To have a little fun?'

In a panic now, Heloise struck out at his devilish mask with her fan. He caught her hand easily, his reflexes surprisingly quick for a man whose slurred speech indicated he was heavily inebriated.

She could not think how to get rid of him. Admitting she was a respectable married woman would do no good.

He would not believe her. Respectable married women did not come to places like this. Not without their husbands.

If he knew she was the Countess of Walton, with a husband renowned for his vengeful nature, he would stop trying to paw at her like this! But she could not betray Charles by using his name! Nobody must ever know that she had disgraced him by coming to a place like this!

In desperation, she mentioned the only threat which she thought might hold sway with the drunken buck.

'I am not here alone! I am here with my…' Even if she mentioned her brother-in-law, it might give her assailant a clue as to her true identity. In spite of his domino and mask, it was impossible to disguise the full nature of Robert's injuries. Anybody who knew anything about the upper classes would have heard of the maimed soldier who lived with his half-brother and the French wife. 'My lover!' she declared, hoping this man had not seen Robert limp off towards the far side of the stage.

'Lover, is it?' the stranger hissed. 'Pretty careless of him to leave you here unprotected, then, wasn't it?' He placed his arm along the back of her chair, propping his leg up against the door of the box as he did so, effectively penning her in with him. 'I don't think he would care all that much if I stole a kiss or two…not if he's the fellow I saw going to the refreshment room with the little tart in the pink domino a moment or so ago.'

Heloise's breathing grew ragged. Robert could *not* have abandoned her! He would not do such a thing!

'You lie! He would die for me! And he was a soldier. If you dare to touch me he will kill you!'

The man's eyes glittered coldly through the slits in his mask. 'He would have to catch me first,' he sneered. 'Is that how you came to be his lover? He fought in France? Is that it? And brought you back with him? Spoils of war…' Almost casually, the hand which was not gripping her shoulder fumbled its way under the silken folds of her domino.

'*Non!*' she cried, trying to push his hand away. 'It was not like that!'

'What was it like, then?' His hand headed unerringly towards her breast. She couldn't believe how strong he was. It took both her hands and all her determination to prevent him from reaching his destination, and even then she was not convinced he hadn't stopped for some obscure reason of his own.

'It is none of your business!' she panted, seizing his wrist as his questing hand altered the angle of its exploration under the concealing folds of her domino, this time sliding to the low neckline of her gown, from whence he slipped it inside her bodice. 'Stop this! Stop it at once!' she shrieked, leaping up out of her chair with such haste that the neckline ripped. 'Oh!' she sobbed, pressing herself to the back of the box, her hands clutching at the torn edges of her gown. Thank heaven Sukey was utterly loyal to her. She would never be able to give a satisfactory explanation to Charles if he ever found out she had come home with the front of her gown torn. 'You will pay for this!'

'Since I'm paying, I may as well get my money's worth,' the man said, lunging at her.

He grasped her by the elbows, his body pressing hers into the thick crimson curtains that shrouded the shadowy depths of the box as his mouth crashed down on hers.

It was an angry, demanding kiss, and quite terrifying. Outraged, Heloise struggled against him with all her strength.

Until something quite unexpected happened. As the stranger's hands embarked on an assured exploration of her feminine contours, she began to compare him with Charles. He was of the same height and build, and though his voice was coarse, and his clothes that of a much poorer man, the eyes which glittered from behind the devilish mask were of a similarly cool blue.

If only Charles would kiss her like this. She groaned, and then, for a few crazy seconds, found herself pretending this man was her husband, and that he wanted her. She stopped struggling, sagging back into the suffocating folds of the drapery, her whole body trembling with a kind of sick, guilty excitement.

If only Charles would caress her like this! Would be so wild with desire for her that he would kiss her in a public place, even peeling the torn fabric of her dress away and pressing his lips to the exposed skin beneath as this man was doing now. She moaned. Oh, if this man did not stop soon, she would fling her arms round his neck and kiss him back!

And why should she not? Charles was doing something like this, maybe at this very moment, with the beautiful Mrs Kenton!

At the thought, a whimper escaped her throat.

The stranger's head jerked back. For a moment he simply stood, gazing down at her, his chest heaving with each hoarse breath he took. And then he astounded her by reaching out, almost tenderly, to brush away a tear that was trickling down her cheek.

She did not even know at what point during the assault she had started to cry.

'Aren't you going to slap me?' he mocked, withdrawing slightly.

Heloise grabbed the chair back as the world seemed to lurch crazily, flinging her completely off balance.

'*Non,*' she grated, shaking her head. 'I deserved it.' She

had just responded lustfully to a drunken stranger's lecherous groping! 'I am a slut,' she gasped in shock. Sinking to the chair, she buried her face in her hands and burst into tears.

Chapter Nine

Heloise flinched when a large male hand landed clumsily on her shoulder.

'Oh, Robert!' She sighed in relief on recognising it was his form looming out of the shadows, and not her assailant's. 'P...please take me home!'

She was still shaking with reaction, unable to form coherent replies to any of Captain Fawley's questions until they were safely shut inside the coach and on their way home.

On hearing the bald facts, Robert became so angry it was all she could do to prevent him turning the coach round and hunting the man down.

'It was my fault—all my fault,' she insisted. 'I never want to go to such a place again.'

'I did not want to go in the first place,' he retorted. 'From now on let me decide where we go, if you must go out with me and not your husband!'

As if she had any choice! The mere mention of her husband's neglect sent her into fresh floods of tears. When they reached Walton House she was in no state to argue when Robert steered her into his rooms, sat her firmly on the sofa, and pressed a drink into her hands.

'If you think you fared badly,' he drawled, easing himself onto a chair opposite her, 'you should hear what I suffered at the hands of the Pink Domino.'

She was sure that he was inventing more than half of the amusing story he went on to tell her, but by the time he had finished, and her drink was all gone, she had stopped shaking.

She even managed a wavering smile for him when, a little later still, she reached the half-landing and looked down to see him standing in the hallway, watching her with a troubled frown.

'I will be fine,' she assured him.

Though she did not believe the lie herself.

From then on, guilt and shame hung over her like a pall wherever she went, no matter how gaily she forced herself to smile.

If it were not for the importance of pushing Robert back into the circle of friends who were restoring him to health and vigour, she would have stayed in her rooms. Preferably in bed, with the covers drawn up over her head.

But she could not let him down too. She might be useless as a wife, but at least she was doing Robert some good.

She glanced across the crowded, stuffy room to the group of young men surrounding him tonight, earnestly discussing the latest news from France. Surreptitiously she crept away to find a quiet corner, where she could nurse her bruised spirits in relative peace.

Heloise did not notice the malevolent look Mrs Kenton arrowed her way, but the Honourable Percy Lampton did. Swiftly he made his way to Mrs Kenton's side.

'We have not spoken before—' he began.

'I am free to speak to anyone,' Mrs Kenton interrupted him, 'since I broke with Walton.'

Percy Lampton was a younger scion of the side of the family she had been strictly forbidden by Charles to have anything to do with, if she valued her position.

'Even his wife?' Lampton said snidely. 'I don't think he would like to hear how you've been tormenting her.' He clucked his tongue reprovingly. 'Letting her think you are still in his keeping. In fact, I wonder at your daring. It can only be a matter of time before Walton finds out what you have been about, and when he does…'

'Are you threatening me?' She wrenched her eyes from Heloise to glare at him.

'Far from it.' He sidled closer. 'I am just wondering how far you would be prepared to go in your quest for revenge. It is revenge you want, is it not? Though why you feel entitled to seek it…' He shook his head in mock reproof. 'You must have known he would marry eventually. And that it could never be to a woman like you.'

Tears of chagrin stung her eyes. 'It would not have been so bad if she had been beautiful, or wealthy, or even from a good family. But to think he cast me off for *that*!' She gesticulated wildly in Lady Walton's direction.

Snagging a glass of champagne from a passing waiter, Lampton drew Mrs Kenton into a small antechamber.

'And what am I left with?' she continued, having downed the drink in one gulp. 'I was completely faithful to him, let other opportunities slip through my fingers for him, and now I have to start all over again…'

'In direct competition with nubile young nymphs like Nell.' He nodded sympathetically.

'I am still an attractive woman!' she spat at him.

All he did was raise one eyebrow, and she subsided. They both knew her career was in terminal decline.

'If it is any consolation to you, I happen to know that

Walton married as he did purely to spite my family. Before he took off for Paris there were moves afoot to bring him back into the fold.' He smiled wryly. 'We had exactly what you described—a beautiful young woman of good family, who was also incidentally in our pockets—lined up to marry him. Is it so surprising he went off and married the first plain, poor foreigner he came across? She is Walton's little rebellion, nothing more. It must be obvious to you that Walton has no strong feelings for her personally. He has done the bare minimum required to stem speculation by arranging her presentation and squiring her to a few *ton* events. But on those occasions the chilliness of his demeanour towards her has been marked.'

'Has it?' Mrs Kenton had never actually seen them together, since she did not have an entrée to the upper echelons of society.

'Most marked.' Lampton grinned. 'And can you wonder at it? She is teetering on the verge of social ruin, coming to places like this. All she would need is one little push…'

Her eyes flashing with malice, she purred, 'What do you want me to do?'

'May I join you?'

Heloise looked up in annoyance. Just because she was sitting on her own, why did men assume she would welcome their attention? Did she have a sign pinned to her gown, saying 'This woman is a slut. Feel free to insult her?'

'I would prefer you did not,' she huffed, snapping her fan open and waving it before her face.

'Ah, I see you recognise me,' the man said cheerfully, taking the vacant seat beside her. 'But don't you think it a little silly to carry the feud so far? I can understand why

Walton should not wish to have anything further to do with his mother's relatives, given their shoddy behaviour towards his brother,' the man persisted, 'but I had nothing to do with all that. I had not even been born!'

'You are of the family I am not supposed to acknowledge?' she guessed, examining his face properly for the first time. There was a strong resemblance, now she was looking for it. He was of the same height and build as Charles, though a good few years younger. His eyes were the same clear, pale blue, fringed with golden lashes. As they rested steadily on her, something about the coldness of his regard began to make her feel uneasy. And then, over his shoulder, she noticed Nell looking from one to the other of them, before scuttling off, wringing her hands in distress.

'Come, my lady,' he said, leaning closer. 'Why shouldn't we be friends? It is not as if your husband even has to know. I dare say he does not know the half of what you get up to, hmm?'

The knowing tone of his voice, the way he slid one arm along the back of her chair while extending one leg so that she felt trapped by his body, was jarringly familiar. Could this be the man who had kissed her at the masquerade?

'I am sure he does not know you attend bachelor parties alone, or that Captain Fawley has introduced you to gaming hells, does he?'

His smile was predatory, chilling her to the core. He must have been watching her every move, just waiting for the opportunity to strike.

'P…please, sir,' she begged him. 'Do not persecute me like this!'

'Oh, Lady Walton—there you are!' a female voice cut in.

Looking up, Heloise saw Mrs Kenton standing over them, with Nell hovering anxiously behind her.

'I have been looking for you everywhere. Have you forgot you promised to partner my friend at cards?'

'Oh, yes,' she replied, jumping hastily to her feet. She glimpsed a scowl marring the stranger's handsome features as she made her escape.

'Have you no sense?' Mrs Kenton hissed, as soon as they were far enough from her persecutor for him not to hear. 'Consorting with your husband's enemies? Don't you know how foolish it is to antagonise a man of his temperament?'

'I didn't know who he was when he sat down!' Heloise protested. 'And anyway, I tried to make him go away.'

'That was not what it looked like from where I was standing,' Mrs Kenton sneered. 'He had his arm round you! And you just sat there!'

What was she supposed to have done? Heloise had no experience of men approaching her with such determination and lack of respect.

Mrs Kenton would have known exactly how to put him off, a little voice whispered in her head. No! No, she would rather die than ask That Woman for advice. It was bad enough to suffer the humiliation of having to thank her for coming to her rescue. Which she could scarcely bring herself to do.

'I did not do it for you,' Mrs Kenton replied. 'But for Nell. She seemed to feel it was her fault Percy Lampton had cornered you. But if you will choose to loiter in secluded corners, what can you expect? Look, if you don't want predators like Lampton pawing at you, the thing to do is stay in full view, preferably in the company of several other people, engaging in some innocuous pastime like playing cards.'

She dragged Heloise into the card room, indicating the small knots of players grouped around the various tables. Plastering an alluring smile to her face, she approached two gentlemen who appeared to be waiting for her.

'Good evening Lord Matthison, Mr Peters,' she said, ushering Heloise towards the green baize table. 'I hope we have not kept you waiting too long?' Smoothing her skirts, Mrs Kenton took a seat opposite the older of the pair, a florid-faced, bewhiskered gentleman with a claret-stained cravat.

His companion, a dark, lean young man, regarded Heloise through world-weary eyes. 'May I hope you are at least a competent player?'

Heloise shrugged as she took her seat opposite him. Much as she hated to admit Mrs Kenton was correct, she would feel safer waiting for Robert in here, pretending to play cards, than falling prey to men like Lampton. 'I do not know. What game do we play?'

'Whist,' the whiskered gentleman grinned. 'And Lord Matthison boasted he could beat me, no matter who Mrs Kenton found to partner him!'

'Oh,' she sighed in relief. If her partner was such a good player, her lack of skill would not matter. 'I have never played whist before, my lord. Is it difficult to learn?'

Lord Matthison gave Mrs Kenton a hard look, before going through the rules with Heloise. They seemed fairly simple, and for the first few hands Heloise did not let her partner down too badly. She even managed to win a few tricks.

But then Lampton strolled into the room, a drink in his hand, and took up a position by the fireplace, from where he could observe her play at his leisure.

The looks he sent her were lascivious enough to make her squirm in her seat. She no longer doubted he was the man from the masquerade—the man to whom she had responded so shamefully! The longer he stood there, leering at her, the more worried she grew that he would use that interlude against Charles, somehow.

But what could she do to stop him?

'I think it is time to call it quits,' she eventually heard Lord Matthison drawl. 'It serves me right for not specifying that I could win were I partnered with any male. In future, miss,' he growled at her, 'you might try to remember that if you lead with a trump, your partner will assume you have a fist full of them. My congratulations, Peters—' he bowed to Mrs Kenton's partner '—on rolling me up so effectively.'

'Did I make you lose a lot of money?' Unsure of the value of what they had just lost at cards, Heloise began to chew at her lower lip.

'No more than I can afford,' he said shortly. 'And I hope the same goes for you. Though, judging by the pile of vowels Peters is holding, you may have to pledge your jewels until you can wheedle the cash from whichever poor sap paid for that expensive gown you have on.' Flicking her one last contemptuous look, Lord Matthison strode from the room, leaving her cringing on her chair.

He thought she was someone's whore! She hung her head. What else was a man to think, when it had been Mrs Kenton who had introduced them?

'Your bracelet,' she heard Mrs Kenton urging her in an undertone. 'Leave that as security until you can raise the ready.'

Still cringing at what she had led her whist partner to think, she peeled off the bracelet and dropped it onto the mound of IOU's she had written.

'How much is the total?' she asked.

'Five hundred guineas!' Mr Peters beamed.

'What the deuce—?'

At the sound of that voice, Heloise looked up to see Robert limping towards her, his face drained of colour.

'Heloise, you have never lost your bracelet at play?'

'It is just a pledge against what I owe,' she protested. 'I will get it back when I pay this gentleman.'

'You will oblige me by giving me your address,' Robert grated. 'I will deal with the matter on the lady's behalf.'

'With pleasure.' Peters grinned, scribbling on the back of a scrap of paper.

Robert did not speak to her again until they were safely tucked into Walton's closed carriage.

'I can't believe you dropped that bracelet on the table like that!'

'But I had run out of money. And I did not like to put any more vowels down. It is not as if the bracelet is all that valuable…'

'Not valuable! You little idiot! It is a family heirloom. A totally irreplaceable part of the Walton parure!'

'Y…yes, I suppose it would be difficult to match those funny yellow crystals…'

'They're not crystals, Heloise. They're diamonds. Extremely rare, extremely fine yellow diamonds.'

'I had no idea,' she admitted, beginning to feel a bit sick. 'But I have not really lost it. We can get it back when you pay Mr Peters what I owe.'

Robert subsided against the squabs, looking relieved. 'That's right. God!' He laughed. 'I wondered how on earth you had the nerve to wear those baubles at some of the places I took you to! I thought it was because you wanted to make Mrs Kenton jealous…' He shook his head ruefully. 'When all the time you had no idea…' He grinned. 'Never mind—it could be worse, I suppose. How much did you lose tonight, by the way?'

'Five hundred guineas.'

Robert went very still.

'What is the matter? Is that a great deal of money? I am not perfectly sure how many guineas there are to the pound, but I know it is not twenty. That is shillings…' She faltered. 'Or is that crowns?'

'I had thought I could bail you out,' he grated, 'if you had any difficulty raising the cash. But there's nothing for it now. You are going to have to go to Walton and make a clean breast of it. You have lost a small fortune at play, and left a priceless heirloom as security against the debt. Only a man of his means will ever be able to redeem it. My God,' he breathed, 'he'll kill you. No, he won't, though—he'll kill me! He'll know you've no more notion than a kitten how to go on in society. It's all my fault for not taking better care of you. I've taken you to the lowest places, let you consort with prostitutes—and not just any prostitutes, oh, no! He will think I did this on purpose. And just when… Oh, hell.' Suddenly he looked very weary.

'Then we must not tell him!' She could not let Robert take the blame because she had been such a fool. 'There must be some other way to find the money. I have an allowance which I draw from Cummings. He might let me have an advance against next quarter!'

Robert shook his head. 'The only way to get hold of that kind of money in a hurry would be to go to a money lender. And for God's sake don't do that! Once they get you in your clutches, you'll never get out. No, there's nothing for it. We'll have to throw ourselves on Walton's mercy.'

'No,' she moaned, burying her face in her hands. It was not just a question of the gaming debt and losing the bracelet. She knew, once Charles looked at her in that cool, superior manner of his, that it would all come tumbling out. How jealous she was of his relationship with Mrs Kenton. This was precisely what her mother had warned her she must never do—behave like a jealous, possessive wife! And she had promised, too, that she would never cause him any trouble. She had broken the terms of their agreement twice over. He would never forgive her.

The carriage drew to a halt and a footman let down the steps. Her heart was in her mouth as they entered the hall together. It seemed the inevitable end to a disastrous evening when, just as she had taken off her cloak and handed it to a servant, the door to Charles' study swung open and he appeared in the doorway.

'Tell him now,' Robert murmured into her ear. 'The sooner you get it over with, the better for all of us.'

'Tell me what?' said Charles, advancing on them. 'Whatever it is you have to tell me had better be told in my study.' He stood to one side, inviting them into his domain with a wave of his arm.

Robert limped forward immediately.

'Care to join us, Lady Walton?' said Charles.

She had never felt so scared in all her life. But it would not be fair to let Robert face her husband alone. It was not his fault she had been stupidly goaded into gambling away a fortune by Charles' mistress. It had been her own stubborn pride that had done that. Not that she should have known who Mrs Kenton was, anyway. And Robert was right. Charles would blame him for that, too. There would be another fight between the two men, and the rift between them, which had begun to heal, would be ripped even wider. She could not let it happen.

Garnering all her courage, she followed Robert into the study, and joined him beside the desk.

Charles took the chair behind it, and gazed upon them with cool enquiry.

Neither of them could tell how fast his heart was beating as he braced himself to hear what he assumed would be the confession of their affair. He had not needed to question Heloise for long when he had trapped her in that box at the masquerade. She had confessed that Robert was her lover. Though she'd clearly felt guilty, bursting into tears and castigating herself for her loose morals, hearing the confirmation of his suspicions from her own lips had stunned him. He had reeled away from her in agonising pain and found himself somehow back here—waiting, as had become his habit, until he knew she was safely home.

They had both gone to Robert's rooms, rather than parting at the foot of the stairs as they normally did. It had been some considerable time before she had emerged, with a little smile playing about her lips as she floated up the stairs. Robert had stood in the hallway, gazing up at her, with a calculating expression on his face.

'Well?' he rapped out, when they had stood shuffling their feet and exchanging guilty looks for several minutes.

'I have taken Heloise to several places you would not like—' Robert began.

'The truth is,' Heloise blurted out, determined not to let him sacrifice himself for her, 'that when we went to that horrid masquerade some man assaulted me!'

Robert turned to her with a look of exasperation on his face. 'Hang on, Heloise, that's not—'

'No, Robert! Let me tell this my own way!'

With a shrug, he fell silent.

'Robert only left me for a minute or two unprotected, I

promise you. It was not his fault. It was mine. I insisted that he ask a young lady to dance, since he had the idea that no woman will ever accept him with the injuries he has taken. And while he was engaged with her this man, whom I have never seen before, took me in his arms and… kissed me.'

'Did you enjoy the experience?' Charles enquired coldly.

Heloise gasped as though he had slapped her.

'What sort of question is that?' Robert put in, aghast. 'She was naturally terribly upset! The point is, I had no business taking her to such a place…'

'Is this all?' Charles enquired politely, looking down at a sheaf of papers on his desk. Frowning, he moved the top sheet, as though something of interest had caught his eye. Certain that they were about to confess what had gone on between them behind closed doors, under his very roof, he was filled with such cold fury he could not bear to look at either of them. The only hope left to him was that he might be able to salvage his pride by masking his true state of mind while he waited for the blow to fall.

'Yes, that is all!' Heloise flung at him, her face white with fury. 'Come, Robert. You can see that to him it is nothing!'

She flounced out, Robert hard on her heels.

'Heloise! Wait!' Robert cried.

She paused halfway up the stairs and glared down at him.

'I told you we would have to find another way!' she whispered, aware that the door to Charles' study was not properly closed.

'You haven't confessed the whole yet—'

'What would be the point? I would die rather than tell him what happened tonight. Besides, if he finds out I have thrown away something you say he values so highly, he will banish me to the country—or put me aside altogether…'

'No, he won't. A gentleman doesn't divorce his wife over—'

'Gentleman! I do not even know what you mean by that term any more. Except that it is a nature that is cold and proud and unapproachable! I will not beg him to rescue me ever again! I wish I had not done so in the first place! Du Mauriac is dead, after all, and I would have been able to stay with my parents, who, though they think I am an imbecile, at least let me draw what I wish!'

While Robert's brow pleated in perplexity at this statement he found incomprehensible, in his study Charles clutched his head in his hands.

He had known from the start that she should not have carried on with the marriage once Du Mauriac was out of the picture.

Stifling a groan, he went to the study door and closed it.

'I will find a way to raise the money myself!' Heloise declared defiantly, storming off up the stairs.

In his study, Charles paced the carpet, too agitated even to pause to pour himself a drink. It would not soothe him, anyway. Nothing could ever ease the agony of hearing Heloise declare she wished she had never married him.

He had done all in his power to reconcile her to her position. To demonstrate she need not fear him he had allowed her more freedom than even the most besotted of men would accord their bride. He had put no pressure on her to conform to his requirements, imposed no restrictions on her movements, no matter how close she had sailed to the wind. And for what?

As he passed the window, he caught sight of his reflection in the panes of glass. Could this wild-haired, wild-eyed man really be him? Within two months of being married his wife had reduced him to this?

He should never have kissed her. That had been his greatest error. Now that he knew what she felt like under his hands, his mouth, he could more readily imagine his brother's hands shaping her breasts, his brother's mouth plundering her soft, responsive lips.

A strangled cry escaped his throat as he whirled away from the reflection of a man whose blood was infected with a form of madness. For no sane man would experience such rage, such despair, such self-disgust! Where was the cool, untouchable man who had always believed that to give way to strong emotion was a sign of weakness?

He flung himself into his chair, dropping his head to his hands. He had to get a grip on himself.

Straightening up, he drew several long, deep breaths through flared nostrils.

He *must* look at this situation dispassionately. The facts were these: his wife, for whom he felt more than he had ever imagined he could feel for any woman, did not return his affection.

Second, in spite of his forbearance, she had decided to humiliate him by taking a lover before providing him with an heir.

Decided? He shook his head. Heloise was too impulsive a creature to decide upon such a course of action. She had just followed her heart. She had been brought up by parents who had eloped in the teeth of opposition, and had applauded her sister for jilting him for the sake of her 'true love'. She had not meant to betray him. In fact, letting him know she was going to that masquerade could have been a cry for help. She had known she was on the slippery slope to adultery, and her tender conscience had been troubling her.

But as for Robert… His fist clenched on the arm of the chair. Robert was getting the perfect revenge. Cuckolding his despised brother under his own roof, secure in the knowledge there would be no divorce to expose him for the scoundrel he was. And if Heloise fell pregnant Robert's child would inherit the property from which he had been excluded. For Walton would be obliged to acknowledge the bastard as his own if he wanted to shield Heloise from disgrace.

And he did. He lowered his head, his face contorted with anguish. He would not permit her to run off with Robert and live a hand-to-mouth existence as the whore of an invalid on a meagre army pension.

He got to his feet and strode to the door. He must tell her, and tell her now, that he would not permit that. Though she might not think so, she would do far better to give up her foolish dreams and accept her lot. She was staying with him!

He took the stairs two at a time, flung open the door to her suite, and crossed the darkened sitting room to her bedroom.

When she saw him, her eyes widened with apprehension. It infuriated him to see her draw the sheet up to her chin, as though he were the villain of the piece! Losing control of the ragged edges of his temper, he strode to the bed, ruthlessly yanking the covers from her fingers.

'You are my wife—' he began.

'Yes, I know, and I am so sorry! I never meant to—'

He laid his fingers to her lips, stopping her mouth. He did not want to hear her confess what he had already worked out for himself. She had only followed where her heart led.

'I know you couldn't help yourself.'

Beneath his fingers, her lips parted in surprise. 'You are not angry?' Had Robert told him everything after she had left? 'Oh, Charles,' she sighed, tears of remorse slipping down her cheeks. 'Can you forgive me?'

Cupping her face between his hands, he brushed those

tears away with his thumbs. Could he forgive her? Wasn't that asking rather too much? With a groan of anguish, he gathered her into his arms and buried his face in her hair.

And suddenly he knew, with blinding clarity, that if he could have her once—just this once—then his future would not be so unbearable. For he could make himself believe that any child she bore might be his.

And so he pushed the nightgown from her shoulders, grating, 'Just this once. Just tonight.'

'Yes,' she sighed, winding her arms about his neck and sinking back into the pillows.

It was her guilt that motivated her to offer him this comfort, he was sure. But he was desperate enough to take whatever he could get. Swearing to himself that he would never take advantage of her in this manner again, he followed her down and for the next few moments let his hot need of her sweep aside all his scruples. He forgot everything but Heloise: the sweetness of her lips, the softness of her skin, the heat of her breath pulsing against his throat.

And then, searing his soul like a whip cracking into naked flesh, the sound of her agonised cry as he took her virginity.

Chapter Ten

Charles could not credit that he had been so wrong about her.

'I beg your pardon,' he said lamely. Where was the rule of etiquette to cover an occasion like this? 'If I'd had any idea you were a virgin…'

She had been lying beneath him with her eyes screwed shut. Now they flew open, full of disbelieving hurt, as though he had struck her.

'Of *course* I was a virgin!' How could he think she would break her marriage vows? Didn't he know she would rather die than be disloyal to him in any way?

The shuttered expression on his face only added to her feeling of humiliation. She had imagined that he had finally come to her bed because he had begun to find her desirable.

Instead it had been an expression of his contempt. He thought she was the kind of woman who…

'Ooh!' she cried, pummelling at his shoulders. 'I hate you! I hate you!'

He reared back, appalled at the mess he had made of things.

Pausing only long enough to snatch up his clothes, he fled from her bedroom, chastened, sickened and shaken.

He might just have destroyed whatever slim chance there had been to make something of their marriage.

He sank to the floor, his back pressed to his bedroom door, his clothing bundled up against his chest.

'Heloise,' he groaned. 'My God, what have I done?'

Alone in the dark, Heloise rolled onto her side, drew her knees up, and let the tears flow.

He must have heard rumours about the places she had been, the company she had kept, and jumped to the worst possible conclusion.

And why wouldn't he? It was only what Lord Matthison had deduced within minutes of meeting her.

Dawn found her gritty-eyed from weeping. When Sukey came in with her breakfast, her throat was so hoarse she could barely croak a dispirited dismissal.

How could she eat anything, when she'd just had her last shred of hope ripped from her? And what was the point of getting dressed and going out, acting as if her life had meaning any more? He had come to her bed. For whatever reason, he had finally decided to make her his wife in fact as well as in name—and what had she done? Lashed out at him. Told him she hated him. Driven him away.

She lay under a black cloud of despair until noon, when Sukey came back, bearing yet another tray of food.

'I told you to leave me alone,' she sighed wearily.

'Begging your pardon, my lady, but His Lordship insisted you had something to eat when I told him you wasn't getting up today.'

His feigned solicitude ground her spirits still lower. Even though he regarded her as an infernal nuisance, he would always fulfil his responsibilities towards her in the most punctilious fashion. Appearances were everything to Charles.

He would not want the servants to know there was anything amiss between them. He most definitely would not want her confiding in Sukey that she wished she had never set eyes on him.

Forcing her lips into a parody of a smile, she murmured, 'How thoughtful,' and propped herself up on the pillows so that Sukey could place the tray across her lap.

For appearances' sake she picked at the food while Sukey drew back the curtains, tidied the room, and poured water into her washbasin. The sound made her aware of how sticky and uncomfortable she felt. She could at least cleanse herself, put off her ruined nightgown and dress in clean clothes.

In some ways, she thought some time later, sitting down at the dressing table so that Sukey could comb out her tangled hair, this would be the perfect time to go to him and confess what a scrape she was in. It was not as if he could possibly think any worse of her.

Could he? Her heart twisted into a knot at the prospect she could sink any lower in his estimation.

No, she would not tell him about the bracelet. Somehow she would get it back. She lifted her chin and met her own eyes in the mirror. He would not divorce her. Robert had been adamant about that. So she had a lifetime to reverse the poor opinion he had formed.

And, judging by the way things had gone between them so far, a lifetime would be how long it would take.

Still, Robert was so much better. She need not go anywhere with him again. Though most of his friends were completely respectable, if not of her husband's elevated status, women like Mrs Kenton hovered on the fringes of his world. She had no intention of locking horns with her again. She would just stay in her rooms if Charles did not require her presence at his side. If she grew really bored she would take the occasional walk in the park, with Sukey. And a footman for good measure. She would put Mrs Kenton right out of her mind, and concentrate on being such a model of rectitude that even Charles would be able to see he had misjudged her.

And in the meantime she would cudgel her brains until she came up with a way of raising enough money to pay off her gambling debts and recover the bracelet. Before Charles noticed it had gone missing.

She dismissed Sukey, needing to be alone to think. After pacing the floor fruitlessly for a while, she went to her desk and pulled out her supply of paper from under the layers of petticoats in the bottom drawer. 'Five hundred guineas', she scrawled across the top of a fresh sheet. How on earth could a woman honestly raise such a sum without going to money lenders?

As her mind guiltily replayed the way she had accumulated the debt, her hands instinctively began to portray that fateful game of whist. She drew herself first, as a plump little pigeon, being plucked by a bewhiskered gamekeeper with a smoking gun at his feet. In the background she added a caricature of Percy Lampton as a pale-eyed fox, licking his lips from his vantage point in a hedge whose leaves bore a marked resemblance to playing cards.

Suddenly she came out of that reverie which often came over her when she was sketching. People—artists like Thomas Rowlandson, for example—made a living by selling cartoons. She had seen them in bound copies in

Charles' library, and lying around the homes of Robert's
bachelor friends. Depictions of sporting heroes, or lampoons
of political figures were very popular. She recalled how
amused the ladies from the embassy in Paris had been by the
sketchbook that Charles had forced her to burn.

Her heart began to beat very fast. She dropped to her
knees and scrabbled through the second to bottom drawer,
where she stashed her finished works. Whenever she
returned from an outing with Charles, she sketched the
people who had particularly amused or annoyed her. Politicians, doyennes of society, even the occasional royal
duke had all fallen victim to her own very idiosyncratic
interpretation of their foibles. If only she could find
someone to publish them, she was sure she could make
money from her drawings!

She pulled them all out and rolled them up together,
then went to the fireplace and tugged on the bell to
summon her maid. She would need string, brown paper,
and a cab. She was most definitely not going to turn up at
a prospective employer's door in the Walton coach, with
her husband's family crest emblazoned on the panels. Not
only would that advertise her predicament, but his driver
would be bound to report back to Charles where he had
taken her. She hoped Sukey would know where to find a
print shop, so that they could give an address to the cab
driver.

Oh, Lord, she was *still* engaged in activities of which
he would disapprove. She pressed her hands to her cheeks,
taking a deep, calming breath. It would not be for much
longer. Once she had paid off this debt she would never
do anything Charles might frown at. Never again.

Charles twirled the pen round in his fingers, staring blindly
at the rows of leatherbound books which graced the wall

of the library opposite his desk. He had never felt so low in his life. Until now he had always been sure that whatever he did, no matter how harsh it might seem to disinterested observers, was the right thing to do.

He could not understand now, in the clear light of day, what had driven him to act in such a reprehensible, nay, criminal fashion last night.

If only he could go to her and beg her forgiveness. Wrap her in his arms and at least hold her while she wept. And he knew she was weeping. Sukey had whispered as much to Finch, the youngest of his footmen, when she had taken the untouched breakfast tray back to the servants' hall. He could not bear to think of her lying up there alone, with no one to comfort her. But he was the very last person she would wish to see this morning.

At midday he had insisted Sukey check on her again. To his great relief Heloise had nibbled on some toast and drunk most of a cup of chocolate. She had then risen, washed her puffy eyes in cold water, and donned her long-sleeved morning gown with the apricot lace flounces. Finch had yielded this information to Giddings, who had informed His Lordship when he brought a cold collation— which Charles had not ordered—to the library, from where he could not find the energy to stir.

Mechanically, he bit into the slice of cold mutton pie Giddings had slid onto his plate, only to leap up at the sound of small feet crossing the hall, followed by the noise of the front door slamming.

Wiping his mouth with his linen napkin, he strode into the hall, Giddings at his heels.

'Where has she gone?' Charles barked at Finch, who froze in an attitude of guilt by the console table.

'I am sorry, my lord, I do not know.'

'She did not order the coach,' Giddings mused. 'She must not intend to go far.'

Charles was barely able to restrain the impulse to race upstairs and check her cupboards, to see if she had packed her bags and left him. Good God, losing Felice was as nothing compared to what it would be like if Heloise should desert him.

Barely suppressing the panic that clutched coldly at his stomach, he fixed a baleful stare on the hapless Finch, and asked, 'What was she carrying?'

'Umm…' Finch thought for a moment. 'Well, nothing as I can recall. Though Sukey had what looked like a long sort of tube thing.' He frowned. 'Might have been a parasol, wrapped up in brown paper.'

A parasol? A woman did not run away from her husband armed only with a parasol, whether she had wrapped it in brown paper or not. He ran a shaky hand over his face as he returned to the relative sanctuary of his library. He could not go on like this. Whether she could believe in his remorse, whether she could ever forgive him, or even understand what had driven him to say what he had, was beside the point. He had to tell her he would accept whatever terms she cared to name so long as she promised not to leave him.

It was late when she returned. He decided to give her only sufficient time to put off her coat and take some refreshment before going up to her room with the speech it had taken him all afternoon to perfect.

Five more minutes, he thought, snapping his watch closed and returning it to his waistcoat pocket.

He looked up, on hearing a slight noise from the doorway, to see Giddings making an apologetic entrance.

'Begging your pardon, my lord, but there is a man who

insists you will want to see him. When I informed him you were not receiving, he told me to give you this.' Giddings laid a rolled-up piece of paper on the desk, concluding, 'He is awaiting your answer in the small salon. I would have left him in the hall, but he insisted that the matter was of the utmost delicacy, and that he did not wish Her Ladyship to see him.'

Charles' hand shot out to unroll the single sheet of drawing paper. He could see, after one glance, that it was his wife's work.

It was the night he had taken her to the theatre. The boxes that overlooked the stage were populated by various creatures, though the one which leapt out at him was a sleek black panther, with one paw upon the neck of the sheep who shared his box. It was Lensborough to the life, and the sheep undoubtedly the silly young lightskirt he currently had in keeping. The stage was populated by a flock of sheep, too, with ribbons in their curly fleeces, and all of them with wide, vulnerable eyes. The audience that filled the pit comprised a pack of wolves, their tongues hanging out as they eyed the helpless morsels penned on the stage.

Was this what Sukey had been carrying this afternoon when she had gone out with Heloise? Not a parasol, however disguised, but this picture, rolled up just as Giddings had presented it to him? And, if so, where had she taken it—and who was the man who had brought it back to him?

For the first time that day Charles recalled that Heloise had other troubles than being married to a man she'd grown to hate. Last night Robert had tried to make her tell him what they were. Instead of listening to her, he had totally lost his head and driven her away, confirming her opinion that he was 'cold and proud and unapproachable'.

'Send the fellow in,' he ordered Giddings. Seating himself behind the desk, he schooled his features so that they revealed nothing of his inner turmoil. That this man had one of his wife's sketches and had dared to use it as a calling card was enough to set his back up. If the scoundrel was in any way connected with whatever it was that was troubling his wife, he would soon learn he had made a bad mistake. Charles would destroy him. Slowly, painfully and completely.

'Mr Rudolph Ackermann,' Giddings announced, somewhat surprising Charles. This man was a reputable publisher, not the sort he would have expected to dabble in blackmail.

'Thank you for agreeing to see me,' Ackermann said, coming to stand before the Earl's desk. 'I apologise for the unorthodox method I employed—' he indicated the sketch that lay on the desk between them '—but I needed to get your attention.'

'You have it, sir,' Charles replied. 'State your business.' He did not invite the man to sit. Nor did he ask Giddings to bring in refreshments before dismissing him.

'Your wife came to my offices on the Strand this afternoon,' Ackermann began, the second the door closed behind Giddings. 'I would not have admitted her had she not brought her maid along. Indeed, at first, I assumed she wanted to make a purchase.'

He ran a finger round his collar, clearly growing uncomfortable under the Earl's hostile scrutiny.

'Instead, she produced a bundle of her own work, and asked me if I would pay her for them, and for as many more as would be needed to make up a volume for public sale. Since she was clearly a lady of quality, I thought it best to humour her by pretending to examine her drawings.

I was amazed at how wickedly comical they were. For a while I got quite carried away with the notion of actually bringing out a book along the lines of *The Schoolmaster's Tour.* We even discussed calling it *The French Bride's Season...*' His voice faltered under the Earl's wintry stare.

'Of course,' he blustered, 'I came to my senses almost at once.' He sighed, looking wistfully at Heloise's sketch of her night at the theatre. 'I realised that such a scheme would be abhorrent to a man like you.' He cleared his throat. 'Not that she told me her real name. Indeed, I was only completely sure of her identity after my clerk returned—that is, the lad I sent to follow her home—and he told me the address of the house she came into.'

The Earl's eyes bored into Ackermann's. 'You say my wife brought you a bundle of her work? I assume you are now going to tell me you hold the rest in safekeeping?'

Ackermann looked relieved. 'Precisely so. If I had not persuaded her that I would buy them all she would simply have taken them to another publisher. Someone who might not share my scruples.'

'Scruples?' the Earl repeated, his lips twisting into a cynical sneer.

'Yes.' Ackermann's face set in implacable lines as he finally understood what the Earl was implying. 'My lord, my business relies on the goodwill of men of your class. If I were to expose your wife to scandal I know full well you would break me. I have taken what steps I could, in good faith, to prevent Lady Walton's actions from coming to light. I gave her a modest payment, to ensure she would not think of going to someone who might enjoy seeing you humiliated...'

'A modest payment?'

'Five guineas.'

'You make a poor sort of blackmailer if all you require of me is five guineas.'

Ackermann looked as though he was hanging onto his temper by the merest thread. 'Whoever may be blackmailing your wife, it is not I. Though she is clearly trying to raise a large sum of money in a hurry.'

Charles stroked his chin thoughtfully. He took another look at the sketch, then at Ackermann's indignant posture, recalling his wife's distress in this very room the night before.

'How much money did she say she wanted?'

'Five hundred guineas.'

For several minutes Charles said nothing.

Heloise was in need of five hundred guineas, but she found him so unapproachable she would probably rather die than ask him for anything. Especially now.

And yet... He tapped on the arm of his chair thoughtfully. If he could somehow supply her with the funds she needed, in such a way that he did not appear as the tyrant of her imagination...

'Take a seat, Mr Ackermann,' he said. 'While I spell out exactly what I wish you to do for me.'

Chapter Eleven

⚬⚭⚬

Heloise did not know whether to massage her aching wrist or rub at the frown that felt like a hot knife welded between her eyebrows. She had sat up all night, putting finishing touches to any half-started sketches she could find, so that she could impress Mr Ackermann with her industry at this morning's interview.

Although if he was only going to give her five guineas per drawing, she had realised just as she was climbing into the cab, she would have to sell him another ninety-nine to clear the debt. It would take her months to raise five hundred guineas this way. Even if he agreed to buy everything she ever drew, which was hardly likely.

She slumped back into the grimy leather seat, chewing at her lower lip. She still had Felice's emerald ring. Charles had said it was quite valuable. Since she was never going to wear it, it might as well go the way her sister had originally intended.

And, since she was never going out again, she would not be needing all the expensive gowns Charles had bought her. In Paris she had thought nothing of going to peddlers of second-hand clothes. There was bound to be a similar market in London. Particularly for beautifully embroidered creations from the salon of Madame Pichot.

By the time the cab reached its destination Heloise was drawn tight as a bowstring. Since it was a bad business tactic to reveal her state of nerves, she pulled her shoulders down and raised her chin as she took a seat in Mr Ackermann's office. The drawings she had left with him the day before were already spread across his desk. He took her latest offerings, slowly perusing every single page.

Little shafts of hope streaked through her every time his lips twitched in amusement. He hovered for the longest time over her depiction of her presentation. At first glance it looked as though she had drawn a lily pond, surrounded by reeds amongst which elegant herons were poised, eyeing the fat carp drowsing in the shallows. The puffed-up toads squatting on their lily pads were easy enough to identify. It took him a little longer to work out which personage each fish or bird represented.

'Is this all you have?' he eventually asked her.

'Yes, but I promise you I can produce as many as you wish. I will work every hour of the day and night…'

'No, no.' He held up his hand to stop her. 'I shan't need any more.'

When her face fell, he swiftly explained, 'I am willing to give you five hundred guineas for what we have here.'

She gasped, pressing her hands to her cheeks as he slid an envelope across the desk towards her. 'You are giving me all the money now? Just like that?'

'Just like that,' he replied, with a wry twist to his mouth.

She grabbed the envelope before he changed his mind, and tried to stuff it into her reticule. It would not fit. Even folded, it was far too bulky. She clutched it to her bosom, bowing her head as a wave of faintness washed over her. It was terrifying to have so much money on her person. What if she lost it? She had to get home and hand it over to Robert at once. She leapt to her feet and made blindly for the door.

Once there, she turned back, gasping, 'I am sorry if I appear rude, but so large a sum of money…'

The strangest look flitted across his face. It was almost as though he pitied her. But his brisk, 'Good morning,' as he began to tidy her drawings from his desk-top was such a businesslike dismissal she decided that in her nervous state she must have imagined it.

As soon as the door had closed behind her, the Earl of Walton emerged from his place of concealment. Sparing only a second to nod his acknowledgement to Mr Ackerman for playing his part so well, Charles set out in hot pursuit of his wife.

He hated resorting to following her like this. But how else was he to find out why she needed five hundred guineas? He had abandoned the idea of simply demanding an explanation almost as soon as it had occurred to him. He would not give her any further grounds for accusing him of bullying her.

It was not long before it became apparent she was going straight home. He bit down on a feeling of frustration as he watched her climb the front steps. He might have to shadow her movements closely for some time before discovering what she intended to do with the money.

He slipped into the hall so soon after her that the footman did not even have time to close the door behind her.

And saw her disappearing into Robert's rooms.

She had flown straight to him!

It always came back, somehow, to Robert.

A series of images flitted in rapid succession through his brain. Heloise embracing Robert in this hall, telling him he was her only friend. Heloise wafting up the stairs with a smile playing about her lips after the masquerade.

Given her family's propensity for eloping at the drop of a hat, he could only draw one conclusion.

Thrusting his hat into the hovering footman's out-stretched hands, he strode across the hall, pushing Linney aside as he plunged into his brother's rooms hard on his wife's heels.

And caught her holding out the envelope containing the money—his money—to Robert.

They both froze, looking at him just like two children caught with their hands in the biscuit barrel.

A vision of her in some French farmyard feeding chickens flashed into his mind. Robert emerged from a shadowy doorway, put his arm about her waist and kissed her cheek. She smiled up at him, the picture of contentment...

Charles could not bring himself to say a word. He felt as if he was teetering on the edge of an abyss, and one wrong move would send him hurtling eternally downwards.

Until this moment he had not really believed she hated him. She had said it once before, in the heat of the moment. When she had calmed down, she had admitted she had not really meant it.

But here was the evidence she could not bear to spend another moment as his wife.

It was his own fault. He had treated her abominably. He had left her shaking and crying at the masquerade. No wonder she had turned to Robert for comfort. He had practically driven her into his arms. And, worse, he had flung his mistrust in her face at the worst possible moment…

He drew in a ragged breath. This time, no matter what it cost him, he would hold his anger in check until he had learned the truth. All of it. Whatever it might be.

Only then would he deal with it—or rather find a way to survive losing both his brother and his wife in one fell swoop.

Like an automaton, he crossed the room to the fireplace and propped himself against the mantel, folding his arms across his chest.

Eyeing Robert, who was reaching for the crutches that were propped on the arm of the sofa on which he sprawled, he ground out, 'I think it is high time someone told me exactly what is going on.'

'Tell him, Lady Walton,' ordered Robert, letting the crutches fall.

'I cannot!' Heloise stood rooted to the spot, the money clutched in her hands, large tears welling in eyes that stared at him piteously from a pinched white face.

'Then I will,' Robert declared, pulling himself to a more upright posture. 'It's no use trying to hide it from him any longer. The game's up.'

'Robert!' she cried, rounding on him as though he had betrayed her.

'It is far better for Charles to act for you in this matter,' he went on mulishly. 'I said so from the start.'

Act for her? These were not the words of a man contemplating eloping with his brother's wife. Nor was his exasperated tone in the least lover-like. A great weight seemed to roll from Charles' shoulders.

'Perhaps you would find it easier to confide in me if I were to tell you that I know you were trying to sell your drawings, and that it was, in fact, I who supplied the publisher with the five hundred guineas in that package?'

Heloise let out a strangled cry, dropping to a chair and covering her face with her hands. She should have known no businessman would pay so much money for the dozen or so drawings she had given him. They were probably not worth a sou!

'I can see I have been even more stupid than usual,' she said, turning the packet over in her hands.

She would have to tell Charles everything. And then he would be so angry with Robert. He would say things that might alienate them from each other for ever. They were both of them so deucedly proud! Insults, once spoken, would not be easily retracted or forgiven by either. And it would all be her fault.

Perhaps if she could tell Charles alone, and he had time to calm down before confronting Robert...

'Robert,' she said, getting to her feet and dropping the mangled package onto the cushion beside him, 'you know what to do with this. Charles—' She turned to him, lifting her chin. 'If you will spare me a few moments, I will tell you the whole.' She took a few steps towards the door. 'In my sitting room.'

To her great relief, not a second after she quit Robert's rooms, she heard Charles' tread on the staircase behind her.

'Please—won't you sit down?' She waved him to a chair to one side of the fireplace once she had dismissed Sukey. Nervously, she perched on the one opposite. 'I p...promised you before we married that I would not be any trouble to you at all, but I have got into such a terrible mess! I do not know where to start.'

'Start with the pictures,' Charles said grimly. 'I should

very much like to hear why you felt obliged to run round town selling your work for a paltry sum…'

'It is not a paltry sum. Robert said it was a small fortune!'

'Well, I have a large fortune at my disposal. For heaven's sake, Heloise, am I such an ogre that you cannot even apply to me for funds when you need them?'

'It is not at all that I think you are an ogre. But that I have broken my word and did not want to admit it. Nor why I broke it! I have done all that is reprehensible. And then I lost all that money at cards…'

'Gaming debts.' Why had he never considered that she might have been fleeced at cards? He shook his head. 'I have even made you think I would not meet your gaming debts,' he said bleakly.

Wringing her hands, she plunged on. 'I am the imbecile. Maman warned me I must not mind about your mistresses, but when I saw her, with those rubies you chose for her, and her air of such sophistication, while I had only those horrid yellow stones… But then Robert said they were diamonds, and priceless, and I knew how angry you would be that I was such a ninny—but how could I know?' She got to her feet then, pacing a few feet away before turning to exclaim, 'You said you had got them cleaned, and handed them to me as though they meant nothing. I thought you could not bother to go out to a jeweller and buy anything just for me. I did not know,' she sniffed, dashing a solitary tear from her cheek, 'I swear I did not know how valuable that bracelet was, and if I had known what a vile place the Opera House was I would never have made Robert take me there. He warned me, but I would not listen, so it was entirely my own fault that horrid man kissed me—'

'Just stop right there!' Getting to his feet, Charles crossed the room and took hold of her firmly by her shoulders.

He had considered once before that there might be only one way to stop his wife when she was in full flow.

He employed it now. Ruthlessly, he crushed her lips beneath his own, knowing she would not welcome the kiss, but completely unable to resist. When he thought how close he had come to accusing her of infidelity again… He shuddered. Thank God he had managed to rein in his abominable jealousy!

'Ch…Charles,' was all she could manage, in a strangled whisper, when he finally pulled away. Why had he kissed her when he was clearly very angry with her?

As he looked down into her distraught face, he knew he still had a long way to go. Though she had not been planning to run off with Robert, he had still been the one she had run to in a panic, assuming she had nowhere else to turn.

Gently, he tugged her to sit beside him on one of her prettily brocaded sofas.

'Heloise,' he explained, 'anyone can get badly dipped at cards. You should have just told me.'

'I was too ashamed,' she admitted. 'I knew I should not have been playing at all, when I am so useless at counting, but when Mrs Kenton looked at me with such contempt I felt I had to prove I could be as good as her at something! And then, because it was the house of one of Robert's respectable friends, and not a gaming hell like some we had been to, I was not on my guard. And nobody told me a guinea was worth more than a pound!' she complained, as though the injustice of this had just struck her. 'Why must you English have crowns and shillings, and guineas, and everything be so complicated?'

'That is the second time you have mentioned Mrs Kenton,' Charles said sternly. 'Would you mind telling me how you came to make her acquaintance?'

Determined to protect Robert as far as she was able, Heloise said, 'Nell introduced us.' When Charles looked puzzled, she explained, 'Lord Lensborough's mistress. They are friends.'

'Yes, but how came you to be acquainted with a woman like Nell—if that is her name?'

'Why should it not be her name? She is entitled to a name, like any other person. Just because to earn her living she has to—'

Charles took the only certain method of silencing his wife once again.

'If you cannot keep to the point, madam wife, I will have to keep kissing you, you know.' He wanted more than anything to rain kisses all over her dear little face. But her reaction told him she would not be receptive to such a demonstration of affection.

She disentangled herself from his arms, her cheeks flushing mutinously. So he kissed her to punish her, did he? A perverse excitement thrilled through her veins. She only had to defy him, then, and he might kiss her again! Oh, if only she were not so determined to clear her name and prove she was not the amoral hussy that Englishmen all seemed to assume, just because she did not follow the stricter rules their society imposed on Englishwomen.

While she was still dithering between his kisses and his contempt on the one hand, or his respect with coldness on the other, he said, quite sternly, 'Heloise, you should not be socialising with women like Nell and…Mrs Kenton…'

'No, Maman warned me that I must pretend not to know about your mistress. But this was absurd when we walked into each other. How am I supposed to ignore a woman who is standing right in front of me?'

Felice would have done it with relish, he reflected. She

had a way of cutting people, a haughty tilt to her head sometimes when she took offence at something said to her, that had made it easy for him to envisage her as his Countess. She would have had no trouble ripping his discarded mistress to shreds. She could easily have become the sharpest-clawed of all the tabbies in town. He swallowed suddenly on the frightening prospect. But Heloise—his sweet, good-natured, straightforward little pea-goose—needed his support and his care in a way Felice would never have done. A feeling of hope warmed his veins. She had based at least some of her actions on a couple of misapprehensions about him. If he could clear those up, perhaps he could begin to redeem his character in her eyes.

'Heloise,' he said, steeling himself for the kind of conversation a man as fastidious as himself should never have to have with his wife, 'Mrs Kenton is not my mistress.'

'Don't lie to me, Charles! Everyone knows those rubies she flaunts were a gift from you.'

'She *was* my mistress. That much is true. But, for your information, those rubies were my parting gift. I gave them to her before I left for Paris. And now we will not mention her again. In that I have to agree with your *maman*. I should not have to discuss my mistress with my wife.'

Heloise did not question how she knew he was telling the truth.

But that cat had deliberately made her think the relationship was current!

Indignantly, Heloise leapt to her feet, pacing back and forth as she assessed how the woman had deliberately played on her insecurities, taunted her into playing beyond her means, and finally goaded her into parting with the bracelet she must have known was priceless.

'Oh!' she cried in vexation, flinging herself back onto the sofa. 'She has made a complete fool of me.' Suddenly sitting up straight, as another thought occurred to her, she exclaimed, 'And *he* was in it too! Percy Lampton!'

'Lampton?' Charles grated, his hackles rising. He might have known the Lamptons would do their utmost to hurt his chosen bride.

'Yes—he persecuted me until Mrs Kenton and her game of cards seemed like a perfectly reasonable means of escape. And he kissed me, too!' she concluded, remembering the assault at the Opera House.

'He *what*?'

A shiver of dread ran down his spine. Apparently Lampton would stop at nothing. Oh, he no longer feared Heloise would stray into an adulterous affair. He must have been mad to suspect her integrity for so much as a second! But a ruthless swine like Lampton would only have to get her into a compromising position, arranging things so that there were witnesses, and his wife's reputation would be in tatters.

It was no use hoping she would suddenly start trusting him enough to listen to any warning he had to give her. The only sure way to keep her safe would be to remove her from that man's reach altogether.

'We will have to leave London.'

He would take her down to Wycke, his principal seat. And while they were there he would make sure she spent at least some part of each day in his company. There were so few other distractions to amuse a city-bred girl like Heloise that she would soon welcome any company—even his. He would rein in his absurd jealousy, treat her with the kindness and consideration a young bride deserved, and maybe, just maybe, she might come to regard him as a patient, devoted husband rather than the unapproachable tyrant of her imagination. God, how he wanted to kiss her again! If only she didn't freeze whenever he took her into his arms, and then look at him with those bemused, wounded eyes when he let her go.

'I just need to clarify one point,' he said. 'Will the money you gave Robert today clear all your outstanding debts, or is there anything else I should know before we leave town?'

'Th…that is all,' she stammered, amazed that he was taking it all so calmly.

He nodded, relieved that she had at least had someone she could turn to for help—but, dammit! He swore to himself, rising to his feet. He should have taken better care of her!

She tensed as he turned his back on her. Did that outward calm only conceal a deep disgust of her failings?

'I am sorry, Charles—' she began.

He rounded on her, a strange gleam in his eye. '*You* are sorry?'

Her heart sank as she saw he was not going to accept her apology. He was not going to give her a chance to prove she had learned a valuable lesson and would never behave so foolishly again. He was just going to pack her off to the country, where she could not do his reputation any damage.

'I suppose,' she muttered mutinously, 'I should thank you for not threatening to cast me off without a penny.'

He flinched as though she had struck him. 'You are my wife, Heloise. A man does not cast his wife off for being a trifle expensive. I might scold, or preach economy, or…' Manfully, he strove to gentle his voice. 'The truth is, you are the least expensive female I have ever—' He broke off, cursing himself for this tactless turn of phrase.

But it was too late.

Stiffening proudly, Heloise replied, 'Yes, in that I should have listened to Mrs Kenton. She told me how generous you are.'

Damn Mrs Kenton, he thought, slamming himself out of the room. If she was here now, he would be sorely tempted to wring her neck!

Heloise watched a Dresden shepherdess on a console table beside the door rock dangerously before settling on its plinth. Could she never learn to control her tongue when she was with Charles? He had told her it was not suitable to speak about his mistress, and what had she done? Dragged her straight back into the conversation again.

No wonder he felt he had no option but to pack her off to one of his country estates. It was she, after all, who had put the notion into his head when she had suggested they should get married! She had actually *offered* to go and live in the country and keep chickens.

Uttering a cry of pure vexation, she seized the hapless shepherdess and flung her against the closed door, shattering her into hundreds of tiny shards. Nobody would ever be able to glue her back together again.

She knew her eyes were puffy from weeping. She knew her face was blotchy. She would much rather have stayed in her room than face her husband's disapproval so soon after that last devastating scene.

But Giddings had told her they would be dining *en famille* in the small salon tonight. And once Charles had deposited her in his country house and come back to town it might be months before she saw him again. As hard as it was to endure his presence, writhing inside as she was with humiliation, it would be far worse to sit alone in her room, knowing he was in the house and still, ostensibly, within her reach.

Charles and Robert were already there, standing on either side of the fireplace, so engrossed in conversation they did not appear to notice she had come in.

At least her time in London had not been a complete waste. When she had first come to England they had barely been able to stand being in the same room. Now, as they fell silent, turning to look at her with almost identical expressions of distaste on their faces, she could see that disapproval of her flighty, irresponsible ways had united these two proud men in a way that perhaps nothing else could have achieved.

'I am pleased we are all able to dine together tonight,' Charles said, as Finch proffered a tray containing a single glass of the sweet Madeira wine she had recently developed a taste for. 'This may be the last time we are all three together for some time. I am taking Lady Walton down to Wycke as soon as all the travel arrangements are in place,' he informed Robert.

'Sloughing me off?' his brother replied bitterly. 'Not that I can blame you, I suppose.' Eyeing Heloise with open hostility, he tossed back his drink, then held his glass out to Finch for a refill. 'Oh, don't look at me as though you're some puppy dog I've just kicked,' he growled, when her eyes filled with hurt tears. After downing the second drink, he sighed, rubbing his hand wearily across his face. 'Best sit down to dinner and forget I said anything.'

A wooden-faced Giddings pulled out her chair, assisting her to take her place when, in response to Robert's remark, Charles gave the signal to commence dining.

They ate their minted pea soup in silence. Heloise could think of nothing to say that wouldn't make everything ten times worse. She kept stealing glances at her handsome, enigmatic husband, a sense of awful finality lining her stomach with lead. While she had been dressing for dinner she had analysed every aspect of his behaviour towards her. She could better understand his attempt to consummate the marriage now she knew he had not, after all, been availing himself of Mrs Kenton's services. Assuming she was experienced, he had decided he might as well try her out 'just the once'. But, from the rapidity with which he left the room afterwards, it was clear she had fallen way short of his exacting standards.

And the fact that he did not seem to mind too much about the gambling debt must be because he was glad she had finally given him the excuse he needed to send her away. He had said they must spend some time in London just at first, to silence gossip. Well, now that time was at an end, and who could wonder at him taking her to the country and leaving her there?

He was only just recovering enough from his disappointment with regard to Felice to be thinking about having another woman in his bed. But once she was installed at Wycke he could come back to London and trawl through the women thronging Covent Garden, just as the other men of his class did.

She briefly wondered what he would look like with pea green soup dripping down his supercilious face. Perhaps fortunately for her, Giddings cleared away her bowl before she had summoned up the courage to indulge her vengeful daydream.

Linney leaned over Robert's plate to cut up the collop of veal that comprised the second course, provoking Robert into thumping his one clenched fist on the tabletop. His wine glass went flying, splattering scarlet liquid all over the pristine white tablecloth, onto his plate, and into the nearby dish of béchamel sauce.

'Dammit, dammit, *dammit*!' As he tried to push himself to his feet, Finch, who had sped to the scene with a cloth to mop up the spill, inadvertently blocked his clumsy manoeuvre. Linney caught him as he bounced off the strapping young man's frame, deftly deflecting him back into his seat. Then, without so much as a raised eyebrow, calmly carried on cutting up his master's veal.

'You'll feel much better, if you'll forgive me for saying so, sir, once you've got on the outside of some meat,' Linney observed. 'Been overdoing it today, he has, my lord.' He addressed Charles. 'Dashing all over town, knocking himself up, and getting into a pucker over the news.'

'Thank you, Linney. When I want you to speak for me, as well as cut up my food and put me to bed,' Captain Fawley stormed, 'I'll let you know!'

For the first time since she had come into the salon Heloise stopped thinking about her own problems and noticed that Robert looked really ill.

'Robert, what is the matter? Why have you been dashing all over town? Oh, please say it was not on account of my—'

'The news which has upset Robert, I believe,' Charles interrupted, hoping to avoid having his wife's gaming debts discussed before the servants, 'is—'

'Hell and damnation! Will you all stop trying to speak for me as though I'd lost my tongue along with an arm and a leg and my looks!'

'I beg your pardon,' Charles replied, calmly cutting up a portion of his own meat and spearing it neatly with his fork. 'By all means, repeat before my wife the news you related to me earlier.'

'Well, dammit, so I will!' he retorted. 'Grey lost the vote,' he told her. 'The government has finally decided to send British troops to support the forces the Prussians, Russians and Austrians have already assembled to put a stop to Bonaparte's ambitions. Britain is, in effect, at war with France again.'

He glared at her so ferociously that Heloise felt obliged to say, 'I know I am French, Robert, but I am not your enemy…'

He snorted in derision. 'But you're the only French citizen I'm likely to get anywhere near. Wellington and Bonaparte are finally going to meet, every able-bodied ex-soldier is volunteering, and what am I doing? Running errands for a French-born—'

'I think you have said enough,' Charles said.

Robert struggled with himself. 'Lady Walton,' he eventually said, 'it is not your fault you are French. I dare say the truth is that Linney is right. I have done too much today—knocked myself up. But if you had heard the way those fools were prating in the clubs! Laying odds on the chances of Wellington beating Bonaparte as though it was a cockfight! And all my friends, joining up and saying their farewells, and I'm stuck here—a useless wreck of a man. I just want to hit someone! I don't particularly care who. And I can't even do that,' he finished, glaring down at the empty sleeve which Linney had pinned neatly out of the way for dinner.

'Truth of the matter is I'm not fit company tonight, and I should never have come to this table,' said Robert, signalling to Linney to help him from his chair. 'I'll return to my rooms and stop casting a blight on your evening. Lady Walton.' He bowed to her. 'I carried out your little commission, as you requested. I gave the package to Charles.

I apologise for my filthy temper, and my boorish manners. And I trust you will enjoy your visit to Wycke.'

Heloise's mind began to race. 'Charles,' she said, turning to him the minute Robert had left, 'it cannot be good to go away just now and leave Robert all on his own. He might sink back to the way he was when I first came here.'

If she could postpone her exile, even for a few days, surely she could come up with some way to prove to Charles that he need not banish her? Even if it was only a stay of execution, she would at least have had a few more days with him.

'No,' he said, with such finality it dashed all her hopes to the ground. 'My mind is made up.' He had to remove Heloise from the dangers London posed for such an innocent. 'We will leave in the morning.'

She sat like a stone, picturing her lonely, loveless future, while the servants efficiently cleared away Robert's place-setting. In a space of minutes it was as if he had never been in the room. Even his chair was removed and placed against a wall, where it blended in amongst its fellows. Charles would no doubt have his servants eradicate all traces of his errant wife from this house just as efficiently.

'Do you require any help with your packing?'

She blinked. Charles was set on his course. She had no doubt that if she tried to resist he would order these efficient minions of his to pack her things for her. She had a brief vision of Giddings wrapping her in brown paper, securing her with string, and stuffing her into a trunk.

'No,' she said, folding her napkin neatly and placing it beside her still half-full plate. 'But what of Robert?' It had occurred to her that her exile might be easier to endure if she had a friend to share it. 'I cannot bear to think of him alone in those gloomy rooms. Could he not come with us?'

Charles set down his knife and fork. If Robert came with them it would ruin everything! He wanted Heloise to himself.

'Robert has a standing invitation to view Wycke any time he pleases. He is my heir, if you recall. But he does not care to go,' he warned her.

Heloise went cold inside. Charles had just reminded her he had no further use for her—not even to provide him with an heir. He wanted Robert to succeed him.

Frantically she grappled for something, anything, that might still win her a tiny place in her husband's good graces.

What if she could get Robert to travel to Wycke? Would that not please Charles? It had to be worth a try. For as things stood she was never likely to set eyes on him again. Once he had settled her into her new home he would feel free to pick a fresh, pretty new mistress, and within a month he would have forgotten all about her.

'I am finished here,' she said, pushing herself to her feet.

On legs that felt like cotton wool she left the salon and wove her way across the hall to pound on Robert's door. She had to persuade him to come to Wycke. It was her last chance to show Charles she had some worth as a wife.

Chapter Twelve

'Goodness!' Heloise exclaimed, leaning over Robert to peer through the window on his side of the carriage. 'How much land does Charles own?'

'More than half of Berkshire, I believe, besides swathes of land just outside London, and several minor estates dotted about the country.'

She sat back, a troubled frown on her face. 'I only meant how big is this estate of Wycke? It has been more than ten minutes, I think, since we drove through the lodge gates.'

'We have been driving through Walton's lands for the past hour and more,' Robert explained.

'All those farms and fields...the village we just passed through...'

'Did you not notice the name of the inn? The Walton Arms? The very vicar of the church is in your husband's pocket.'

He owned a village. And paid the priest. He was—she shuddered—the local *seigneur*. Just like her infamous grandfather.

She had always known Charles had a grand title. He had

told her he had a vast fortune. But she had never fully comprehended what it all meant until this moment.

Feeling very small, and very helpless, Heloise turned to look out of her own window, so that she could keep her feeling of shock from her travelling companion. And caught sight of Charles, mounted on his favourite hunter, breaking away from the cavalcade that was winding its ponderous way along the carriage drive and making for a belt of trees on top of a small rise. Did the house lie in that direction? In the middle of a forest?

She swallowed down a feeling of panic. He was going to abandon her here in the middle of all this countryside, with not a soul to talk to for miles.

The carriage wound round a right-hand bend, revealing yet another feature of Wycke's extensive grounds. On her side of the carriage the ground sloped down to a shimmering silver lake, containing an island complete with yet more trees, and a ruined castle.

It was a relief when the coach veered away from what looked suspiciously like the very sort of place a man would lock away an unwanted wife, and rolled along an avenue bordered by neatly clipped shrubbery.

The house itself was huge, naturally, and built of stone the colour of fresh butter.

'Oh, hell,' muttered Robert.

Following his gaze, Heloise registered that in order to reach the front door they were going to have to ascend a flight of about twenty steps.

By the time they stepped through the glass-paned double doors and into a bright, airy lobby, Robert's face was the colour of whey.

'Walton,' he gasped, addressing the figure emerging

from a green baize door to the rear of the hallway. 'Beg leave to inform you…'

But before he could finish, his eyes rolled back in his head. With a grunt, Linney took his dead weight, lowering him gently to the cool, marble tiled floor. Heloise dropped to her knees beside them, her hands frantically tearing away Robert's neck cloth.

'Finch! Wilbrahams!' Charles barked.

Heloise briefly lifted her head, registering her husband striding towards them with his jacket flying loose, his riding crop in his hand, closely followed by two footmen in the familiar blue and silver livery.

'Get Captain Fawley to his rooms!'

With Linney's help, the footmen manhandled Robert's dead weight towards a set of mahogany doors to the right of the grand staircase.

When Heloise scrambled to her feet and made to follow them, Charles caught her by the arm. 'Leave him to Linney,' he snapped. 'Your duty lies elsewhere.'

For the first time she noticed that the hall was crowded with servants, all of whom were watching her with avid curiosity.

From among them stepped a grey-haired lady, severely garbed in black bombazine.

'The staff wish to extend a warm welcome to your new bride, my lord,' she said dropping a respectful curtsey, though the expression on her face did not match her words.

Heloise was suddenly aware that as she had knelt to help Robert her bonnet had come askew, and that in rising she had caught her heel in her skirts, tearing loose a flounce. Her face felt sticky after the journey, and she was convinced there must be at least one smut on it.

'This is Mrs Lanyon, our housekeeper,' Charles said, his

fingers curling more tightly round her arm. He guided her along the line of servants as the housekeeper proceeded to name each and every one, along with their position.

Charles could not seriously expect her to remember the names of an entire regiment of household staff? Could he? Never mind the additional brigade of grooms and gardeners.

'And now I shall conduct you and your personal maid to your suite of rooms, my lady,' Mrs Lanyon intoned. 'There will just be time to refresh yourself and change for dinner,' she added, sweeping up the dark oak staircase. 'We have held it back against your arrival on this one occasion, although normally, of course, we do not keep town hours at Wycke.'

Heloise meekly followed, mortifyingly aware of the staff nudging each other and whispering behind their hands.

'I trust this is to your satisfaction, my lady?' Mrs Lanyon said, upon showing her into a set of rooms on the second floor.

'I am sure it is,' Heloise replied, loosening the ribbons of her bonnet. There had been something in the woman's tone that almost dared her to make any criticism. 'If you would show me where I may wash?'

Mrs Lanyon led the way across what Heloise had to admit was a very pretty, feminine sitting room, and opened a door. 'Your dressing room.'

'What a lovely washstand,' Heloise said inanely.

The top was of pink-veined marble. Standing upon its gleaming surface was a floral-patterned washing set, comprising ewer and basin, and a dish holding a cake of soap sculpted into the shape of a rose. Pristine linen sheets were draped in readiness over a free-standing towel rail.

'I shall feel so much better after a wash,' she said,

removing her bonnet and unbuttoning her spencer in the hope that Mrs Lanyon would take the hint and leave her in peace.

'Shall I send up some refreshments?'

'A glass of lemonade would be very welcome.'

'Lemonade,' Mrs Lanyon echoed faintly. Then, as though pulling herself together, 'If that is what you wish…'

'It is,' Heloise insisted, barely resisting the urge to stamp her foot. It had been a horrible day. Charles had been in one of his most unapproachable moods all day, the coach had been hot and stuffy, making the journey extremely uncomfortable, and she had discovered that her husband was not just Charles at all, but a man as important and influential as a French *seigneur*. This woman's thinly veiled disappointment in her new mistress was the last straw.

Only when she heard the door shut behind her did she permit herself to sink onto a striped day bed and toe off her sweat-stained pumps.

'Oh, Sukey,' she groaned, pressing her fingers to her throbbing temples. 'Did you ever see such a place? Or so many servants?'

'No, my lady,' she agreed, in a voice that was slightly muffled since she was peering into the wardrobe. 'Shall I pour the water for your wash now?' she asked, shutting it, and running her hand reverently over the beautifully carved door panels.

'You had better,' Heloise replied, prising herself from the sofa and padding to the dressing room in her stockinged feet. 'I dare not be late for dinner. You heard what that woman said. "We don't keep town hours at Walton."'

Sukey giggled as Heloise imitated the woman's voice almost perfectly.

'What shall I lay out for you to wear?'

'Whatever looks the least crumpled,' Heloise replied as Sukey went to work on the hooks of her gown. 'Oh, that feels so much better,' she sighed, as she peeled gown and stays from her perspiring body.

It felt better still to sponge herself all over with cool, delicately scented water. When she went back into the sitting room, wrapped only in a linen bath sheet, she found a tray containing lemonade and a plate of freshly baked biscuits on a little occasional table. Both were delicious, and very welcome.

'I've laid out that light yellow silk gown for dinner,' Sukey said, emerging from another door, which Heloise could see led to a bedchamber. She felt a queer tightening in her middle at the possibility there might be a door somewhere that connected her suite to her husband's rooms, just like in London. Should she ask Sukey? Or just go and look for herself later on? So it would not seem as though she had given the matter any thought?

'Since it has been such a hot day, I thought you would want something cool to wear.' Sukey explained her choice. 'But I've put the gold silk shawl out as well, in case it gets chilly later on.' She picked up Heloise's hairbrush. 'Shall I start on your hair while you finish your drink, to save time? And if I bring the plate of biscuits to the dressing table you can carry on eating, too.'

'A good idea,' said Heloise, settling on the low-backed chair.

'It's going to take me a month of Sundays to remember the names of all the people who work here,' Sukey muttered through a mouthful of hairpins.

'Me also,' agreed Heloise with a rueful smile.

'And have you ever seen so many trees? Not but what we don't have trees in London, but at least they are in nice straight lines along the side of the road, where they give shade in the summer,' she grumbled, swiftly working the brush through Heloise's tangles. 'I reckon they must be downright gloomy when it rains.'

'Do you dislike it so much here?' Just because she was doomed to misery, it was not fair to condemn her maid to the same fate. She felt a flicker of panic. 'If you want to return to London…'

'I dare say I will get used to it!' Sukey said hastily. 'I didn't mean to complain. I'd much rather be a lady's maid, even if it is stuck out here in the middle of all this nothing, than go back to blacking the fires in London!'

'I don't expect you will go back to blacking fires—not now you've become a lady's maid,' Heloise reproved gently. 'You have learned to do it so well! At least, I think you have.' She frowned. Then, seeing Sukey's downcast expression in the mirror, she explained, 'You see, I never had a maid—not before I married Lord Walton. In Paris I shared a room with my sister, and we used to help each other dress and do each other's hair.'

Absentmindedly, she nibbled on a biscuit. She had no experience with servants at all, if truth be told. In London, once she had discovered that Charles disliked her chatting to Giddings as though he were a real person, she had tried to ignore them. They had all helped her by taking care to be as unobtrusive as possible. They had certainly never all stood in one place at the same time, and stared at her as though she was some kind of fairground exhibit. Why had he not warned her they would all turn out to greet her like that? And why had he not told her what she should say? She had seen the expression of disapproval on his face when she had been struck dumb by the onslaught of all that curiosity. And she had felt the scorn emanating from Mrs Lanyon's stiff back as she had led her way up the stairs.

'I hope you won't leave me, Sukey,' she said, suddenly reaching for her maid's hand over her shoulder. She needed at least one ally amongst all these strangers.

'Of course I'll stay. It's not as if we'll be down here for ever, is it? Old Giddings was explaining to me that though His Lordship comes down here regular, he never stays for long. We'll soon be back in town, dressing you for parties and the theatre and the like!'

Charles never stays for long. She sighed, replacing her half-eaten biscuit on the plate. But she doubted very much whether she would ever see London again.

Just when he'd thought the day could not possibly get any worse, Charles discovered dinner had been laid out in the state dining room.

Nothing could have been more daunting to a woman like Heloise. His place was at the head of the table, while she sat at its foot, some twenty feet distant. There was no point in even attempting any sort of conversation.

He barely managed to stifle the irritation that had dogged him all day, reminding himself that the staff had clearly gone to a great deal of trouble to impress his new Countess. The meal was a culinary triumph. And he was sure Mrs Lanyon had not intended to intimidate Heloise the minute she stepped through the front door. It was just, he realised, that his guardians had inaugurated a devilishly formal atmosphere at Wycke. And he had never bothered to dismantle it. When he was in residence his focus was on the land, and his tenants. He did not care enough about household management to bother altering a routine into which he fell without thinking.

He should have given Heloise a hint, though, about how to deal with that welcoming party. He had meant to, but when he had gone out to the coach and seen Robert sitting in it he had been so angry that the only way to avoid an unpleasant scene had been to have his hunter saddled up and claim he preferred to ride in such warm weather. So instead of spending the journey warning Heloise that their housekeeper liked to do things 'properly', he had flounced off in a right royal huff. He should have been pleased that she had somehow cajoled Robert into finally accepting an invitation to come and view the place where he should have grown up.

All he could think of was that his plans to get Heloise to himself had been ruined. He would have to divide his time between wooing his reluctant bride and initiating his recalcitrant brother into the ways of Wycke. And in giving way to anger he had done them both a disservice. Not only had Heloise's inadvertent recoil offended Mrs Lanyon, but he had not taken sufficient care of a man who was still far from well. It would probably take Robert days to recover from the journey down here.

He rose to his feet when Heloise left the table, morosely noting how swiftly she fled his presence.

He had the devil of a job on his hands with both Heloise and Robert. And, he reflected, gulping down port that should really have been sipped and savoured, he was damned if he knew how to proceed with either of them.

Heloise took the stopper from the perfume bottle she had found on her dressing table and sniffed tentatively. It was floral, but with an underlying hint of musk that was quite sensual. She dabbed a little onto each wrist, and behind her ears. Then, feeling very daring, between her breasts.

She had already dismissed Sukey, claiming with complete honesty that she would not need her any more. For seducing her husband was a thing a woman had to do for herself.

During dinner she'd had ample opportunity to study her distant spouse and form a plan. He seemed very much at home here, in this house that ran with the precision of a clockwork toy. He was not the sort of man to break any habit he had formed without good reason. So she could probably expect him to come and bid her goodnight.

Gazing along the length of polished mahogany that had symbolised the vast gulf that separated them, she had noted that he was able to enjoy the meal for which she had little appetite. He was a healthy man in his prime, with healthy appetites—at least one of which had not been met since they had married, so far as she could tell. And they were miles from anywhere. And he was not the sort of man to dally with the housemaids.

Which was why she had got Sukey to fetch her most revealing nightdress under the pretext that it was a very sultry night. And doused herself with the only perfume she could lay her hands on.

Finally, with great daring, she arranged herself in what she hoped was a seductive pose on top of the covers.

And waited nervously for Charles to come to her.

It was hard to resist the instinctive desire to preserve her modesty by pulling the covers over herself when she heard the knock that presaged his arrival. Her sense of vulnerability increased when he strode into the room fully dressed.

His reaction was not what she had hoped for either. He glanced only briefly to where she knew her nipples were just visible through the filmy fabric of her nightgown, then, his jaw tightening, fixed his eyes firmly on her face.

'I must apologise,' he said, sitting on the chair beside her bed and crossing his legs as though he had not noticed she was barely decent, 'for the reception you received from the staff. Mrs Lanyon meant well. I was remiss in not preparing you for the formality with which things are done here,' he added, thinking of the dreadful atmosphere at dinner. 'Mrs Lanyon has ruled the roost for a long time.'

Far too long. It was well past time some changes were made. Mrs Lanyon presided over the routine his guardians had inaugurated. But he could remember that Wycke had had a far more relaxed, happy atmosphere when his father had been alive.

'I hope you will make whatever changes you feel are necessary to make this a comfortable home.'

Heloise bit her lower lip. Before they had married he had told her that his staff were efficient, and that he did not want her altering anything. That had been before he had discovered she was such a liability he would not be able to tolerate living in the same household. That he was now granting her permission to make whatever changes she wished here at Wycke, so that she could be relatively comfortable in her exile, was a generous concession on his part.

'You must be tired,' he said. 'It's been the devil of a day.'

He kissed her swiftly, and left so abruptly he might just as well have slapped her.

It was only after he had gone that she worked out what she should have done. When he had bent to kiss her she should have put her arms about his neck and kissed him back. Not on the lips, she had not the courage to be so brazen. For if he had recoiled from such a kiss she would have died of the humiliation. But she could have given him an affectionate peck on the cheek. She frowned. Though he had warned her he did not like displays of affection.

Oh, damn the man! She knelt up and flung a pillow at the door through which he had retreated. Then buried her face in her hands. The barriers which separated them were impenetrable. Especially since he bolstered them every way he could. She should just give up before she totally humiliated herself.

Charles' mood the next morning was even blacker than it had been the night before. Heloise had looked so tempting, lying on her bed in that confection of lace and moonbeams, that it had been all he could do to keep his hands off her. The wary look on her face had reminded him just in time what a disaster that would have been. The speech he had spent so long carefully preparing had evaporated like morning mist at the sudden hot flare of lust he'd had to disguise by sitting down quickly, crossing his legs, and clasping his hands in his lap.

He'd spent a sleepless night, remembering how she had looked reclining on that bank of pillows and wishing he could be beside her. Racking his brains to think of some way he could achieve that goal.

While he had been shaving, he'd had a brainwave. For a couple of days he would have Heloise to himself, while Robert was recovering. He could make a start by showing her over the house. And while he was doing that he would persuade her that it might be a good idea to learn to drive the estate gig. The narrow seat of the two-wheeled vehicle could only accommodate a driver and one passenger. They would have to go out on their own. He would have to take hold of her hands to teach her how to use the reins. She would get used to him touching and holding her, under the guise of accepting instruction, and slowly she would cease to feel threatened by him. When they reached that point he would slide his arm about her waist, or her shoulder. He would inform her that her bonnet was most becoming, and drop a kiss on her cheek…

A less contained man than he would have whistled on the staircase as he went down to breakfast.

And would then have thumped Giddings for informing him that his bailiff was already waiting for him in the estate office.

Why had he forgotten that he always spent his first day at Wycke going over the estate accounts? And damn the place anyway, for its relentless routine which ground any hope of spontaneity into the dust!

Heloise checked on the threshold of the breakfast room when she saw the thunderous expression on his face. A stickler for good manners, he got to his feet and bade her a gruff good morning, but it was evident he had not expected her presence at the breakfast table.

The room was far nicer than the one where they had dined the night before. It was smaller, for one thing, and the floor-to-ceiling windows gave a view over a gravelled parterre in the centre of which an ornamental fountain played. The table was round, and lacked formal place-settings. If Charles had not retreated behind his newspaper, indicating his preference for solitude, she could have sat next to him.

'I had thought you might like a tour of the house this morning,' he said, as she helped herself to some chocolate from a silver pot which stood on a sideboard. 'Unfortunately I have pressing estate business to see to, else I would have taken you around myself.'

'It is of no matter.' Heloise shrugged. She would have years to explore this horrid house, and would probably come to detest every inch of it. 'I will go and make a visit with Robert, see how he does. And after I shall take a walk through the gardens.'

'I have another suggestion,' he put in hastily. He had to wean her from the habit of turning to Robert. 'Have Mrs Lanyon take you over the house this morning. She knows far more about its history than I, in any case. She has made quite a study of it. And, you know, it would be a good opportunity to get on terms with the woman.' They had not got off to a good start. 'You are going to have to deal with her on a regular basis…'

Yes, Mrs Lanyon was to be her jailer! Breaking open a bread roll with rather more force than was necessary, Heloise considered her husband's advice. It was bad enough that she was going to have to live in this wilderness, let alone with a woman who despised her. One who wielded such immense power over the staff as well.

'You are right,' she sighed.

'Then I shall arrange it. Also,' he added in a deceptively casual tone, 'one day soon, since the estate is so large and you do not ride, I shall teach you to drive a gig. Then you will be able to get around more independently.' He studied her downbent head with a growing feeling of disquiet. It was almost as if she sensed his suggestion was merely a ruse to get her alone, and was thinking of excuses to put him off. 'It would be a great pity to be restricted to the house when there are so many delightful vistas just a short drive away,' he went on, in some desperation. 'Once you become proficient I should not object to you driving yourself into the village on occasion—provided, of course, you took your maid.'

Heloise could hardly swallow her bread and honey for the lump which formed in her throat.

He might not be able to feel any affection for her, but

he was clearly not going to leave her here until he was fairly sure she had the means to be comfortable. He was intent on smoothing her way with the formidable Mrs Lanyon, and had come up with a plan to ensure she had a degree of freedom when he was no longer there.

Though he did own a village, and held the lives of so many people in the palm of his hand, he was by no means a tyrant. His strict sense of duty ensured he looked out for the welfare of all his dependants, be they tenants or injured and estranged brothers, or ill-chosen wives. How could she help loving him?

She sighed. It would take a remarkable woman to earn his regard. She did not know why she had even thought it was worth trying.

There was no point in her wearing transparent nightgowns and dousing herself with perfume to try to titillate his manly impulses. Or trying to worm her way into his busy life by interrupting him at the breakfast table when he clearly would much rather be reading his paper. She would revert to the routine they had set in London and keep out of his way, as she had initially promised.

She lifted her chin, laying what remained of the honeyed crust on her plate.

'You do not need to teach me to drive. I shall get Robert to do it. It will do him good to get out in the fresh air. Besides, I am sure he wants to explore the estate, but nothing would let him admit as much. If he has the excuse of having to look after me, it will mean he can get out as often as he wants.'

He was still groping for some objection to her very logical suggestion when she rose from her chair and glided from the room without a backward glance. Somehow she had managed to slip through his fingers yet again.

* * *

'And now we come to the portrait gallery,' Mrs Lanyon intoned.

She certainly knew a great deal about Wycke, and the family who had lived there since it had been built, in the latter days of Queen Elizabeth. She liked nothing better, she had confided on collecting Heloise from her rooms, than showing interested parties around.

Wycke was mentioned in guidebooks, and visitors to the county always put it at the very top of their itinerary, she had further declared, with pride.

'This is the first Earl,' she said of a life-sized portrait of a man with a ruff round his neck and a fierce expression on his face that put Heloise in mind of Robert.

Each successive Earl and Countess Mrs Lanyon introduced her to gazed down at her with varying degrees of disdain.

'The late Countess of Walton,' Mrs Lanyon said, jerking Heloise out of her introspection.

'Which one?' she dared to ask, her interest reviving for the first time since 1724.

'I mean to say, is it the Earl's mother, or his stepmother?'

Mrs Lanyon drew herself up to her full height before saying frostily, 'His mother, naturally. She was the grand-daughter of the Duke of Bray.'

She looked as though she might have been, Heloise mused. The weight of generations of breeding sat heavily on the slender shoulders of the young woman who looked out of her gilded frame with a somewhat pained expression. The glossy curls which peeped from under the brim of her hat were of a similar colour to Charles' hair, and her eyes were blue, but her mouth had a petulant droop to the lips that she would never associate with him.

'My grandfather,' Heloise blurted in a spirit of rebellion, 'was among the very first to go to the guillotine.' Her father might be only a government functionary, but her mother's blood was as blue as any of these ancestors of Charles'.

'Dreadful!' gasped Mrs Lanyon, her hand flying to her throat.

'Yes, he was. He doubled the taxes during a period of famine, causing great hardship to the peasants. Something that Charles,' she declared with conviction, 'would never do.'

Having finished her tour of the house, Mrs Lanyon handed her over to Bayliss, the head gardener. Thoroughly oppressed by so much history, and aware she had spoken too controversially for Mrs Lanyon's comfort, Heloise was glad to get out of doors.

To her dismay, the Walton family, and in particular the ladies, pursued her through the grounds. A knot garden was the work of the first Countess; a rose garden was the inspiration of the third. She could see why the place attracted visitors, for it contained a great deal that was beautiful. But it was more like a museum than a home.

Spying a familiar figure lounging on a south-facing stone terrace, Heloise escaped from her guide.

'Robert!' she cried, running up the steps and bounding to his side. 'You are better today, yes?'

'Just sitting out enjoying the fresh air,' he groused. 'Don't go pestering me to go anywhere today, because I have no intention of stirring from this terrace. Which is mine, by the way.'

'How do you mean, yours?' She sat on a wooden bench next to him, her eyes alight with curiosity.

'I mean just that. The windows behind me lead directly into my rooms. Nobody is supposed to disturb me out here. Do you know you have to walk across I don't know how many lawns to get to those steps you ran up?'

'Only too well!' she snorted. 'For I have walked across them. Oh,' she said, suddenly registering what he had said, 'you wish me to leave you alone.' From his eyes she met the hostility of generations of Waltons. 'I understand.'

Leaping to her feet, she ran back down the steps and, without knowing where she would end up, headed away from the house. Anywhere, she fumed, blinking back tears, as long as she was out of everyone's way! She blundered through a dense shrubbery to emerge on the lip of an embankment. To her amazement she discovered she had come out just above the curving carriage drive, and that beyond it a flower-sprinkled meadow undulated down to the lake.

Perhaps the grounds were not so large as she had first assumed. She would never have guessed, when she had driven along this particular stretch of the drive the day before, that she was so near the house.

She eyed the ruined tower on the island in which she had imagined Charles might lock her away. He might just as well. The servants had despised her on sight, and now even Robert, whom she thought of as a brother, had said he wanted her to stop pestering him.

Very well! She would not pester Robert to teach her to drive after all. She would get one of the grooms to do it. And prove to Charles that she did not need him—no, not for anything.

And then he could go back to London and forget all about her.

And she…no, she would never forget Charles. She would spend every minute of her long, lonely exile wondering what he was doing.

And who he was doing it with.

Chapter Thirteen

Charles paused in the doorway of the state dining room, which tonight was looking its most magnificent. The staff had polished the massive epergnes to mirror-brightness, filling them with banks of freshly cut flowers that filled the air with their perfume. A footman was going round lighting the candles already. Once he had finished, the china and crystal would glitter like jewels set against the yards of spotless damask linen tablecloth.

'It all looks splendid—as ever,' he said to his house-keeper. Within a week of his arrival Mrs Lanyon had reminded him that he always sent out cards of invitation to his neighbours. It was just one more tradition he wished he had never allowed to become set in stone. 'Though in future you should expect Lady Walton to oversee events of this nature.'

Fortunately for her, Mrs Lanyon refrained from making the comment which would have brought her instant dismissal. Though the way she pursed her lips told him exactly what she was thinking. Heloise had played no part in the organisation of this dinner whatsoever. Whenever Mrs

Lanyon had consulted her, she had replied she must do exactly as she wished.

Though it hurt to think she disliked him so much she could not even pretend to show an interest in his social life, he could not be angry with her. Being on display for his neighbours would be an ordeal for a woman of her shy, retiring disposition. If he could only have thought of a way to cancel the dinner without insulting his neighbours he would have done so. But in the end he had decided it would be better to just get the thing over with as soon as possible. Far better for them to find out that his wife was a little gauche than for them to imagine she was unfriendly.

He had never been so irritated by the number of obligations his position brought him before. But since they had come down to Wycke every chance he might have had to get closer to Heloise had been thwarted by estate business in one form or another.

Still, he had dealt with all the most pressing business now. And once this annual county dinner was over he could devote himself almost exclusively to wooing her.

As he went along the corridor to the red salon, he wondered what lay behind her decision to get Grimwade, the head groom, to teach her to drive rather than Robert. Strolling to the window that overlooked the carriage drive, he rubbed his hand across the back of his neck. To his knowledge, Robert had not stirred from his rooms since his arrival, although Linney assured him his master was recovering nicely from the journey. He barely repressed the urge to fling the window open. Though the room felt stuffy, the air outside was even hotter, and heavy with the threat of an approaching storm. He hoped it would not break too soon. The last thing he wanted was for his guests to be stranded, so that he would be obliged to offer them hospitality.

* * *

'Do I wear the Walton diamonds?' Heloise was anxiously asking Sukey. 'Or will it look as though I am showing off?'

One did not dress so elaborately in the country. Even she knew that. Which was why she had chosen the simplest evening gown she had. But, since she had no other jewellery, it was either wear the Walton parure or nothing. She did not think Charles would wish her to look dowdy.

Though how could she look anything else? She had neither Felice's emerald eyes, nor the voluptuous figure of Mrs Kenton. With a small cry of distress, she whirled away from the mirror.

'Don't be nervous, my lady,' Sukey said brightly. 'You are the highest-ranking lady in the district, and nothing anyone might think will alter that.'

She was right. The women she'd seen wearing the Walton diamonds in portrait after portrait might disapprove of her, but she was as much the Countess as any of them. Because Charles had married *her*. Not the graceful Felice, nor the experienced Mrs Kenton, but plain, naïve little Heloise Bergeron.

Anyway, these hard cold stones were all she had to prove this marriage was real. Especially since the arrival of her monthly courses, a few days earlier, had robbed her of even the faint hope that she might have conceived a child during that one brief coupling.

Straightening her shoulders, she walked across to the table on which the ancient jewel case squatted. 'I will wear the diamonds,' she said. 'All of them.'

She did not care if anyone thought she was overdressed. She clipped the earrings to her earlobes with a grimace. Though she wanted to make a good impression on the people who would form her new social circle, she had an even greater need to bolster her flagging self-esteem.

Before long she was ready to join Charles in the red salon, where Mrs Lanyon had told her he always greeted his dinner guests.

He looked magnificent in his evening clothes. He was always so immaculately dressed, so correct in all his behaviour. She itched to reach up and tousle his neatly brushed hair, to mar that perfection which threw all her own faults into stark relief. When his guests started to arrive, and saw them standing side by side, they were bound to wonder at the Earl having made such a mismatch.

The breath hitched in Charles' throat as she trailed slowly across the room to join him beside the empty hearth. She was so lovely. The simply cut gown she had chosen became her slight figure far more than some of the fussy creations he had seen adorning the so-called leaders of fashion in London. And with the diamonds glittering about her throat and wrist she looked every inch the Countess.

He was on the verge of telling her so, when she began to twist her hands together at her waist. He had got used to seeing her drooping disconsolately about the place, but this new symptom hurt him abominably. She could not bear to come within three feet of him!

He turned from her abruptly. It took him a moment or two to get himself in hand. And then he found he was standing by the sideboard. He did the only thing that came to him which might just help her. He poured a small glass of Madeira and carried it back to her.

Heloise tossed it back, wondering in what way she had failed to measure up this time, for him to walk away from her with such a grim expression. Had it been a mistake to wear the full parure? Had it reminded him of how very nearly she had lost part of it? Or did he just think she was overdressed? And if he thought so what would his guests think? Perhaps she should run back upstairs and change? Oh, but there was no time. The front door was being opened, she could hear Giddings greeting someone, and already there was the sound of more wheels crunching over the gravel drive.

Her heart pounding against her ribs, she held out her empty glass to Finch.

'Get me another,' she pleaded, avoiding her husband's gaze. It was bad enough knowing she disappointed him without encountering the full wintry blast of his eyes.

The room rapidly filled with about thirty people who had known Charles and each other all their lives. There was only one person amongst them who did not totally overwhelm her. Her name was Miss Masterson, and her father was a retired colonel. Heloise empathised with the way she sought out a corner away from the more ebullient guests, and made sure the circulating footmen did not overlook her. When Charles had gone back to London she would call on the girl, who looked as if she was of a similar age, and see if she could make a friend of her. If, that was, she could bear to enter the house of the Colonel and his bulldog-faced wife.

'Hoped to be able to meet your long-lost brother,' Colonel Masterson was booming at Charles, as though he was yards away across a parade ground. 'Military man, ain't he? Was hoping to have a jaw with him about developments in the Low Countries. Wellington's been given charge of the allied armies, d'you know? Got it from Viscount Brabourne on his way through to his hunting box in Wiltshire. Damned shame we're at war with your wife's country again. Though I'm sure,' he said turning towards her, 'you want to see Bonaparte brought to book, eh? Must support the Bourbons. Walton wouldn't have married you unless you was a Royalist, now, would he?'

'You are mistaken,' she replied, cut to the quick by his barely concealed speculation as to what on earth could have induced an Earl to marry her. 'I am very far from being a Royalist.'

She did not realise that she should have taken the time to explain she despised fat Louis and his inept government almost as much as she detested Bonaparte's ruthless efficiency until she heard the Colonel confide to his wife, in what he must have thought was a whisper, as they were processing to the dining room, 'Outrageous! He's brought a Bonapartist amongst us!' His wife managed to hush him, but she could not stop him casting suspicious looks her way throughout the meal.

Lord Danvers, who was sitting to her right at the foot of the table, opened the conversation over the soup by enquiring if she hunted.

She made the fatal error of confessing that she could not ride at all.

'Not ride?' He looked at her as though she had confessed to a crime.

Swiftly she tried to vindicate herself. 'It is considered unpatriotic, in my country, to keep a horse. Like our sons and brothers, they belong to the army of France.' The malevolent glare this comment drew from Colonel Masterson suggested he now believed she must have come to England for the sole purpose of winkling state secrets from her husband. Now he would never allow her to befriend his daughter.

After that, the conversation at the foot of the table became painfully stilted. And yet Heloise dreaded the moment when she would have to rise, signalling it was time for the ladies to withdraw. While they were confined to their seats and occupied with their food only the nearest handful of guests could attack her. She had the feeling that once she got to the music room it would turn into a free-for-all.

Lady Danvers fired the opening salvo.

'Do you play the pianoforte, Lady Walton?' she cooed. 'Or perhaps the harp? Or have you arranged something particularly French—' she tittered '—to entertain the gentlemen when they join us?'

'No,' she replied bluntly. She did not ride, she did not play any musical instrument, and she did not have a lively personality. She sighed. And if only it were true that she had ensnared her husband by the sort of French naughtiness this abominable woman implied.

With a triumphant gleam in her eye, Lady Danvers went to the sofa where Lady Masterson was sitting, settled beside her, and murmured something in her ear that caused the older lady to regard Heloise with even deeper hostility.

'Perhaps our dear Countess has other talents,' suggested the vicar's wife. 'We are all good at something. Even if it is only the art of putting the poor at ease when visiting. Or the clever arrangement of flowers. Or embroidery. Or…' Looking more and more desperate as Heloise shook her head at every suggestion the kind lady put forward, she eventually subsided.

'You mean to tell me you have no accomplishments whatever?' Lady Danvers drawled.

'I do not tell you that at all,' Heloise snapped, her patience finally running out. 'I am an artist!'

'An artist?' Lady Danvers quirked one eyebrow in distinct mockery. 'You mean you dabble about with paint?'

'No, I draw,' she replied, her heart suddenly plunging to her dainty satin slippers. Charles would hate it if these people ever found out she had tried to make money from the sale of her work. Work of which he strongly disapproved.

'But I do not have a portfolio to show you. It was lost…' Well, at least most of it was 'lost', burnt, actually '…when I left France.'

'Oh, how disappointing,' drawled Lady Danvers sarcastically. 'I am sure we have missed a rare treat.' She exchanged a knowing smile with Lady Masterson.

Heloise gasped. The woman was accusing her of being a liar to her face!

Lydia Bentinck, one of a trio of elderly spinsters, sniffed loudly before saying, 'There is more to being a lady of quality than being able to draw, or play the piano, or ride a horse. I have always held that good manners are an absolute prerequisite.' She looked pointedly at Lady Danvers. 'So sadly lacking in many these days.'

Lady Danvers' eyes snapped with fury. While she struggled to find a suitably cutting come back, Diana Bentinck turned to Heloise and enquired, 'What sort of drawings do you do?'

'People. I do sketches of people.'

'Oh, how charming. Would you do a sketch of me and my sisters? I should love to have a likeness. Or would it take too long?'

She was on the point of refusing, out of deference to Charles' views, when she caught sight of Lady Danvers' lip curling in derision.

'I would be glad to sketch you,' she declared defiantly. 'Please to take seats close together, while I find some materials.'

By this time one of the other ladies, a Mrs Goulding,

had taken a seat at the piano, and while Heloise unearthed some sheets of writing paper from a desk drawer she began to pick out the bare bones of a Haydn sonata. From her reticule, Heloise produced the sliver of charcoal which she was never without. While the Bentinck sisters fluttered about the three chairs they had decided to pose on, arguing as to which order they should sit, either by age or by size, and whether one should stand behind the other two to make an interesting group, Heloise's nimble fingers flew across the page. By the time they were settled she was able to walk over to them, holding out her finished work.

'Why,' exclaimed Lydia, 'this is quite remarkable!'

Three grey heads bent to examine the sparse lines on the creamy vellum. They could see Lydia standing over her two seated siblings. Diana was holding out her hand, palm upwards, while Grace had her head tilted to one side, a pensive frown knitting her brows. Though each pose denoted a certain amount of conflict, each woman was also expressing a strong affection for the other two, so that the overall impression was one of harmony.

'I cannot believe you did that so quickly!' Diana Bentinck cried.

'It was not so quick.' They had been bickering gently for several minutes, and she had always found it a simple matter to reproduce an accurate physical likeness.

'I am sorry that it is only on writing paper…' she began.

But, 'Oh, no!' the three sisters cried simultaneously. 'This paper has the Walton crest on it. What a lovely reminder it will be to us of a delightful evening spent at Wycke!'

The vicar's wife had now sidled up to her. 'Oh, I should love to have a sketch drawn by you, Lady Walton,' she gushed.

'As you wish,' Heloise replied, picking up her charcoal.

Fortunately, she had not had time to study these people too closely, and so link them inextricably in her mind with some member of the animal kingdom. So she managed, with some application, to repress her imagination and stick to a strictly literal likeness of her next subject. The resultant sketch was exclaimed over, passed round, and generated such excitement that several other ladies asked if she would do their portraits too.

She became so deeply absorbed that she noticed neither the passage of time nor the arrival in the music room of the gentlemen. All she did see, when she handed Miss Masterson her finished sketch, was the smile which lit up her face.

'Do I really look like that?' the girl exclaimed, running a finger wonderingly over the smudged lines of her portrait. Her face clouded. 'I think you must have been flattering me.'

'Not in the least,' Charles said, startling Heloise. She'd had no idea he was standing behind her chair. 'My wife never flatters her sitters. She has the knack, though, of putting something of the subject's personality in beyond the physical likeness. Perhaps that is what you recognise in your own portrait, Miss Masterson?'

Heloise did not know what to make of this remark. Perhaps his oblique reference to the way she habitually portrayed people as the animals they reminded her of was a warning to behave herself?

'You must do my son,' Lady Masterson said. 'Now that you have managed to make my stepdaughter look so fetching.'

Heloise hesitated. She would have been thrilled at winning over one of her major opponents so easily, were she not so scared of offending Charles. Warily, she looked to him for guidance. But his expression gave her no clues.

She pulled a fresh sheet of paper from the drawer of the writing desk as young Thomas Masterson took the seat his older sister had just vacated.

Why did she never think about the consequences before acting? she berated herself. It had been just the same in that stupid card game. Only tonight it had been Lady Danvers who had goaded her into losing her temper and acting in a way that was guaranteed to displease Charles. Gripping the charcoal tightly, she paused to examine the young man's features for a moment or two before setting to work.

Charles watched in fascination as her fingers flew across the paper. He had never seen her drawing before. She had pitched her work this evening in a way that was guaranteed to please their guests. His heart swelled with pride. She could so easily have taken revenge for the various snubs she had borne earlier, by accentuating the uglier aspects of her neighbours. Instead, she brought out the best in them. She had even managed to make the dreary Miss Masterson look interesting, transforming her habitually vacant stare into the dreamy reverie of a *savant*.

She was so talented. He ached to tell her so. He pondered how best to word the compliment, savouring the knowledge that it was the very one he could pay her that would please her.

And while they were on the subject he must ask her pardon for forcing her to burn that sketchbook. If she could forgive him that one transgression… His heart-rate picked up dramatically. Had he finally found the key that might unlock his wife's heart?

He could hardly wait for the last of his tedious guests to leave so that he could make his declaration.

'I am sorry you did not have an easy time of it this evening,' he began, his expression sobering as he recalled

Colonel Masterson's rudeness, and imagined the barbed comments he was sure the spiteful Lady Danvers must have let fly. 'But I believe most of our guests went away having been tolerably well entertained.'

His words struck at her like a blow from a fist. Though she had very nearly disgraced him, he seemed to be saying, his neighbours had been gracious enough to overlook all her inadequacies.

'Then may I go to my room, now?'

'Very well,' he conceded, battening down his eagerness to put his new plan of action in train. He followed her into the hall and watched her ascend the stairs. He would give her a few minutes before following her, and then…

'A word, if you please, Walton!'

Robert's harsh voice abruptly shattered his fantasies. He turned to see his half-brother emerge from the shadows beneath the bend in the great staircase.

'Ashamed of me, are you?' Robert began, with no preamble.

'I beg your pardon?' Why did he have to pick such an inappropriate moment to pick a quarrel? 'You'd better come into my study.'

Striding past his brother, he flung open the door and went in. He was not going to participate in any kind of a scene in the hall, where angry words would echo up to the rafters.

'What is it?' he said with impatience, going from habit to the side table on which rested a decanter of fine cognac and several glasses.

'I want to know why you excluded me tonight,' Robert began, stumping angrily along in his wake. 'Why the devil drag me down here if all you do is shut me away like some…?'

Abruptly his words petered out as he caught sight of the portrait that hung above Charles' desk.

'That's my mother!' he exclaimed in indignation. 'Why have you got a picture of my mother in your study? Why isn't she up in the gallery with all the reputable Waltons?'

'When have *you* been up in the picture gallery?'

Robert looked a little discomfited, but did not admit that he had bribed Finch to show him round at times when he knew neither Giddings nor Mrs Lanyon nor Charles would discover he had done so.

'Well, I am glad you have been exploring your home, though had I known you wished to do so I would gladly have been your guide...'

'Oh, would you?' he sneered. 'When you hide me away from your neighbours as though you are ashamed of owning such a brother!'

'I have done no such thing! I had nothing to do with the arrangements. Heloise...' He frowned. She had left the whole thing to Mrs Lanyon. Did the housekeeper have a problem with Robert's presence in the house? Might she even have some lingering loyalties to the Lamptons?

'Oh, hell,' said Robert, casting himself into a chair and easing the position of his wooden leg with his good hand. 'My cursed temper! I've upset her. I wondered at the time...though normally when I rip up at her she gives it me back threefold.'

'Here.' Charles pressed a glass of cognac into his hand and settled behind the desk.

'I wish you wouldn't be so damned reasonable all the time,' Robert grumbled. 'If only you would shout back at me just once in a while, instead of being so...icily polite, I shouldn't feel so...so...'

Charles shrugged one shoulder. 'My guardians did a

sterling job of raising me after the pattern of my own mother's irreproachable forebears. Although...' he swivelled in his chair to gaze at the portrait that hung there '...when I gaze upon your mother's face I can remember a time when things were very different here at Wycke. It was only from the day they ousted her it became this cold, inhospitable mausoleum. They told me she had abandoned me.' He took a large gulp of the cognac. 'I was eight years old. She was the only mother I had ever known. She had always seemed warm and loving, to both me and my father. Suddenly it was as if I had never known her at all. How could a woman turn her back on a child who had just lost his father?'

'She didn't!' Robert defended her. 'They sent her back to her family and then threw all their weight into crushing her spirit!'

'For which crime I shall never be able to forgive them.'

His eyes grew so cold that Robert took a swig of his cognac to counteract the chill that pervaded the whole room.

'You should have grown up here, with me. We should have climbed trees, fished in the lake, and played at Knights and Saracens in the ruined tower. If your mother had been here she would have made sure I went to school rather than being walled up here with a succession of tutors.'

'I never appreciated you may have felt like this.' Robert frowned into his glass. 'I always assumed that the quarrel you started with the Lamptons when you came of age was to do with money...'

'Money! Oh, no. They were always scrupulously honest when it came to my finances. It was something far more valuable they robbed me of.' His eyes returned to the portrait of the dark-haired woman smiling down at her boys. 'Something irreplaceable. My childhood.'

After an awkward pause, Robert managed to mumble, 'Grown up in the habit of hating you, but I have to concede of late you have been very generous to me…'

Charles made a dismissive gesture with his hand. 'I have done nothing but restore what should always have been yours. How our father managed to make such a botch of his will…'

It was the opening he had longed for since the day he'd discovered he had a brother. As the level in the brandy bottle steadily dropped, the two men managed to discuss, for the most part relatively cordially, the woman they had both called mother, and the events that had led up to her tragic demise.

By the time Charles went upstairs and softly entered his wife's room she was fast asleep.

'Oh, my darling,' he murmured, bending to kiss her sleep flushed cheek. 'Thanks to you, my brother has been restored to me.'

Gently, he brushed one stray lock of hair from her forehead, before retreating to his own room. If she did not come down for breakfast in the morning he would send a note, requesting she join him in his study as soon as she was awake. He had learned a valuable lesson from his long, and painful interview with Robert. His brother had attributed nefarious motives to all his actions. It was not until he had spelled out exactly why he had taken what steps he had that Robert had finally managed to let go of years of resentment.

He needed to have just such a conversation with his wife.

Heloise stared at the curt little note she held in her hand with a sinking heart. Charles requested her presence in his study as soon as she woke. Pushing her breakfast tray to one side, she swung her legs out of bed. He must be so angry with her for flouting his wishes the night before. She did not wish to make him any angrier by keeping him waiting. She went straight to her washroom, pulling off her nightgown and tossing it aside in her haste to begin her toilette.

'Please to lay out my clothes while I wash,' Heloise said, when Sukey gaped at the sight of her mistress pouring water into the basin for herself. 'My green cambric walking dress.'

She was halfway down the stairs before she wondered what on earth she was doing. She could well imagine what he wanted to say to her. He was ready to go back to London. And, since she had let him down so badly, he had no intention of taking her with him. She had lived in dread of this moment ever since they had got here.

She stood, clutching the banister for support, as tears began to roll down her cheeks.

Stifling a sob, she hitched up her skirts and, instead of meekly going to the study, she ran down the passage that led to the back of the house and fled into the gardens.

And she kept on running. From her pain, from her loneliness, from her sense of utter failure. Across the lawns, through the shrubbery, down the bank and across the meadow. Only when she reached the lake did she veer from her course, following the shoreline until her strength gave out and she crumpled to the ground, giving way to the misery she had bottled up for so long.

She had no idea how long she lay there, curled up like a wounded animal, her utter misery cloaking her in a dense shroud of darkness.

It was only when the first great fat drops of rain began to strike her back that she sat up, suddenly aware that the darkness was not only inside her. The storm which had been hanging over Wycke for days had finally broken. She gasped as rain struck the ground around her like a hail of bullets, spattering her dress with sandy ricochets.

Her first instinct was to seek shelter. But she could not bear to go back to the house. She could see herself standing before Charles' desk, her hem dripping water onto his polished floor, her hair hanging in rats' tails round her face, while he informed her, his lip curling with disdain, that he never wished to set eyes on her again.

She pushed herself to her feet and made her way back to a wooden footbridge she remembered running past. It led across a narrow strip of water to the island on which stood the ruined tower. She would wait there until the storm had passed.

Maybe by then Charles would already have left Wycke, so that at least she would be spared the ordeal of suffering his dismissal in person.

Stumbling over a large piece of masonry half hidden by nettles alerted her to the fact she was nearing her goal. She lifted her head, brushing back the streamers of wet hair clinging to her face. The tower stood defiantly amidst the mounds of crumbling stones, all that remained of what might once have been an impressive set of fortifications. It still possessed a door, though it was almost completely obscured with a tangled growth of ivy. Grabbing the iron ring that served as a latch, Heloise turned it and pushed with all her strength.

The door yielded by perhaps two feet, grating over the stone-flagged floor within. She squeezed inside, grateful to have found shelter so quickly. It was dry inside, though almost pitch-black. Only the faintest glimmer of light filtered in from a source far above her head. It originated from the head of a wooden staircase, set into the outer wall of the tower.

She wrinkled her nose at the smell of decay that hung in the air. What was she doing in this dark, dirty ruin, when she could be sitting before a nice warm fire in her pretty sitting room, sipping hot chocolate? She could at least be comfortable, even if she would not feel any less miserable.

She wrapped her arms round her waist as a shiver racked her body. The rain had soaked right through her dress and flimsy indoor shoes in a matter of seconds. Charles would think she was an idiot for running in here instead of returning to the house.

Well, she *was* an idiot! She had been told as much for as long as she could remember. She sniffed. But the most foolish thing she had ever done was fall in love with a man that even a child could see should never have married so far beneath him!

And the worst of it was she had no right to admit she was miserable because he did not love her. Love was never supposed to have been part of the bargain they had made.

She wiped her hand across her face, not sure if it was rain or tears that were running down her cheeks, as a gust of wind blew in through the partially open door. She retreated from the storm, deeper into the gloom, and felt a sharp stab of pain in her shin as she stumbled over a broken chair which was lying on its side next to a battered wooden trunk.

Perhaps she would be better off up on the next floor, where it was a bit lighter. And there might not be so much rubbish lying about, she thought, making for the stairs. There was a metal railing fixed into the wall, onto which she clung as she tentatively began to climb. After only a few steps the air began to feel fresher, and as her head came onto a level with the upper floor, she saw that the room was indeed a great improvement on the rubbish tip the ground floor had become. Though the floor was a bit dusty, there were several pieces of quite sturdy-looking furniture, arranged to face a floor-to-ceiling window which, though grimy, was fully glazed.

She was just congratulating herself for making the decision to explore, when without warning the step upon which she had just placed her foot gave way with a sharp crack. Her foot went straight through, and if she had not been clinging to the handrail she would have fallen. Shaking with shock, she pulled her leg carefully up through the splintered tread.

Then realised, with horror, that it was not just her body that was shaking. The whole staircase was quivering under her weight.

And then, with a sound that reminded her of the ship's timbers creaking as the craft had plunged its way across the Channel, the whole structure parted company from the wall.

Chapter Fourteen

Charles pulled his watch from his pocket and frowned as it confirmed what he already knew. It had been three hours since Sukey had put his note into Heloise's hands, and still she had not come to him.

'You sent for me, my lord?'

Charles looked up to see Giddings standing in the doorway.

'Yes.' He snapped his watch shut and tucked it back into his waistcoat pocket. 'Have luncheon served in the breakfast parlour, and send someone to find out if Her Ladyship will be joining me.'

Perhaps she was unwell. Although, if that were the case, surely she would just have replied to his note with one of her own, apprising him of the fact.

No, he could not shake the conviction that this prolonged silence was a message in itself. He sighed. It had been too much to hope that he could put things right with his brother and his wife on the same day.

He went to the window, leaning his forearm on the sash as he gazed out at the rain which had begun to fall not long after Robert had left in the family coach, bound for London. He accepted that Robert needed time on his own, to come to terms with the new understanding they had reached in the early hours of the morning. And when Robert had haltingly given his reasons for wishing to return 'home', his heart had leapt, knowing that this was at last how he thought of his rooms at Walton House.

He turned at the sound of a knock on the door.

'Begging your pardon, my lord,' said Giddings. 'But Sukey does not seem to know Her Ladyship's whereabouts. Apparently she dressed in a great hurry and left her rooms quite early this morning, as soon as she received the note Your Lordship sent her.'

Charles felt as though a cold hand had reached into his chest and clamped round his heart. It could not be a coincidence that Heloise had disappeared the same morning his brother had returned to London.

'Will that be all, my lord?'

'What? Oh, yes—yes,' he snapped, dismissing his butler with a curt wave of his hand.

He had been standing in this very room, he recalled, the last time he had received news that had rocked his world to its foundations. Though he had only been a child, and standing on the other side of this desk, when his maternal uncle had told him he was never going to see his stepmother again. He stared blindly at the desk-top as he felt that same sense of isolation closing round him all over again.

His stepmother had kept a little singing bird in a cage in the sitting room that now belonged to Heloise. He had been able to hear it singing clear up to his schoolroom. But not that morning. When she had left she had taken it with her, and a dreadful silence had descended on Wycke.

And now, though Heloise had never really belonged to

him, her absence would reverberate through every corner of his existence.

How could she have betrayed him like this? How could Robert?

He drew in a deep breath, forcing himself to sit down and consider his situation rationally.

Though jealousy would have him believe his wife was the kind of woman who would run off with another man, his saner self knew her better than that. Though she had made her marriage vows in haste, and soon come to regret them, he could not believe she would break them so easily. Her conscience was far too tender. Look how she had berated herself for supposed lack of morals that night he had kissed her at the masquerade, when she had still been a virgin!

No, if she had left with Robert, it was not to embark on an affair.

She could not do it.

The only thing that would ever induce her to break her marriage vows was if she fell in love with someone else. And there was no evidence to indicate she had done so.

And as for Robert... No, he could no longer believe that he would deliberately conspire against him either. What he could imagine was Heloise going to him and begging him to take her back to London, where she would be safe from her cruel husband. A man would have to have a heart of stone to refuse her.

He would give her a few days' respite from his loathsome presence before following her to London. Though follow her he would. For he would not be able to rest until he could look her in the face and tell her...

He sucked in a sharp breath as the truth hit him. He had fallen in love with his wife. Fallen. He groaned. What an apt term! A fall was something you had no control over. It happened when you least expected it. It shook you up, and took your breath away, and it hurt. God, how it hurt. Especially when the woman you loved could not bear to be in the same room—nay, the same county!

What was he to do now?

Why, he mocked himself, take luncheon as if there was nothing the matter, of course. It was what he did best—act as though nothing touched him.

He went to the breakfast parlour, sat down, and methodically worked his way through the food that was set before him.

When at last he rose from the table, he went to the windows. For a while he just watched the rain trickling down the panes, observing how it was drowning his entire estate in tones of grey. But at length something impinged on his abstracted mood. There was a thin plume of smoke rising from the trees on the island. Who on earth would be foolish enough to try lighting a fire, on his private property, in such weather as this?

His heart quickened. He knew only one person foolish enough to be outside at all on a day like today. He could not begin to imagine what Heloise was doing out on the island, nor did he question how he was so certain she was the one responsible for raising that defiant plume of smoke. He only knew he had to get to her.

Flinging open the French windows, he strode along the parterre, vaulted over the stone parapet, and broke into a run. He sprinted across the lawns and through the shrubbery, skidding down the slope and landing in an inelegant heap on the carriage drive.

He scrambled to his feet and pounded his way across the bridge, not stopping until he reached the foot of the tower, from which, he had soon realised, the smoke was rising.

'Heloise!' he roared as he forced his way through the half-open door. 'What the devil do you think you are doing in here?'

'Charles?'

He looked up to see her head and shoulders appear over the lip of the upstairs landing. It took him only a moment to work out what must have happened. All that remained of the staircase was a heap of rotten timbers scattered across the floor.

Heloise's face looked unnaturally white, and her hair was plastered to her face. Just how long had she been stranded up there, alone and afraid? When he considered how he had tucked into a hearty luncheon, bitterly imagining her guilty of all manner of crimes...

'I'll soon have you down from there!' he vowed, looking wildly about for something he could use to climb up to her. He had to get her to safety, take her in his arms, and wipe that agonised expression of dread from her face.

There was a chest which he knew contained croquet hoops and mallets, a table kept specifically for picnics on the island, and several chairs and other boxes used for storing all manner of sporting equipment. Hastily he piled them up against the wall where the stairs had been, and began to climb.

'Oh, take care!' Heloise cried, when the pyramid of furniture gave a distinct lurch.

'It is quite safe, I assure you. Give me your hand and I will help you climb down.'

She shook her head, backing away. 'Charles, I don't think I can...'

He was just about to offer the reassurance he thought she needed when his improvised staircase separated out into its component parts. The chest went one way, the chair another, and he gave one last desperate push upwards, to land sprawled at his wife's feet on the upper landing.

Before he could do more than push himself to his knees, Heloise had flung her arms around his neck.

'Oh, thank heaven you made it safely! I was so afraid you were going to fall,' she said, pulling back just far enough to be able to gaze up into his face. Her eyes were full of concern.

Charles looked down into her tear-streaked face with a sense of wonder. She cared about him. Oh, maybe not as much as he cared for her, but nevertheless…

Taking ruthless advantage of her momentary weakness, he wrapped his arms about her and hugged her to his chest.

'I am fine,' he said, and in fact he could not remember when he had ever felt better. 'But what about you? Are you hurt?'

'Only a graze on my leg where my foot went through the stairs.'

'Let me see.' As he pulled her onto his lap, he suddenly registered that she was wrapped in what looked like a large, dusty sheet.

'What on earth is this?' he asked, pushing a swathe of material away from her leg. He winced as he saw the gash on her shin, and the blood which smeared her skin right down to her toes. Her bare toes.

'It is a curtain. I hope you do not mind, but I was so wet and cold, and I did not know how long it might be until somebody came to rescue me, and then I found the tinder box, and there was already some kindling in the grate, and I am sorry, but I also smashed one of the chairs, but only the littlest one, to get a fire going…'

Looking over her shoulder, he saw various items of feminine attire draped over a semicircle of chairs arranged

in front of the fireplace. A muddy gown, a dripping petticoat, torn stockings…

His hand stilled.

'Are you completely naked under that curtain?' he
asked throatily.

She nodded, her cheeks flushing. 'That is why I could
not have climbed down to you. I was going to explain that
if I let go it would just fall away, for I have no pins to
secure it, nor a belt…'

She had simply wrapped the curtain round her shoulders like a cloak, and was maintaining her modesty only
with the greatest difficulty.

'Your feet are cold,' he said, having forced his hand to
explore in a downward direction, when all it wanted to do
was slide upwards, underneath the curtain. Her ankles
were so slender, he noted, gritting his teeth against the
sudden surge of blood to his groin. He could almost
encircle them with his fingers.

The rest of her was not cold at all—not any longer, she
thought. As his hand gently stroked her injured leg, it sent
fire coursing through her veins, making her feel as though
she was melting from the inside out.

'And I fear I am making you wet again,' he said,
suddenly pushing her off his lap.

Guilty heat flooded her face as she wondered how on
earth he could know what his touch was doing to her. But
when he stood up and stripped off his jacket she realised
he had not been saying what she thought he had at all.

For as he draped it over the back of the chair which
already held her stockings, he remarked, 'My waistcoat is
a little damp, too, but apart from my neckcloth—' which
he deftly unwound and hung beside her petticoat '—my
shirt is quite dry.'

Her mouth went dry when he untied the laces and pulled it over his head.

'Here,' he said, holding it out to her. 'Put this on. You will be more comfortable and...er...secure than wrapped in that curtain. Which looks none too clean, by the way.'

She got up and moved towards him. The flickering firelight seemed to caress the planes of his face, the powerful sweep of his shoulders. His hair was a little mussed from having pulled off his shirt, his shoes were caked in mud, and his breeches were grass-stained. For the first time since she had met him he did not look in the least forbidding.

As her eyes strayed to the enticing expanse of male flesh bared to her avid gaze, her lips parted. Instead of taking the shirt he was holding out, she found herself reaching out to touch the very centre of his chest. The hair which grew there was coarse and slightly springy. His body was so intriguingly different from hers. Where she had soft mounds of flesh, he had slabs of hard muscle. Her hand slid over, and down, until Charles abruptly stopped her exploration by clamping her hand under his own.

'What are you doing?' he rasped.

Shocked at her own temerity, she tried to pull her hand away. But he would not let it go. Keeping it firmly pressed to his waist, he declared, as though in wonder, 'You want me!'

She could not deny it. But nor dared she admit it, only to suffer the humiliation of being rejected all over again. She turned her face away, biting down on her lower lip as she wondered how on earth she was going to come up with an explanation for what she had just done.

'You don't need to be shy with me. I'm your husband,' said Charles, taking her chin firmly between his thumb and forefinger and turning her face upwards. 'If you really do want me, I will be only too happy to oblige.' He smiled, and lowered his head to kiss her.

His mouth was so gentle. For the first time he was kissing her as she had always imagined a lover would kiss his woman.

And it was all she could ever have dreamed of. As he let go of her hand to pull her closer she slid it up his side, finally feeling she had permission to explore the rugged contours of his body. He was so big, so powerful. Yet so gentle as he lifted her and laid her down on a rug by the hearth.

She basked in the wonder of his touch, not even registering the moment he unwound the curtain from her body until he reared up to gaze down at her nudity.

It was too much for her. Shyly, she pulled a corner of material over her hips, stammering, 'I cannot…we cannot… it is broad daylight! Somebody might discover us!'

'Nobody will even think of beginning to search for us until we do not appear for dinner,' he pointed out. He could not bear it if she were to draw back now. 'We have hours. Hours and hours…' he murmured, bending to kiss her into submission again. But she was no longer so pliant under his ministrations.

Eventually he knew he would have to make some concession to her shyness. In desperation, he got up, went to the window, and tore down the one remaining curtain.

'Here,' he said, draping it over them both as he lay down beside her. Though he would have enjoyed being able to look at her while they made love, the most important thing was that he got her past this first hurdle.

She wrapped her arms tight about his neck, pressing her lips to his throat as though in gratitude, and he sighed with contentment.

She had been so scared when he had got up and walked away, a frown on his face as though he had grown impatient with her. It was such a relief when he came back she could have wept. She would make no more foolish protests. Whatever he wanted to do, whatever he asked of her, she would comply.

Even though to begin with she felt a little shocked that there were so many places on her body he wanted to kiss, or lick, or nip with his teeth, or pluck at with his clever, sensitive fingers.

But before long he'd roused such a tide of sensation in her that it swept all modesty aside. She writhed and moaned, kicking the curtain away as her whole body throbbed with heated pleasure. Then his fingers plucked once more, sending her shooting high into a realm of such exquisite sensation she cried aloud at the glory of it.

'Ah, yes,' he murmured into her ear. 'You liked that.' He was elated by her response. He had hoped she might grant him some concessions eventually, after a long period of wooing. He had been prepared to play on her sense of honour, reminding her she had a duty to give him heirs, if nothing else worked. Yet she had just yielded completely. And it was typical of her to give so much when he deserved so little. Especially considering how he had insulted her on the night he had taken her virginity. He should have been gentle and considerate of her inexperience. Instead of which…

'I was less than chivalrous last time,' he ground out. 'I will not be so careless of your needs in future, I promise you.'

She was so beautiful, lying in sated forgetfulness in the aftermath of what he knew must have been her first orgasm.

'But I have needs of my own,' he said, moving over her and into her, revelling in the soft warmth of her welcome.

Her eyes fluttered open as he began to move gently, her hands lifting to his waist as, unbelievably, she began to respond to him all over again.

He forced himself to go slowly, introducing her to the next level of lovemaking with an entirely different repertoire of moves.

'Charles!' she cried, and he felt her throbbing with release.

Hearing his name rise to her lips as she came to completion was all that was needed to send him tumbling over the edge. And, when he was spent, a feeling of such intense peace washed over him he dared not say one word for fear of shattering their first experience of harmony.

It took Heloise quite a while to come back down to earth. Charles had given her such intense pleasure. She could never have imagined her body was capable of anything so wonderful.

She turned her head to look at him. He had fallen asleep. Not surprisingly, she smiled. For he had done all the work.

'He likes to have the mastery between the sheets,' she remembered Mrs Kenton gloating, fanning her face, and just like that her joy was snuffed out. He was always like this in bed with a woman. It was nothing special to him.

And, she recalled, a feeling of sick dread cramping her stomach, he had only done this to 'oblige' her. She had approached him, blatantly stroking his chest, with her mouth hanging open at the sight of his semi-nudity. He knew they would not be rescued for hours, so it had seemed like as good a way to pass the time as any other. And he had needs, as he had pointed out as he had taken what was on offer.

She turned onto her side, pulling the curtain up over her shoulder, wondering why she should feel so cross. After all, not many nights ago she had worked out for herself that he would need a woman soon, and then made that spectacularly unsuccessful attempt to seduce him. She should be crowing in triumph, not blinking back tears. For she had got what she wanted, had she not?

It made her feel even more cross when he awoke with a smile on his face. When he saw that she was sitting hunched in front of the fire, the curtain clutched to her chin defensively, he cheerfully broke up another chair, tossing the pieces onto the fire until it was ablaze. It annoyed her that he was so much more successful at coaxing warmth from a fire she had only managed to get smoking damply. And it made her resentful when he began to tell her all about how this room had been used by former countesses to take tea, since it overlooked a particularly pleasing view of the lake, as though she were a guest he had to entertain.

It was a relief when, as dusk fell, she heard footsteps approaching the tower. Charles went to the landing, informing the servants who had come looking for them what had happened, and telling them to fetch a ladder. Hastily, while his back was turned, she fumbled her way into her damp clothing under cover of the dusty curtain.

Charles wished there was something he could do to ease his wife's discomfort. He could see she felt guilty for having enjoyed herself so much with a man she did not love. She had only married him to escape the horrific subjugation she would have suffered at Du Mauriac's cruel hands. It was futile to point out that plenty of people enjoyed the sexual act without any emotional involvement whatsoever. What they had just shared fell far short of her ideal.

She had succumbed to a fleeting moment of desire. Probably brought on by relief at surviving a frightening ordeal. He had disrobed before her, she had already been naked, and nature had taken its course.

He wanted to tell her that this mutual attraction was only the beginning. That love could grow from here. But she did not look as though she would be receptive to anything he had to say—not yet. She was clearly quite annoyed with him for taking advantage of her moment of weakness.

But he was not in the least repentant. They were lovers now, and there was no going back. She could not pretend his touch repelled her any more. They could have a good marriage. For even if she did not love him, he loved her— more than he had thought it was possible to love any woman, he reflected, as he helped her down the ladder. He would show her, he vowed, sweeping her up into his arms when she made to leave the tower on her own two feet, how good marriage to him could be. No bride would ever be as spoiled as she would be.

Ignoring her shocked gasp, and the amused looks of the two footmen who were holding the ladder, he kissed her, lingeringly, full on the mouth. And quelled her feeble protests that she was capable of walking back to the house.

'You are far too weak to make the attempt. You have not eaten anything all day. And you spent the entire afternoon making love.'

She subsided into his arms with that mutinous little pout he was beginning to love so much, saying not a word until he laid her down on the sofa in her own sitting room.

And then, when she drew breath to make the first of what he was sure would be a litany of complaints, he forestalled her.

'Sukey! See that Her Ladyship has a hot bath, and tend to the grazes on her shins. Then put her to bed and bring her some hot soup, bread and butter, and some of that apple pie she enjoyed so much at dinner the other night, if there is any left. And don't forget a pot of hot chocolate. I,' he said, dropping a kiss on his wife's parted lips, 'will return when I have had my own bath and a shave, and put on clean clothes. And, Giddings?' He turned to address the butler, who had followed them up the stairs on seeing the bedraggled state of his master and mistress. 'No visitors for the next two—no make that three days.'

'Very good, my lord.'

'And don't glare at me like that,' he advised Heloise. 'I have dealt with all the most pressing estate business, I have given my duty invitation to the neighbours to meet my Countess, and now I am entitled to enjoy my bride.'

Heloise let out one cry of vexation as Giddings turned, red-faced, from the room. First he had made it obvious to those two grinning footmen what they had spent the afternoon doing, and now he had scandalised Giddings with a statement of what he intended to spend the next few days doing. Where had all his rigidly correct behaviour gone, just when she could have done with it to spare her blushes?

Though in many ways she enjoyed his attention over the following week, just as much as he seemed to be enjoying hers, she never quite got rid of the feeling that it could not last. In desperation she grabbed what happiness she could, whilst privately waiting for the axe to fall.

It fell one morning while they were at breakfast, and Charles was reading one of the newspapers he had couriered up from London daily.

'My God,' he breathed, his eyes scanning the printed columns. 'There has been a battle.' Though he lowered the paper, it was as though he was looking straight through her. '*The* battle—the decisive battle. The losses have been disastrous.'

'Wh…who won?'

'Nobody.' His face was grim. 'The cost in human life was too great to call it a victory for Wellington. The losses from Robert's regiment alone…' He appeared to pull himself together. 'I will have to return to London. He should not be alone to deal with this.'

She went cold inside. He was going back to London. Just as he had always planned.

She could not let him walk out of her life like this. Not without a fight! Before they had become lovers she had fled out into the gardens rather than humiliate herself by confessing he was the centre of her universe. But now the thought of trying to survive without him was even more unbearable than the prospect of begging for a tiny place in his life.

'Please,' she began hesitantly. 'Please let me come with you.'

She saw disbelief in his eyes, and her heart began to thunder. She was breaking the terms of their agreement.

'Yes, I know I promised I would never cause you any trouble. But really, truly, I will not get in your way. I might even be able to help you,' she argued in desperation. 'I managed to help Robert before when nobody else could! Surely I could be of more help in London than stuck down here in the middle of nowhere? Please, Charles, let me try. Let me come with you. Don't leave me here alone!'

Chapter Fifteen

'Leave you here?' Charles frowned. 'Why would I do that?'

'B...but that was why you brought me down here! Because I had become too much trouble in London...'

'Because you had been *having* too much trouble in London,' he corrected her. 'I hoped that by the time we returned we might have come to a better understanding. So that you would feel you could come to me when you were in a scrape.'

'You never planned to leave me here?' Her eyes filled with tears. 'Truly?'

'I have never lied to you, Heloise,' he replied sternly. 'I never will.'

'But you were so angry...'

'Yes, I was angry the day we travelled down here. But that was not your fault.'

'Oh, but it was. I promised I would never give you any trouble, and I was in such a tangle...'

'I hold myself responsible for that. I should have taken better care of you. I knew there would be people that would try to hurt you in order to score off me, and I did nothing to protect you. Can you forgive me?'

'F...forgive you? There is nothing to forgive!'

He felt shamed that she should take such a generous attitude. Most women who'd found themselves tied to such an unsatisfactory husband would have done nothing but complain. Some would even have taken a lover—for consolation if not revenge.

Yet she seemed to be poised for him to mete out punishments for the most trifling faults... He blinked, remembering the day she had first come to him with her proposal. She had assumed from the very first that he would find her so irritating he would end up beating her.

She had no idea of her own worth.

And as yet he had done nothing to demonstrate just how much he valued her.

But all that was about to change...

'Well, now we have that misapprehension cleared up, we should make all haste to leave. Both of us,' he said firmly.

She scurried from the breakfast room as though his remark contained some kind of threat. She was so ready to believe the worst of him, he sighed. Just as Robert had been.

She had declared she found him cold and proud and unapproachable.

It was true that he had an abhorrence of expressing his feelings, especially when they were as turbulent as the ones Heloise aroused in him. Fortunately, he had already taken steps to show his regard for her.

But it was not just his reserve or her own lack of self-esteem he had to counter. As he climbed into the carriage beside her, and caught the expression of trepidation on her face, it hit him afresh that her plea to return to London was not in any way due to a wish not to be parted from *him*.

She had only spoken of her desire to help Robert. And when he reflected how miserable she had been during her stay at Wycke, it was perhaps only natural she should want to return to the city. He frowned as the carriage rumbled through the lodge gates and out into the lane. Her dislike of the place was yet another hurdle he would have to overcome. For he had a duty to his tenants and neighbours to visit the place more than once each year. And he was not going to leave Heloise alone and unprotected in London while he dealt with estate business. Besides, his heirs would be born there. And he wanted them to grow up there. He could picture a brood of perhaps three or four, tumbling over their mother's lap under the shade of the yew tree on the south lawn. Heloise would be such a good mother— loving and loyal.

He reached for her hand abstractedly, raising it to his lips and kissing her fingers as he focussed on how he was to bring about a state in their marriage where she would look up and smile as he approached, rather than shrink from him in expectation of a scold, as she did now.

The regime at Wycke would have to change before they visited again. Of that he was certain. He did not know if he should go so far as dismissing Mrs Lanyon, but sadly he feared that might be necessary. She seemed to harbour some kind of grudge against Robert, and, though he had always appreciated her efficiency in the past, he now saw that she was singularly lacking in compassion. A kinder woman would have helped Heloise grow accustomed to her position, instead of increasing her feelings of inadequacy.

He had not been aware how long they had been sitting

in silence until he heard Heloise sigh. It struck him forcibly that if it had been Robert sitting beside her she would no doubt have been chattering away merrily. He turned to look at her, noting the dejected slump of her shoulders. Except for a few brief moments when she forgot herself, in his arms in bed, that air of sadness hung round her like a persistent mist.

He drew in a sharp breath, turning away from her to look out of his own window as he felt a stab of fear that he might never be able to totally lift it. Even if she grew content with what he could offer her, it would never be the grand passion she had so admired her sister for harbouring for that penniless young engraver. Her parents had eloped, too, setting love above their personal safety. Whatever understanding they eventually reached, would it always seem like a poor substitute for the real thing?

Well, he might never move her heart to any great degree, but he could prove his solid worthiness.

He cleared his throat. 'When we return to London, things will not be between us as they were before.'

She turned to look at him, a little frown pleating her brow.

'There is no need to look so alarmed. It is your well-being that I am thinking of.'

He would need to deal with Lampton and Mrs Kenton in person before he could permit Heloise the same degree of freedom she had enjoyed before.

It was not just the personal vendetta the Lamptons held against him that might prove dangerous to her, either. After the losses incurred at Waterloo, there might well be some antagonism towards her simply because of her nationality. Until he had tested the waters for himself, and made sure she would be absolutely safe, he was not going to permit anyone anywhere near her.

Nor, to begin with, would he be free to escort her anywhere. The political map of Europe was going to change radically, if he was any judge of matters, and, while he had no intention of forcing Heloise to cross the Channel so that he could participate fully in negotiations, he could be busy laying the groundwork for those who would go in his stead.

'It might be a good idea if, just at first, you did not move about too much in society.'

Was there anything more annoying, she thought, than being told to act in a way she had already decided upon for herself? Why, it had been weeks since she had determined to be such a model wife that she would scarcely even venture out of doors! She knew she ought to be grateful that he was permitting her even a tiny place in his life, yet the longer he lectured her about what she was and was not permitted to do, and trotted out excuse after excuse for why he would be behaving much as he had done before, resentment began to smoulder inside her.

Charles noted that the nearer they drew towards London, rather than being reassured by his promises to take far better care of her than he had done before, she looked increasingly strained.

'Is something worrying you?' he eventually asked her.

Smiling determinedly to conceal her increasing feelings of resentment, she replied, 'Of course there is! I worry about Robert. It is for him that we return to London after all,' she reminded herself.

Charles was glad to get out of the carriage when at last it pulled up outside Walton House. He knew she was not in love with Robert, yet to hear of her concern for another man filled him with such unreasonable jealousy that it was all he could do to keep it leashed.

Heloise drooped into the house in his wake. He seemed

so relieved the journey was finally over. Oh, he had tried manfully to be what he seemed to think she would want—holding her hand, forcing himself to make conversation to keep her amused. As though she was a child and he a rather stern guardian, pointing out that he was going to be busy with important matters of state, and she must behave herself until he had a few minutes to spare!

He surged into the house, making straight for Robert's rooms. Just before he reached his door, he turned, as though recalling her tiresome presence, and said, with an exasperated expression on his face, 'I think you should go up to your rooms, Lady Walton, while I see how my brother fares. I cannot say when I may join you.'

She lifted her chin as her heart sank even lower. 'Of course.' Whatever had made her hope he might appreciate having his silly little wife at his side? Or that she might be able to help him through this crisis? He just wanted her to keep out of his way.

'I will see to my unpacking. As long as Robert is being cared for, that is all that matters.'

He turned from her so swiftly she was sure he had already relegated her from his thoughts. As he pushed open Robert's door, she caught a glimpse of booted feet sprawled at ungainly angles, and empty bottles lying on the floor.

She caught her breath. She really was silly to feel slighted because Charles did not dance attendance on her when his beloved brother was going through such a terrible time.

Feeling slightly ashamed of herself, she went up to her rooms.

'There is a parcel for you, my lady,' said Sukey, as soon as she saw Heloise trail in.

Frowning, Heloise went to the bed, on which the flat,

square package lay. She did not think she had any orders outstanding with the modiste. Wondering what it could be, she tore open the brown paper wrapping to find it was a leatherbound book.

She opened it at random, and gave a gasp of surprise. She was looking at one of her own sketches. Crossing to the desk by the window, she laid the book out flat and flipped through the pages.

'These are all mine!' she said to Sukey, who was peering over her shoulder. All the drawings she had left with Mr Ackermann were bound, here within these beautifully tooled leather covers. Just as though they were the work of a real artist.

She turned back to the very first page, and read the words: *'A collection of original watercolours, penned by the hand of Lady Heloise, beloved wife of Charles, 9th Earl of Walton...'*

Beloved wife? She ran a trembling finger over the printed words. This flowery language was not at all the kind of thing Charles would ever say, never mind cause to have written. He must have left the exact choice of words to the printer.

'Charles,' she whispered, wishing with all her heart that the words were true.

It was scarcely half an hour later that he came in and found her sitting on the bed, the book clasped in her arms and tears streaming down her face.

'Don't you like it?' He felt as though an iron fist had squeezed his heart. He had been so sure she would love seeing her work professionally bound.

'Like it?' she raised tear-drenched eyes to his. 'I love it. Did you...?' She stopped, shaking her head. If he had not meant the words, she did not want to hear the denial from his own lips. Far better to cling to the illusion that he felt some affection for her than to have her dreams shattered.

Hesitantly, Charles took a step towards the bed. 'I wanted to do something to demonstrate how sorry I am for forcing you to destroy that other sketchbook. It was quite wrong of me.'

'Oh!' Her head flew up, her eyes looking curiously wounded.

He clasped his hands behind his back. He would have thought his apology would comfort her. Perhaps it had only reminded her what an unfeeling brute he could be.

'I was acting completely out of character that night,' he admitted. 'My state of mind at that time was not... That is, Heloise...' He swallowed, searching for the words that would convince her, once and for all, that he was not the tyrannical bully he had shown himself to be during those few mad days in Paris. 'You have a remarkable skill. I admire it greatly. I have no wish to stifle your talent. I know I made a great deal of fuss, saying I did not want people to see your work, but that is not how I feel about it now. Now I have come to know you better, I know you would not do anything to embarrass me, or the name of Walton.'

'Not deliberately!' she cried, kneeling up and moving towards him, her hands outstretched. 'I did not mean to make a spectacle with your neighbours at Wycke...'

'You did not!' he vowed, taking the final step that brought him within touching distance. Taking her hands in his, he said, 'I was proud of the way you managed to make some of the most cantankerous, narrow-minded provincials look like rational, attractive people. With only a stub of pencil and some rather ancient writing paper!'

'Truly?'

He sat on the bed next to her, drawing her hands close to his chest. 'Heloise, when will you learn that I never say anything I do not mean? In fact, the next time we go to the country I hope you will spend some time making sketches of my favourite vistas. It is long past time that I put up some original artwork in this place.' His gaze flicked round the uninspiring collection of oils that graced her walls, and he grimaced. 'Your work would at least have the bonus of being amusing.'

'I draw people, though, not scenes,' she protested.

He cut her off with a smile. 'You do scenes. And you capture the atmosphere of a place. Have you forgot this?' He leaned down and flicked through the pages of the book until he came to the depiction of their first night at the theatre. 'Looking at it brings back the atmosphere of that night so vividly I can almost smell it.'

'But it is the people that create the atmosphere…'

He shook his head. 'Heloise, you have more talent than you give yourself credit for. I know you focus on the people, and regard the background only as the setting for your caricatures, but even in the few strokes you begrudged the curtains round Lensborough's box you captured the very texture of the velvet. If you wanted, you could capture not just the scenery of my home but its very essence. When you know it better. I feel sure that even now, should you decide to draw the ruined tower…'

Their eyes met and held as they remembered that afternoon they had become lovers. The book slid to the floor, forgotten, and they moved into each other's arms.

'I shall ring and have supper sent up,' Charles said, much later. 'There is no point in dressing for dinner now. And we would be eating it alone, wherever we took it. Robert is in no fit state to appear before you, my love.'

Rolling onto his side, he propped himself on his elbow. 'We had no need to fear that Robert would suffer alone. While the bells rang out all over London to celebrate the nation's victory, those who could not stand the pain of their bereavement gravitated to his rooms and made a valiant attempt to drink my cellars dry. You may be surprised to hear Lord Lensborough himself is one of those currently nursing a hangover down there.'

Heloise was beyond making any response. He had praised her work, taken her to bed in broad daylight, and called her his love. Yet downstairs Robert and his companions were mourning the shameful waste of so many young male lives. It was wrong to experience any measure of happiness when so many were grieving.

'I will visit with him tomorrow,' she declared. Tonight was just for her and Charles.

'Tomorrow will be soon enough,' he agreed, making her heart soar. 'Robert's rooms are no fit place for a lady at the moment. But now he knows we have returned, it may be the push he needs to begin sobering up. And his friends will feel they may safely leave him now that we have come home.'

Her brief moment of joy dissolved. Charles was not thinking of how delightful it would be to have a romantic supper in bed with her. His priority was still Robert's well-being.

'You are not upset, are you, that I will be otherwise engaged tomorrow?'

As if she were a spoiled child who had to be constantly amused!

She lifted her chin. 'I do not need you to dance attendance on me,' she declared proudly. 'Even when I first

came to London, did I not manage to amuse myself?'
Flushing darkly, she added, 'Perhaps that is not such a
good thing to remind you of. But I will do better now. I
will not go to gaming hells, or masquerades, or gamble
with military gentlemen again, I promise you!'

'Even if you should do all of those things,' Charles
declared, 'I should not banish you to the country. If you
get into any sort of trouble you must tell me straight away,
and no matter what you have done I will help you.'

'I have just told you,' she snapped, 'that I won't get
into trouble!'

'Well, we'll see, shall we?'

Crestfallen that he still assumed she would get into
some sort of trouble the minute his back was turned, she
rolled over and pretended to go to sleep.

Over the next few days Heloise was carried along by a determination to prove to Charles that in spite of his misgiv-
ings she *could* behave herself when the need arose.

She usually slept in until quite late. For, although she
scarcely saw Charles during the hours of daylight,
whatever time he came home, he never failed to come to
her bed.

Once she had washed and dressed, she liked to take an
airing in the park, although she made sure both Sukey and
a footman always properly escorted her. When she returned
there was always some little gift from Charles for her to
unwrap—proof that he was appreciative of her efforts to
reform. She spent the hours before dinner either reading
the poetry, or pressing individual blossoms from a posy—
or, once, attempting to put together the cleverly designed
portable easel he had purchased. And she spent the hours
after dinner waiting impatiently for him to come home.

She might even have felt a measure of contentment if only she'd had Robert to keep her company during the long, dull evenings. But whenever she went and knocked on his door there was always already a group of grim-faced young men sprawled about the rooms, and a distinct aroma of alcohol in the air. The fact that all conversation ceased the moment she walked in made her feel increasingly awkward about intruding. He had friends about him. That was the main thing. And who better than those young men, with military backgrounds, who could understand far better than she could what he was going through?

She was selfish to wish he would at least let her in for half an hour, so that she had someone to talk to. She sighed now, picking up the latest novel that Charles had sent her. Did she not have so much more now than the last time she had been in London? She might not go out, but then she had not really enjoyed many of her outings anyway. Particularly not once she had locked horns with Mrs Kenton.

She shivered, applying herself to words that she had a vague recollection of reading before. It was not an easy story to get into, but she wanted very much to be able to tell Charles that she was enjoying it. Even though she was having difficulty working out what the story was supposed to be about, she sighed. Still, though the story itself was not very interesting, she did love the fact that Charles had bought it for her. He was so generous.

'…so generous that it quite makes up for the coldness of his public manners…' she heard Mrs Kenton whispering.

That Woman! The moment her mind strayed in her direction, her words flooded her mind with her poison all over again.

She shut the book with a snap, and went into her

bedroom. She would sketch until Charles came home. That always made her feel better.

But though she sat at her drawing desk, and took the charcoal in her fingers, her mind remained devoid of inspiration. She could not think of a single thing she wanted to draw. She had not been anywhere or seen anyone since returning to London to fire her imagination at all.

There seemed to be nothing but a great emptiness all around her. When Charles came in, far earlier than she had expected, she was so relieved to see him that she flew into his arms. She knew he would not rebuff her these days. On the contrary, he seemed only too keen to strip her naked and kiss and caress every inch of her, until she was mindless with pleasure and he was completely exhausted.

She looked down at him, as he lay sleeping beside her later, a troubled frown creasing her brow. If only she had never met Mrs Kenton. For then she would be completely happy, thinking that the way he behaved was an indication that he felt something for her. But she *had* met Mrs Kenton, and she knew that he took similar pride in his performance in bed, no matter which woman shared it.

And, on reflection, she could not read very much into the fact he sent her gifts every day, either. Mrs Kenton had told her how generous he was to his mistresses.

He had never given her a single thing before he had taken her to his bed. With a pang of shock, she realised that, far from being a mark of his approval, those gifts were more like payment for services rendered.

He was treating her just like he would treat his mistress!

No, on second thoughts he was not even treating her so well as that. At least a mistress got an outing every now and again. She had met Nell in the theatre, and at Vauxhall Gardens, and although everyone said Lord Lensborough was a hard man, even he had given Nell her own carriage and pair to drive about in the park.

She sat up, hugging her knees to her chest as she grew more and more upset. He had said before they married that as his wife she would move in the first circles. But she didn't. She never went anywhere. It was as if he was ashamed of her!

She could barely look at him when he rose the next morning to be about his business. Business which, she thought huffily, he could as well conduct at home, if he had a wife he trusted. If he really was engaged in politics. She sniffed. For all she knew he could be out carousing with his friends, or even trawling Covent Garden for a new mistress.

'Heloise?' he said gently, noting the stiff set of her shoulders under the blankets. 'I can see you are not happy with me this morning.' Or indeed any morning. 'This state of affairs cannot continue.' Fortunately he would be able to conclude his involvement in party affairs today. And then he would be able to devote himself entirely to getting his wife to admit that being a partner in a marriage of convenience was not the end of the world. 'When I return tonight, you and I need to have a serious talk.'

She shut her eyes tight on the wave of pain that assailed her. She had known it! She had known it from the first! She had only ever been a poor substitute for Felice, and now he could not even continue to use her as he would use a mistress. He was tired of her.

Had he already found her replacement? Was that where he went every night, when he said he was engaged in state affairs? *Affaires*, more like! And she, rather than demanding he treat her with respect, had welcomed him into her bed whatever time of the night he rolled in, with open arms, like the lovesick fool she was! She should have known when she'd had to go to such lengths to seduce him that he would not stay faithful for long. If he had ever found her in the least bit desirable he would have made the first move!

'In the meantime, I should like you to have this.' He went to his jacket, which was hanging on the back of a chair, delved into the pocket, and extracted a black rectangular box. 'I had meant to give it to you last night, but…' He smiled wryly at the memory of her flying to his arms, and more or less dragging him into bed.

'Don't remind me!' she flung at him waspishly.

He frowned as he approached the bed, where she was sitting with her knees hunched up, a mutinous glare on her face. He faltered, wishing with all his heart that she did not feel so ashamed of experiencing desire without love.

'Here,' he said, proffering the jeweller's box.

Until now, the gifts he had bought her had been trifling things, meant to amuse her and remind her he was thinking of her, though he could not be with her. But he had never forgotten her face when she had spoken about the Walton diamonds. She had thought he did not care because they were old. She seemed to have thought that if he cared about her he would have bought her something new. And so he had sought to redress that error in the purchase of these pearls. Pearls for purity. For she was the purest woman he had ever known. Besides which, he could not wait to see how the ear drops would look against the glorious silk of her dark hair.

As he opened the box to reveal the long strand of perfectly matched pearls, her eyes widened in horror.

'How dare you?' she cried, drawing back as though he was holding out a snake. 'I won't be treated like this! No— not one minute more! Oh, yes, I know I promised I would not stop you from amusing yourself, however you wished, but I have to tell you that I cannot keep to that stupid bargain we made one minute longer!'

He went cold with dread as he heard her telling him their marriage was over. And all because he had given her pearls? He looked down at the box, lying open in his hand, wondering where he had gone wrong this time.

He was about to find out. Flinging the covers aside, Heloise rose from the bed, completely forgetful of her nudity, and advanced on him, her eyes spitting fire.

'I am your wife! Your *wife!*' She swiped at the box, knocking it from his nerveless fingers. 'And if you think you can pay me off with pearls, when even that Mrs Kenton got rubies, you are the greatest imbecile! And I know you never made *her* stay within doors, not to mingle with your so perfect friends. Even poor little Nell gets trips to the theatre every now and again. And you think, you *really* think, that I will walk out of your life quietly after you give me the kind of jewels that a mother would give to her daughter when she makes her first curtsey in society? Well, I tell you, *no!* I am not going back to Wycke, and I am not going to sit at home any more while you go out and amuse yourself without your embarrassing wife hanging on your arm. And if you think I am going to do nothing while you set up another mistress, then you are very much mistaken. If you dare…if I find out where you are keeping her…I shall…I shall…'

For much of the tirade Charles had been too bemused to take in more than the fact that she was furiously angry and gloriously naked. But at last some of her meaning began to percolate through.

'What,' he said, his heart pounding, 'will you do, Heloise, if you find out where I have set up my mistress?'

'Oh!' She drew back, as though him saying it made it real. Her eyes filled with tears. She began to shake. 'I shall do something terrible,' she whispered, her face grim. 'Of that you can be sure.'

'Thank God,' he sighed, drawing her into his arms. She loved him. She must do to be experiencing such fierce jealousy. It was a feeling he recognised only too well.

'No!' she whimpered, struggling to break free. 'You shall not subdue me with your kisses again. I won't let you. I hate you!' she cried, raising her fists to beat at his chest.

'No, you don't,' he countered. 'You hate feeling weak and helpless under the force of your feelings. But your feelings for me are not hatred. Ah, no—don't cry, my little love,' he crooned, scooping her up and carrying her back to bed. 'I have not set up a mistress. I promise you,' he said, kissing her forehead.

'You…you have not?' she hiccupped, frowning up at him through tear spiked lashes.

'Of course not. Why ever would you think I would do such a thing?'

'Well, I know you are only putting up with me…you only married me, after all, to save face so that no one would know Felice broke your heart. I…I know you will never love me like you loved her.'

'That much is true,' he said dryly. 'For I was never in love with her at all.'

'What? That is not true. When she ran off with Jean-Claude your heart was broken!'

'Actually, no, it was not. Not in the least. The truth,' he said ruefully, 'as you pointed out with such perspicacity at the time, was that she had severely dented my pride. You see,' he said, taking her hand, 'Felice was such fun to be with. I had never met anyone like her before. When I was with her she made me feel as though there was something about me as a person that she valued, since she made no secret of the fact she despised the aristocracy as a class. She was not forever hinting that she wanted me to buy her things, either.' He shook his head, a frown clouding his brow. 'And I was in a peculiarly vulnerable state of mind at the time.'

Though Heloise still seemed oblivious to her state of undress, he felt obliged to reach down and pull the coverlet up, tucking it round her shoulders as he considered the best way to explain.

'I had suffered a series of shocks. Discovering I had a brother. Learning that the men I had trusted throughout my youth had perpetrated a crime against him and my step-mother…and then finding that I was totally unable to escape their pernicious influence!' He laughed bitterly. 'I could cease seeing them, but I could not undo my training. No matter how much I wished it, I could not find the least desire to behave with anything less than complete decorum. And then I took Robert into my home and endured his scorn, while seeing how very much he was valued by his friends… In the end I fled to Paris looking for…well, I don't know what I was looking for, to tell you the truth. I only know that for a while I felt that Felice was the answer. She made me feel as though I could slough off all that I had been and make a fresh start. It was my dreams of becoming a better man she stole, not my heart, Heloise.'

He stopped fussing with the coverlet and looked her straight in the eye as he confessed, 'My heart belongs to you, Heloise. It is a poor, stunted thing, I know. But, such as it is, it beats for you alone.'

'But when…? But how…?' She sat up, an intent expression on her face. 'When you brought me to London you left me utterly alone. After giving me a long list of things I was not supposed to do and people I was not to talk to, as though I was a complete nuisance!'

He took her face between his hands. 'Do you know how much it hurt that you never understood?' He took a deep breath. 'You always put me in mind of a little bird. And when I saw that picture you drew of yourself, chained in an intolerable marriage, I knew I did not want it to be like that between us. I know I said a lot of damn fool things at the start, but once you were mine I did not want you to feel you were caged, or chained. I wanted you to be able to fly free and come to me because you wanted to come to me, not because I compelled you.'

'I…I thought you did not care what I did. And I felt as though my heart was breaking. Because I loved you so much…'

'You said you didn't!' he protested, rearing back. 'When you suggested we get married…'

'I don't think I did—not at that precise moment. Or perhaps I had not allowed myself to, because I thought your heart belonged to my sister. But by the afternoon, once I knew you were to be my own husband, I could not bear the thought that you might want any other woman. And then, when I feared Du Mauriac would kill you, then I was sure. I was so scared! I had to get you away from France to safety, no matter what it cost me!' She reached up and stroked his cheek, her expression full of remembered concern. 'I told myself I would not care if you never loved me back so long as you were safe. Oh, but when we got to London, and you were so cold, I made such a fool of myself trying to win your approval,' she finished ruefully.

'You were trying to win my approval with all that

time you spent with Robert?' he groaned. 'While I was trying to show you how tolerant I could be, letting you do as you liked!'

'Oh, don't be tolerant any more, then,' said Heloise. 'It made me so unhappy!'

'Very well, since you ask,' he growled. 'From now on I shall be the most intolerant—' he kissed her hard on the lips '—jealous—' he pulled her down until she lay flat on her back '—possessive husband that ever drew breath! In fact I will never let you out of my sight again. When I think of the torment I suffered when I thought you planned to leave me…'

She looked perplexed. 'When was that? I never thought of leaving you!'

No… The day he feared she had run back to London with Robert she had in fact been stuck in the tower. And the day he had assumed she was trying to raise money to elope with him she had been trying to sell her pictures to pay off her gambling debts. Even in France, when he had thought she would want to flee an intolerable marriage, she had already been in love with him!

She had never thought of leaving him. Nor had his stepmother, come to that. And at that revelation something inside him seemed to unfurl and blossom. He felt tears prick his eyes. Somewhat appalled, he blinked them away, before burying his face in the silken cocoon of her hair.

'I love you,' he said, for there was nothing else that summed up so neatly the enormity of what he felt at that moment.

Her answer, 'I love you too,' was exactly what he needed to hear.

Some time later, she whispered, 'And you promise you really won't send me away and take a mistress?'

'I would not dare,' he groaned, rolling onto his back and

pulling her into his side. 'Besides, you would not let me—would you?'

'How could I stop you if you really wanted to?'

He chuckled. 'Are you serious? Don't you know how powerful you are?'

'Powerful? Me?' she squeaked.

'Yes, you. You have been able to mould me like putty in your hands from the first moment you set your sights on me. When I had vowed to have nothing whatever to do with your family you persuaded me to marry into it. I had decided nothing would induce me to leave Paris until my lease expired, and scarcely a day later you had me racing for the coast like a lunatic. And worst of all, when I had always believed love was a debilitating emotion from which I would never suffer, you wrung it from my stony heart. Nobody else could have done it.'

'Are you sorry?' she asked in a small voice.

'Sorry?' He snorted. 'I have never been more glad of anything in my life. You are my life, Heloise,' he said softly. 'The light of my life. If you had never bullied me into marrying you I would have been the coldest, loneliest man in London. Instead of which…' He paused, his eyes suspiciously bright with moisture. 'Ah, don't talk any more,' he groaned. 'Just kiss me.'

'With all my heart,' she sighed. 'With all my heart.'

* * * * *

*Harlequin is 60 years old, and Harlequin Blaze
is celebrating!
After all, a lot can happen in 60 years,
or 60 minutes…or 60 seconds!
Find out what's going down in Blaze's heart-stopping
new mini-series,
FROM 0 TO 60!
Getting from "Hello" to "How was it?"
can happen fast….*

*Here's a sneak peek of the first book,
A LONG, HARD RIDE
by Alison Kent
Available March 2009*

"Is that for me?" Trey asked.

Cardin Worth cocked her head to the side and considered how much better the day already seemed. "Good morning to you, too."

When she didn't hold out the second cup of coffee for him to take, he came closer. She sipped from her heavy white mug, hiding her grin and her giddy rush of nerves behind it.

But when he stopped in front of her, she made the mistake of lowering her gaze from his face to the exposed strip of his chest. It was either give him his cup of coffee or bury her nose against him and breathe in. She remembered so clearly how he smelled. How he tasted.

She gave him his coffee.

After taking a quick gulp, he smiled and said, "Good morning, Cardin. I hope the floor wasn't too hard for you."

The hardness of the floor hadn't been the problem. She shook her head. "Are you kidding? I slept like a baby, swaddled in my sleeping bag."

"In my sleeping bag, you mean."

If he wanted to get technical, yeah. "Thanks for the loaner. It made sleeping on the floor almost bearable." As had the warmth of his spooned body, she thought, then quickly changed the subject. "I saw you have a loaf of bread and some eggs. Would you like me to cook breakfast?"

He lowered his coffee mug slowly, his gaze as warm as the sun on her shoulders, as the ceramic heating her hands. "I didn't bring you out here to wait on me."

"You didn't bring me out here at all. I volunteered to come."

"To help me get ready for the race. Not to serve me."

"It's just breakfast, Trey. And coffee." Even if last night it had been more. Even if the way he was looking at her made her want to climb back into that sleeping bag. "I work much better when my stomach's not growling. I thought it might be the same for you."

"It is, but I'll cook. You made the coffee."

"That's because I can't work at all without caffeine."

"If I'd known that, I would've put on a pot as soon I got up."

"What time *did* you get up?" Judging by the sun's position, she swore it couldn't be any later than seven now. And, yeah, they'd agreed to start working at six.

"Maybe four?" he guessed, giving her a lazy smile.

"But it was almost two…" She let the sentence dangle, finishing the thought privately. She was quite sure he knew exactly what time they'd finally fallen asleep after he'd made love to her.

The question facing her now was where did this relationship—if you could even call it *that*—go from here?

* * * * *

*Cardin and Trey are about to find out that
great sex is only the beginning....
Don't miss the fireworks!
Get ready for
A LONG, HARD RIDE
by Alison Kent
Available March 2009,
wherever Blaze books are sold.*

CELEBRATE
60 YEARS
OF PURE READING PLEASURE
WITH HARLEQUIN®!

We'll be spotlighting a different series
every month throughout 2009
to celebrate our 60th anniversary.

Look for Harlequin® Blaze™ in March!

0-60

*After all, a lot can happen in 60 years,
or 60 minutes...or 60 seconds!*

Find out what's going down in Blaze's
heart-stopping new miniseries *0-60!*
Getting from "Hello" to "How was it?"
can happen fast....

Look for the brand-new 0-60 miniseries in March 2009!

REQUEST YOUR FREE BOOKS!

 Harlequin® Historical
Historical Romantic Adventure!

2 FREE NOVELS PLUS 2 **FREE GIFTS!**

YES! Please send me 2 FREE Harlequin® Historical novels and my 2 FREE gifts (gifts are worth about $10). After receiving them, if I don't wish to receive any more books, I can return the shipping statement marked "cancel". If I don't cancel, I will receive 6 brand-new novels every month and be billed just $4.94 per book in the U.S. or $5.49 per book in Canada, plus 25¢ shipping and handling per book and applicable taxes, if any*. That's a savings of 20% off the cover price! I understand that accepting the 2 free books and gifts places me under no obligation to buy anything. I can always return a shipment and cancel at any time. Even if I never buy another book, the two free books and gifts are mine to keep forever.

246 HDN ERUM 349 HDN ERUA

Name	(PLEASE PRINT)	
Address		Apt. #
City	State/Prov.	Zip/Postal Code

Signature (if under 18, a parent or guardian must sign)

Mail to the **Harlequin Reader Service:**
IN U.S.A.: P.O. Box 1867, Buffalo, NY 14240-1867
IN CANADA: P.O. Box 609, Fort Erie, Ontario L2A 5X3

Not valid to current subscribers of Harlequin Historical books.

Want to try two free books from another line?
Call 1-800-873-8635 or visit www.morefreebooks.com.

* Terms and prices subject to change without notice. N.Y. residents add applicable sales tax. Canadian residents will be charged applicable provincial taxes and GST. Offer not valid in Quebec. This offer is limited to one order per household. All orders subject to approval. Credit or debit balances in a customer's account(s) may be offset by any other outstanding balance owed by or to the customer. Please allow 4 to 6 weeks for delivery. Offer available while quantities last.

Your Privacy: Harlequin Books is committed to protecting your privacy. Our Privacy Policy is available online at www.eHarlequin.com or upon request from the Reader Service. From time to time we make our lists of customers available to reputable third parties who may have a product or service of interest to you. If you would prefer we not share your name and address, please check here. ☐

HH08R

BRENDA JACKSON

TALL, DARK...
WESTMORELAND!

Olivia Jeffries got a taste of the wild
and reckless when she met a handsome
stranger at a masquerade ball. In the
morning she discovered her new lover
was Reginald Westmoreland, her father's
most-hated rival. Now Reggie will stop at
nothing to get Olivia back in his bed.

**Available March 2009
wherever books are sold.**

Charles had taken her completely by surprise.

She didn't know what to do. No man had ever kissed her before.

But she didn't want to evade Charles, she discovered after only a fleeting moment of shock. What she really wanted, she acknowledged, relaxing into his hold, was to put her arms about him and kiss him back. If only she knew how!

Uttering a little whimper of pleasure, Heloise raised shaky hands from her lap and tentatively reached out for him.

"My God," he panted, breaking free. "I never meant to do that!"

The fierce surge of desire that even now was having a visible effect on his anatomy was an unexpected bonus. When the time was right, he was going to enjoy teaching his wife all there was to know about loving....

* * *

The Earl's Untouched Bride
Harlequin® Historical #933—February 2009

To my parents, who taught me to love reading.

Praise for Annie Burrows

"Annie Burrows is an exceptional writer of historical romance who sprinkles her stories with unforgettable characters, terrific period detail and wicked repartee."
—*Cataromance*

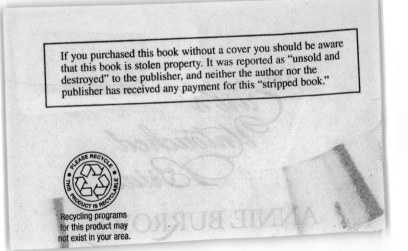